THE ALIEN'S
ALLEGIANCE

NORAKIAN WARRIOR SERIES

CALLA ZAE

PROSE & CONCEPTS

COPYRIGHT

For those loyal to their hearts.

.

.

.

"Your heart knows the way. Run in that direction." — *Rumi*

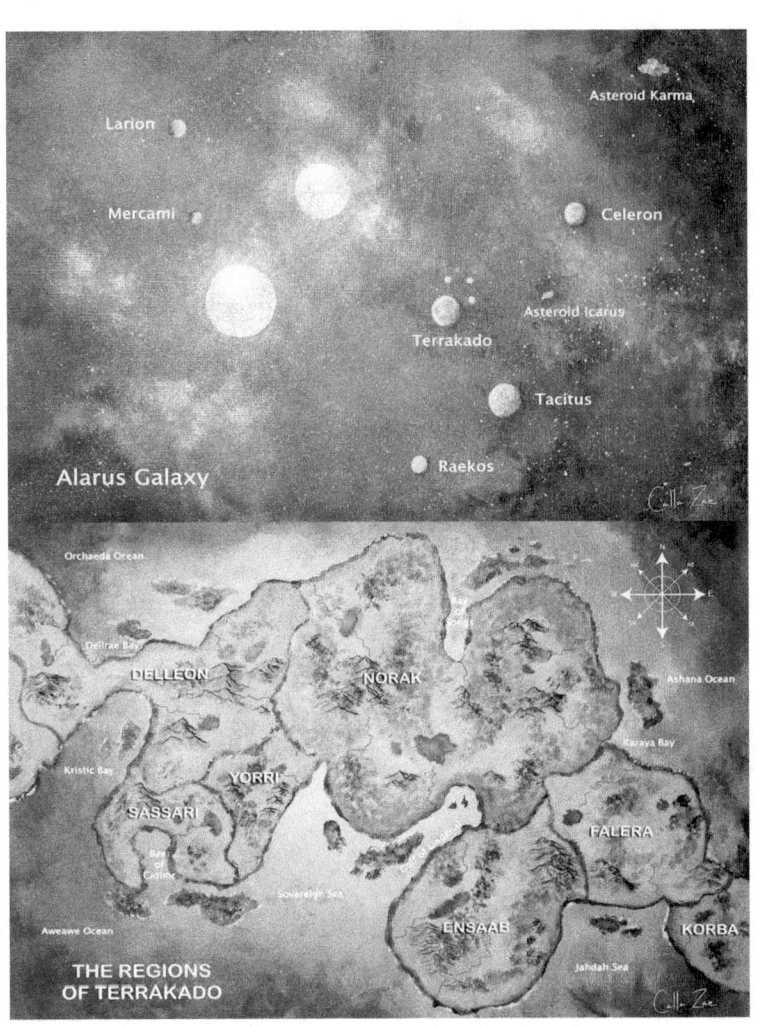

ONE

Kazstrom

THE WOUND SCORCHED Kazstrom's back as pain clung like claws, digging into his mental state. He was exhausted, irritated, and would do anything for ease and rest. But he wouldn't get any of that until he found the Soulstar, a rare moonstone that could heal his poisonous wound. A wound caused by an enemy in a recent battle.

The injury was a setback to his goal and responsibilities. Kazstrom had been spending every minute of his free time building his strength and elevating his fighting skills to a level where no one—and nothing—could keep him from victory. He was going to earn the title of General of the Norakian warriors, a position that had become available after the death of his mentor, General Atreyu.

Kazstrom loved serving the Norakian citizens as their Captain. But as General, he could be more, attain more. More power and opportunities.

There is nothing wrong with having goals and ambitions. Goals produced accomplishments, satisfaction, and self-worth. If more star-beings created valuable missions for themselves, the number of crimes within the Cosmos would be reduced.

And that would make him unemployed, he acknowledged.

All his hard work would mean nothing if he died before next month's assessment.

That was why he landed on Earth two days ago when his monitor had picked up the Soulstar's energy. It led him to the Unites States of America in a city called Springfield, in the state of Massachusetts, before he lost the trace. He docked his *Spectre Seven* spaceship in a large, abandoned parking lot, where he continued his search for the moonstone.

A muscle pulled in his shoulder and inflamed the deep gash that ran across his back.

"Malastrom!" He popped three painkillers into his mouth.

He checked his vambrace for the current reading of the Soulstar. He pulled up several virtual monitors, scouring the nearby areas. Though it was daytime, that didn't matter. Detecting the moonstone's frequency could be done during the day or the night. Still, nothing appeared on the screen.

"Where are you hiding?"

He zoomed out of the vicinity, scanning the city, state, country, and eventually all around Earth.

Kazstrom had visited Earth two other times before. The frequency on Earth was lower than that of his own planet, Terrakado. Yet, there was a strong power, like an innate will that emanated from the human *corra*. He placed a hand to his own corra and felt its power thumping with life and purpose.

He didn't know if the humans understood this power they possessed. Probably not, which was why many of them lived unconsciously, without a purpose. But then again, that reflected any species on any planet.

One reason he enjoyed coming to Earth was that despite the constant conflicts, there was always a seed of hope for humanity. He could feel the planet's pulse from light-years away. That explained why so many other star races came to abduct humans for examination.

Kazstrom wasn't interested in any of that. Furthermore, abduction was illegal according to the cosmic law, created by the Galactic Coalition of Truth. He had no desire to create more issues for himself.

Inside his cloaked spaceship, invisible to anyone in the area, Kazstrom stared out at the empty parking lot. Buildings that once had potential now stood crumbling with broken bricks, smashed windows, and graffiti as decor. Why didn't the humans rebuild their abandoned structures into some amazing architecture?

Broken didn't mean useless. Broken meant potential. At least, to Kazstrom it did.

His childhood had left him in pieces, but he had gathered up those fragments and remade himself.

An individual who reconstructed himself always had standards because he knew what came before. He made sure the living environment was suitable for his citizens by catching, imprisoning, or killing criminals.

Those criminals stole from the innocent and killed their parents, making them orphans.

A dark memory resurfaced and soured his mood, so he shoved it away. He was a warrior now, and he had the power to defend and protect those who mattered to him. He would use all his power to ensure that those who broke the law would pay. There were several forms of punishment; shipping them off to the dark prison on Asteroid Karma was one option.

Nerves surged in Kazstrom's gut and prickled his skin. Was something wrong at home? Concern for his region had him whirling back to his computer station, where several virtual screens gave him a snapshot of Norak. The magnetic field around the Aurora Matrix Bridge appeared steady, which meant there was equilibrium within the region. Updates from his warrior brothers and sisters also showed nothing unusual. Despite that, his gut told him something was off. Maybe he was just overworked and too wounded to understand his feelings.

Then a beep sounded on his vambrace. The Soulstar's energy pulsed on the glowing screen. The way the moonstone's vibration faded in and out seemed strange, as if it was near a source that helped conceal it.

Peculiar energies swirled to the forefront of his mind and activated the cosmic codes within his skin. In shock, he glanced at the skin on his hands where the illumination faded. *What is going on?* He honed in and didn't recognize the feminine energy. Perhaps Earth's energy was toying with his own.

Of all the planets out there, why was the Soulstar on planet Earth? How did it get here? Planetary particles flew all over the place because of cosmic forces, but he couldn't imagine why or how the Soulstar had traveled this far away from its origin. The Soulstar was a moonstone from his home galaxy, Alarus, millions of light-years away from Earth.

He didn't have time to contemplate as another shot of pain stabbed into his muscles.

"Malastrom! Damn it all to void!"

The misery on his back aggravated him, reminding him that finding the moonstone and removing the pain was all that mattered right now. The location of the moonstone wasn't too far from where he was.

"There you are." A smile curved on his lips. "I'm coming for you."

He pressed a button on the other forearm guard. Going out

in public on Earth required a suitable outfit. In seconds, his comfortable smart-tech shirt and high-performance pants became a pair of dark jeans and a blue leather blazer over a cotton t-shirt. His battle boots transformed into a pair of comfortable shoes applicable to human fashion. The Norakian technology enabled him to transform his blue skin to that of a human male that had gotten some sun.

Kazstrom was on a mission that demanded efficiency, not delays. A blue alien dressed for battle and decked with weapons would absolutely attract delays.

"Let's go, my friend," Kazstrom called out to his cat-like pet, Warcat, who woke from a nap on a soft, luxurious rug in the corner. He was composed of half flesh and half metal. The metal legs, ears, tail, and part of the neck were made of the Norakian alloy called fortisium. It was a mix of steel, chromium, and other rare metals combined for strength, hardness, and flexibility. Kazstrom's own warrior attire, blaster, and parts of his sword were made from the same source. Neutronic beads covered parts of Warcat's legs and feet, allowing him to race above the ground when necessary.

With four ears perked, the black and gold jaguar got to its feet and growled, "Where to?"

"To retrieve my remedy." Kazstrom opened the gate and a long energy ramp extended out.

Warcat yawned and stretched. "There's nothing that can cure your bossy and domineering attitude."

He was used to Warcat's complaints, which always occurred after an unsatisfying nap. "This boss treats you very well. Don't forget that." He narrowed his eyes. "You're well-fed and loved. What else do you need?"

"Sleep and rest." Warcat curled his tail and stared up at his master with aqua eyes. "I remember that *someone* needs them more than me." In seconds, he shape-shifted into a magnificent, black motorcycle with gold accents.

Because he didn't have time to waste, and because he understood his friend, Kazstrom ignored the jab. "We can rest after I get my promotion. Now, let's get this moonstone so we can go home."

TWO

Teegan

THIRTY MINUTES until the doors opened. Thirty minutes produced thirty pounds of stress. Thirty pounds of stress made a woman feel as attractive as a cow in a fitted summer's dress. Huffing out a breath, Teegan Moore felt that heaviness as she dragged her anxiety around the bookstore while she made sure all the vendor tables, name tags, and chairs were in place.

But eighty percent of the stress wasn't because of the Artist and Author Fair, which she had spent the last week preparing for. It resulted from her lack of judgment in men. It was her fault for not seeing the asshole as his true self until it was too late. Love had poked her in the eye, and she was now living with the dire consequences.

Her ex-fiancé, Josh, had used her identity without her consent to gain loans, which had put her in so much debt she needed an additional full-time job on top of her profession as a second-grade teacher. It was why she was the manager at Brilliant Books. This supplementary job, which she didn't mind because it was summer vacation, gave her the extra income and kept her mind off of the long to-do list comprised of court dates, lawyer fees, bills, and so forth.

Teegan was split in so many ways and in so many directions, she swore her head, limbs, brain, and heart were all in separate places by the end of the day.

Despite all of this, there was a secret part of her wishing for an adventure. She didn't understand where this desire stemmed from and concluded that it was probably her psyche wanting to escape from responsibilities, betrayal, and heartache. Detach from everything and become free, wouldn't that be nice? She could dream and dream, and maybe one day, it would come true.

That was what she taught her young students. That they should never give up on their dreams, no matter how far-fetched they might seem.

Reach for the stars; you might discover something out-of-this-world.

She should listen to her own advice. But somehow, she didn't have the motivation in her heart to believe in those inspiring words. Was she worthy of all that she wanted? Was it that simple? To acknowledge and move forward, ignoring all her failures and mistakes?

It sucked being an adult. Adults analyzed too much and always came back to the initial thought that always added more anxiety than relief.

Stop it! Teegan scolded herself. *You're better than this. Don't pity yourself. You're a kind and intelligent twenty-seven-year-old woman.*

Everyone made mistakes, she decided. Life was full of them.

So what if she felt a deep calling for adventure? So what if she wanted to scratch an itch that would alleviate all her life's problems? So what if she often heard strange whispers that seemed to echo out of her bones when she was alone? Perhaps it was her parents visiting from Heaven, reminding her to take care of herself and her older brother, Maverick. There were days when she felt she was living in two different worlds, half here and half elsewhere.

Teegan glanced down at her checklist and smiled at her efficiency, at how she could pull off the Artist and Author Fair in a week's time. She'd learned the art of organization from her parents.

God, she missed them so much. They were probably just as disappointed in her as she was in herself. She should have known that love was more than pretty words and a pretty face. She supposed she should thank God for letting her see the truth before she married the jerk.

Putting her clipboard down on the counter, Teegan looked out at the parking lot of the bookstore as a couple exited their car. They held hands as they strode into the nearby bakery. She cursed as the image reminded her of how Josh had also betrayed her in non-financial ways. Teegan didn't have time for childish behavior from a grown man. No more excuses. No more settling for someone who didn't meet her standards. She had ended it.

Why was she still thinking about him? She shouldn't give him an ounce of her energy or time. The best way to move forward was to look the monster in the face. He had betrayed her with his big-breasted trainer and used Teegan's name to sign up for a loan for his lover. These were all glaring reminders that she was done with men.

With relationships.

With trust.

Anger and sadness fractured her heart a little more each time she stared at the facts, so she forced herself to stop and focus on the task at hand. She was a smart and capable woman.

She wouldn't let a few setbacks ruin her life. Nope. Teegan Moore was a survivor.

She didn't need a man telling her what to do, how to do it, or what to be. It was time she focused on her career and what made her happy.

With that thought, Teegan whirled back to examine the event space and smiled at what she had accomplished. Ten authors were setting up their books, giveaways, bookmarks, and so on. Across the room, ten artists did the same with their creations. She waved at her best friend, Steffani Jacobs, who was a participating jewelry designer.

Teegan wiped a bead of sweat from her forehead as she went to the counter and cross-checked the list on her clipboard with the official one in her book. Satisfied that everything was as it should be, she grabbed her bottle of water and sipped, hoping to cool off. The July summer in Springfield was hot, but the air conditioner was working fine inside the bookstore, so why was she so warm?

Steffani approached her. "Are you okay? You're flushed."

"You'd be, too, if you'd been running around like a headless chicken since five in the morning," Teegan replied, straightening out her lilac wrap dress and fixing the braid of her brown hair. Glancing at the mirror on the counter, she noted that highlights would give her hair a new beginning. Maybe next month, when one of several bills would be paid off, she told herself. "How do I look?"

"Beautiful as always," Steffani said and offered Teegan a rectangular gift box. "But you'll look better with this on. I made it for you."

Even though Teegan felt as pretty as a warthog, she didn't want to ruin the moment for her best friend.

"Why? For what?" she asked, smiling. "It's not my birthday."

"It's a just-because gift. You give me those all the time." Steffani pushed back the long, red hair that made her look like a magical fairy queen when paired with her chiffon dress.

Teegan opened the box, and her jaw dropped. "Whoa! This is mesmerizing."

The iridescent raw gemstone was elegantly wrapped with gold wire that twisted into a hook that hung from a gold chain. She ran her fingers over the stone, and a zap traveled up her arm, then all over her body, making her shudder for a moment. "It has compelling energy," she said as she pulled it around her neck.

The pink stone gave off a blue tint when the light hit it at various angles.

"It likes you," Steffani said. "When you have that kind of connection with a crystal, it's special."

"It's gorgeous. I love it. Thank you." Teegan threw her arms around Steffani for a tight hug. "What gemstone is this?"

"Maybe a moonstone? I'm not sure. It was inside that box of old jewelry and knickknacks you gave me. The stone was all brown and covered with dirt, but look at it now, after I cleaned it. That just goes to show you can't judge something by its looks."

Tell me about it, Teegan wanted to say. She'd had no idea what was inside the box of junk she had given to Steffani when Teegan and her older brother cleaned out their parents' garage.

"I really love it. Thank you. You're the best." Teegan held the pendant, adoring it in a way she didn't quite understand.

The soft colors and the way it soothed her were exactly what she needed.

"You're welcome." Steffani stepped back, studying her creation. "It's perfect on you."

From behind the counter, the assistant manager, Lisa, called out to Teegan, tapping her wrist.

Teegan glanced at her watch and realized it was ten minutes until the doors opened. "I've got to go. We'll catch up later."

"You bet." Steffani strode back to her table.

Lisa called over from the window. "Look at all those cars. It's going to be a great fair! All your promotions worked, Teegan!"

"We do what we can to help the community. They've supported us," Teegan said, remembering how much she loved working at the bookstore. She loved the smell of books, of words, and the magic of stories. Books helped her remember her dreams, and that anything was possible. At one point, she even considered opening her own bookstore. She laughed at her silly dreams. But hey, it gave her something to believe in.

Teegan headed over to the Reading Corner, where there was a complimentary water cooler for her customers. She refilled her bottle of water and noticed the moonstone glowed brighter than before. She wasn't sure if it was the sunlight from the window or the light bulbs in the store that made the stone more luminescent. She held up the pendant, and the energy penetrated her skin and coursed through her body. It activated her chakra points as it moved up her spine. She sucked in a breath as the force rushed through her, came to her throat, and exited her mouth with a loud exhale.

A series of melodic chimes rang in her ears. What followed was an odd moment of silence. The soft music that had been playing in the store stopped. She glanced around as people opened and closed their mouths, but she couldn't hear them. Everyone appeared calm and normal, nothing out of the ordinary. Everyone, but her.

What the hell was happening to her? The heat that had been burning her subsided. Still, she took a sip of water, and her ears popped again. A flood of sounds overwhelmed her ears all at once. Her heart drummed along with others. Birds chirped and animals grunted. The wind whistled, and the leaves rustled.

She placed a hand on her forehead, pulled out a chair at the closest table, and sat down. She felt like she had been shoved into some portal and thrown back out like a polished gemstone that was being processed and was never the same again.

This wasn't a panic attack; she knew what those were. She wasn't hyperventilating. She wasn't having abdominal cramps or chest pains. Nor did she have any flashing visions or numbness. She was still in control of the situation.

At least she thought she did until a voice whispered, "Tune in."

She whipped her head around, searching for the source of the voice. Teegan caught Lisa's smile and thumbs up as she opened the door to the store.

Fear crawled up her body as she tried to remain calm. "Who are you?"

Nothing replied as customers flooded in and headed toward the event section.

Chatter crammed the store, but something separated Teegan from the chaos. The moonstone sparkled brighter, confirming it had something to do with this bizarre experience.

Murmurs echoed from all directions, connecting Teegan to multiple conversations.

"Tune in," a gentle female said again. Her voice rose above all the other sounds in the store.

Turning her head, Teegan checked to see who was nearby and didn't see anyone. Nerves pricked her skin. Had she encountered a ghost? "Who are you? What do you want?"

A feather-like gentleness brushed against her ears. "Tune in. Focus."

Her body understood the words before her mind did and

forced her eyes closed to concentrate on the voice. The static sounds faded when she tuned into the correct "radio station."

This time the voice was clear. "Tuck me inside the neckline of your dress. Do it now. Hurry."

Teegan's mouth dropped as she stared at the glowing moonstone that spoke to her. With each word, it glowed.

"Hurry," it repeated with urgency.

There was a motherly calmness to the voice that made Teegan tuck the pendant into her bra.

"Thank you."

Unsure of what was happening, Teegan rose. "You're welcome."

She had to ask Steffani if the stone was some trick. And if not, Teegan wanted to know if Steffani had ever talked to her stones.

As if the day couldn't be any stranger, two men entered the store who looked like they dressed for some sci-fi or fantastical movie with mean faces and long tails. One looked like a green lizard humanoid, while the gray, scaly one possessed two tails. Both creatures looked like they had just stepped off of Planet Scary. Perhaps they belonged to the cosplaying groups from the nearby colleges.

Their shiny clothing appeared modern, with asymmetrical jackets that revealed a purple diamond-shaped tattoo on their chests, right below their necks. In addition to the cosplaying groups, Hollywood often filmed their movies in her town, so she was used to seeing strange characters wandering into her shop.

However, something about the bulky men unsettled her. Goose bumps rose on her arms and neck. Were these men robbing her shop? *They better not.* She wasn't in the mood for them to ruin all her hard work, not to mention all the work from these artists and authors.

Teegan strode over to the event section as the man disguised as the green beast looked through Steffani's jewelry collection.

Their wicked eyes, hideous eyebrows, and angry mouths clawed at her safety. The two beasts—aliens, mutants, or whatever they were supposed to be—exchanged glances and roared with laughter as they picked through the collection. These men had outstanding costumes that looked real with the rows of sharp teeth and long tongue. But as she watched them, their energy slithered around her like venomous snakes. Her body trembled.

The door to the store opened, and in came a blast of fresh energy. The swoosh of fresh air seemed out of place. No one else appeared to notice him. Their eyes were on the gray and green beasts.

He wore a cream-colored shirt under a blue leather jacket with dark jeans. He was well over six feet tall, with chiseled features that were made more prominent from his time in the sun. The sharp cheekbones and strong jawline twisted her stomach in several knots, triggering her sexuality.

Something about him grabbed her and wouldn't let go. Like a leech, it clung and sucked at her curiosity. Perhaps it was the short, dark hair and the determined eyes that held stories that made her want to sit and have a conversation with him. Moreover, it was the way he moved, the way in which he conquered the space in front of him like he owned the place, that made her heart both terrified and excited.

When he spotted the beasts, he moved toward them. For a moment, everything around her appeared in slow motion. The focus on him sharpened, blurring out all other distractions. Her heart hummed, making her blink. The incredible sound it made was like a familiar song she'd heard before. How was it possible that she felt a familiarity about him when she'd never met him?

She held her breath, fearing that if she exhaled, this beautiful man would disappear like a dream. The closer he got, the more sensitive her body grew. Something in her resonated with him on a level she didn't understand.

A strange image flew across her mind. It was too fast and too blurry for her to see. Whatever that image was, it dropped a warmth in her stomach that was heartfelt and instinctive.

"Go with him. Help him," the moonstone whispered.

Teegan glanced down at the pendant. "What? How? What do you mean?"

When it didn't reply, her attention wandered back to the man.

An innate knowing bloomed inside of her. Somehow, she knew this man would change her life. That admission gleamed like a key as the humming in her heart stopped, and the slow motion of time returned to normal.

THREE

Teegan

WHEN THE BEASTS spoke a strange language to each other, Teegan pulled her attention away from the man in the blue leather jacket. At first, the guttural sounds made no sense. But slowly, her brain recalibrated itself, and she picked up on some words: stone, here, and find.

Somehow, her ears and her mind translated the randomness into: "The stone is here. We must find it."

Her eyes widened at the realization of what they wanted and what her moonstone had asked of her. It knew it was in danger. Her heart raced up to her throat. Nausea rose, indicating that something bad was about to happen.

"These your only stones?" the green beast with long hair the color of mud asked with a thick accent. When he reached to look at the jewelry, several silver guns glinted from the inside of his jacket.

Steffani forced a polite smile. "Yes, that's all I've got."

"Liar!" shouted the gray beast with a circular tattoo on his bald head.

When his eyes flared, Steffani flinched back, almost tripping over her own chair.

"Where is it?" He clasped Steffani's arm. "I can feel its energy on you. Don't lie to me."

"Let go of me, you bastard!" Steffani yanked her arm away, but her arm was like a twig compared to his tree-trunk one.

At this point, most of the customers had left the shop except for the few nosy ones who remained to see the situation play out. A few authors and artists tried to intervene, but the green beast pushed them away.

"Get your hands off of her!" Teegan inserted herself between the gray beast and Steffani. She kicked him with her flat shoes. If only she had her killer stilettos on, she'd shove them right up those large nostrils until the sharp heels came out of his eye sockets.

Anger gave her courage, so she clung to that and shouted to the assistant manager, "Lisa, call the police!"

Shock had the beast releasing his grip on Steffani. He reached for Teegan, and she curled her fingers into a fist, trying to punch him before he got to her. He clutched her fist and squeezed.

"Bitch."

Something sharp punctured her skin, but she didn't scream. She let the anger take over. With all her might, she shoved him away with the other hand. To her surprise, he fell two steps back.

His comrade laughed. When embarrassment overcame him, he charged at her.

"I didn't know Artwell from Ensaab enjoys harassing females half his size." The man with the blue leather jacket narrowed his eyes at them.

Artwell and his comrade exchanged a look of surprise that then turned to fear.

"What are you doing here, Kazstrom?" the green beast asked.

Steffani pulled Teegan closer and whispered, "What the hell are they saying? Are we on one of those weird reality television shows? Because if we are, this isn't funny."

"They're looking for something."

Steffani's eyes widened. "What do you mean? You understand them?"

Teegan frowned. Was it possible that she was the only one who could understand them? What language were they speaking? And how was it possible...?

The moonstone.

The stone had activated something in her. She remembered the strange sensation around her throat, ears, and head after she held it. Teegan had so many questions, but no one to answer them.

"What are you doing here, Bartu?" Kazstrom replied, revealing no apprehension.

"We're looking for the Soulstar." The beast that gripped her hand smirked. "My guess is you are too."

The attractive man faced them, his eyes leveled with theirs. "Keep guessing."

Abstract symbols glowed beneath his skin for an instant before disappearing.

As he stood beside Teegan, energy sizzled and would have knocked her off her feet if the bookcase hadn't been in reach. That compelling sensation she had felt earlier returned. For a heartbeat, gravity disappeared and she felt like she was floating from the strong vibration. Did he sense her imbalance? When she stole a glance at him, his expression was unreadable except for his unwavering focus on the beasts.

She'd always been sensitive to energy and had a fascination with mystical things, so she was open to inexplicable phenomena. But this strange event with odd-looking creatures was too surreal for her to accept. She expected a movie director or producer to step forward any minute now.

Despite his magnetism, she didn't forget that beauty often wore a mask. That exact weapon had bruised and broken her. She steadied her breath and joined all the women staring at this beautiful being that was more than a man. She didn't know how that thought inserted itself into her brain. But it made sense.

"We need the Soulstar," Bartu said.

"We all need something." Kazstrom's voice was like honeyed wine accentuated with impressive sexuality. "We all want something."

His gaze met Teegan's, and color changed within his irises. The intensity of his eyes filled her body with a yearning she didn't understand.

FOUR

Kazstrom

WHY DID this human female look familiar to him? He'd never met her before, and yet, his energy recognized hers. Her strong frequency caressed him and had a private conversation with his energy. But right now, he had something critical to deal with.

Kazstrom sensed the Soulstar was in here somewhere. The more he tried to hone in on it, the more dispersed its energy became. It was playing hide-and-seek with him. He had picked up on a strong feminine energy during his search for the Soulstar. Was it hers? He couldn't be sure, as his sensory skills were foggy.

Regardless, this female intrigued him. Not just by her beauty, but by the courageous way she had pushed away Artwell. That was admirable.

Artwell cocked his head and spoke in the universal language, "Why is a Norakian warrior here on Earth? Aren't you supposed to be protecting the Aurora Matrix?"

Not all Ensaab Rebels were stupid, Kazstrom thought. But

he couldn't imagine these rebels wanting the Soulstar for the same reason he wanted it.

"What makes you think I'm not protecting it while I'm here?" Kazstrom smiled and picked up a piece of jewelry. "Why don't we go outside and discuss this further. Do you want me to report you to the Galactic Coalition of Truth? I'm sure they'd love to hear that an Ensaab Rebel is breaking cosmic laws on Earth. I hear that Asteroid Karma has a lot of prison space."

Bartu flared his nostrils. "We don't want trouble with anyone. We're just having some fun with the humans. You know, testing their intelligence."

The brazen brunette with the braided hair who had stood up to Artwell snorted and glared at Bartu. If eyes could tell a story, hers revealed how Bartu and Artwell could die a spectacular death. Kazstrom couldn't help the smile that formed on his lips, nor the increased fascination with this marvelous human female.

But there was no time to digress. He was here for one thing only: the Soulstar. First, he had to convince these Ensaabs that the Soulstar wasn't in the vicinity so he could search for it before another group of aliens arrived. If the Ensaabs knew about it, most likely, other star races would know too.

Kazstrom contemplated if the Soulstar knew it was being hunted and, therefore, had hidden itself. Could a moonstone be that intelligent? He didn't push that idea away; this moonstone came from one of Terrakado's three moons. So, the possibilities were endless.

"The human officials are on their way, so I suggest we get out of here. You don't want your faces blasting all over their TV screens. The Galactic Coalition of Truth would have a field day with the Ensaab government." Kazstrom headed out the door.

"GCOT can go to hell." Bartu muttered under his breath as he followed Kazstrom out.

FIVE

Teegan

WHEN KAZSTROM LEFT with the beasts, a part of her left too. She was delusional or overly exhausted. Or both. She wasn't making any sense at all.

Where did he go with those beasts? What were they up to?

"Are you okay?" Steffani asked while Lisa rushed to lock the front door. "You're pale. Where are the cops when you need them? Why are they taking their damn time, anyway?"

"Probably because they think it's a prank," Lisa commented. She tried to calm down the customers who were still inside the store, while looking out at the parking lot to see if there was a scuffle outside. "It seems they're gone. Good riddance."

Heat hammered Teegan's body while a headache bloomed. "I'm not feeling well."

"Yeah, no kidding. You're paler than a ghost. Why don't you go home? I'll help Lisa close up," Steffani suggested. "I don't think we'll have many customers for the rest of the day. The shoppers who come in will just want to gossip about the event."

Teegan nodded. "You're right. I do need a break."

She wanted privacy to talk to the moonstone. Something told her Steffani had no clue about the moonstone's ability to talk. That stone had come from Teegan's parents' garage, so she scratched her initial idea of asking Steffani.

What did it want from her? Was her brain hijacked by some dark spirits? She'd read about how dark magic could seize control of your body and mind. Was that why she could communicate with the moonstone? Could that be the reason she sensed an inexplicable connection to a complete stranger?

Confusion and anxiety collided and sent her into panic mode. Her chest tightened, and she inhaled several deep breaths to calm her body. Was she going crazy? She had been dealing with extreme pressure, so perhaps everything pushed her into a corner where she was hallucinating. She glanced at her sweaty palms, clenching and unclenching them. She pinched the top of her hand, and pain swelled. She wasn't hallucinating.

But why was all this happening to her? She had so many questions, including how she could understand the beasts' language. She wanted to show that green beast how intelligent she was by ripping off his head and sticking it on a pole for the birds to feast on.

Teegan walked over to Lisa. "I'm heading out. Not feeling well. Steffani said she'll help you close out the store. Are you okay with that?"

"Of course. Please get some rest. You've put in too many hours over the past couple of weeks already. I was wondering when you'd crash."

Teegan tossed her purse into her car and was about to get in when she heard voices from the rear lot. She closed the car door, locked it, and walked toward the voices that came from behind the plaza dumpster. Making sure she was out of sight, she stepped closer and leaned in.

Her mouth dropped open in surprise at the attractive man talking to the beasts. She blinked a few times to ensure the image in front of her was real. Unlike before, the alluring man was now a blue being with vivid abstract symbols that ran down the side of his face and neck. She hadn't been hallucinating about them!

For a moment, she stood in absolute awe as she spied on the three beings. As she listened to their conversations, her mind began to process the reality she was in.

"The Aurora Matrix needs you," the gray beast said with a sly smile. "You should be back home."

Kazstrom angled his head. "Do you know something I don't, Artwell?"

The green beast's eyes glinted. "We know a lot of things. We know that you're wounded and that the Aurora Matrix is damaged."

With lightning speed, Kazstrom wound an arm around Bartu's neck, aiming a silver gun to his head. "Wound or no wound, I can still kill you with ease, Bartu." He pushed the tip of the gun harder into Bartu's head. "Who damaged the bridge? Why? Tell me!"

"Your command means nothing to us. All the Norakian warriors will fall." Artwell glared at Kazstrom choking his comrade. "All of Norak will fall. The rise of the Ensaab Rebellion is here." He spat and charged at Kazstrom.

With a single shot, Kazstrom blasted Bartu's head into bits and leaped away from Artwell's attack. Artwell pulled out a silver blaster, and the two fighters shot at each other. A shot hit the dumpster, and Teegan shrieked and stumbled from the strike.

Artwell's glare raked through her body. She trembled, remembering how she had pushed him. He lifted his blaster and aimed it at her. Frozen by fear, Teegan closed her eyes, thinking she was going to die. Nothing came.

When she opened her eyes, Artwell was on the ground with purple blood pooling beside him. Terror engulfed her, escalating her heartrate. But courage and curiosity pulled her forward. She pushed herself up from the ground and went over to see his body.

Kazstrom flinched and hissed. Had he gotten injured from these beasts?

Artwell choked on his blood, and Kazstrom gave him a few extra blasts to ensure his quick death, then looked over at Teegan. He eyed the moonstone that had become visible around her neck. It glistened in the sun.

Fearing he would yank her necklace off her neck, she covered the stone with her hand. "This belongs to me. You're not taking it."

At first, he blinked, then amusement filled his eyes. "You speak my language? You speak Norakian?"

Did she? It didn't even occur to her what language she spoke.

"I don't know. I'm not sure." Teegan tucked the moonstone back into her bra.

His eyes followed her movement, then he stared past her to something in the sky. Teegan spun around and faced a black double-decker spaceship heading her way. She fell back a few steps and sucked in a breath.

"Is that a real spaceship?"

"Yes."

"Holy shit." She wanted to dismiss the profound image as a special effect usually added in movies, but what floated before her was not part of some Hollywood set.

"You need to come with me. They will kill you for that Soulstar."

"Soulstar?"

Kazstrom pointed at her chest, and the moonstone warmed against her skin.

He let out a whistle, and a black motorcycle roared up to him. The gold accents on the black metal glistened as it purred. The sleek feline shape and headlights resembled a jaguar.

Teegan couldn't just leave with him. She didn't know him. Where would he take her? Would she return unharmed?

The Soulstar warmed her skin again. *Go with him. Help him.*

What did he need help with? Right now, she was the one who needed help.

"That's an Ensaab Rebel spaceship. There are more ruthless aliens than the two I just killed. Come with me."

Aliens, the word echoed in her head.

She never imagined she would ever come face to face with an alien, let alone three in one day. After witnessing the horror from Artwell and Bartu, she didn't want to encounter any more like them. How many aliens were on that huge spaceship? What kind of destruction could they create? If they were anything like the two dead ones, all the people in the vicinity would die. All her friends, coworkers, and neighbors would perish. Her stomach churned at the thought.

Teegan couldn't live with that. Besides, she didn't think the police could protect her if she stayed. Even her FBI brother, Maverick, wouldn't be able to keep her safe.

How would they protect her? Where would they secure her?

Fear and anxiety overwhelmed her like a swarm of bees.

"Hurry, we have little time." Kazstrom reached out his hand to her. Something in his eyes told her to trust him. Something ancient. Something that made the moonstone in her bosom heat once more.

Nerves tumbled inside her as she made her decision. With a trembling hand, she clutched his and swung her legs over the bike. Her arms tightened around his waist as the bike sped off. The warmth from his body embraced her, making her feel safe.

Curiosity had Teegan turning her head, and she cursed herself for doing so. Two more spaceships appeared in the sky like a vicious blemish, desecrating her summer day.

SIX

Teegan

TEEGAN CLOSED HER EYES, trying to squeeze the picture of three spaceships coming after them out of her vision. But the horror clung to her and spider-webbed across her back.

A chill rushed through her body, and she tightened her arms around him. "There are three spaceships."

"I know."

His calmness confused her. When Kazstrom turned slightly, allowing her to see his profile and tight jaw, his assurance portrayed he was used to this kind of danger.

Sirens blasted, and she prayed for everyone at Brilliant Books.

The motorcycle devoured the road. It didn't make the loud noises that accompanied most bikes. Traffic on a Sunday afternoon was light, so the bike sped on easily.

"Where are we going?" Teegan asked.

"To my spaceship, Spectre Seven."

For some reason, the thought of being inside a spaceship

excited her. She glanced back, knowing the enemy had to be closer. It was. A metallic black spacecraft, the size of several buildings, hovered in the sky. It had a purple diamond emblem that resembled the one she had seen on the rebels. This spaceship didn't look like the circular discs that were often depicted in the movies. This had a pointed top and bottom on both levels.

The cars that passed them on the other side of the road didn't appear alarmed. "Can everyone see the spaceships?" Teegan asked.

"No. They made themselves visible to us. They want us to know they're after us."

Kazstrom swerved the bike down a street she didn't recognize. No houses were in sight, just a few buildings in the distance.

"Hold on tight," he told her in a calm and directive voice, like he was used to giving orders.

A loud roar cut through the air as the bike traveled at a speed that whipped her hair everywhere and turned the sky, trees, and ground into a blur. The motion unsettled her stomach, and she fought off nausea. She pressed her face to his back, tightened her embrace, and closed her eyes. For a heartbeat, he smelled like something from a past that had snuck into the present, perplexing her. His scent warmed her body and spoke an intangible love language she couldn't comprehend.

When the bike slowed, she opened her eyes to an outline of what she assumed was *Spectre Seven*, fading in and out of focus. Seconds later, the image cleared, and a magnificent silver spaceship sat on the ground of an abandoned parking lot. It wasn't as large as the terrifying black spaceship that was after them. *Spectre Seven* appeared suitable for at least five passengers, whereas the other one could carry an army.

Teegan glanced back and met any empty sky. "Where are they?"

"Probably went into cloaking mode," he said. "Or they're busy retrieving their comrades' dead bodies."

"They're just giving up like that?" That would be the best outcome.

"No, they're not. They're regrouping."

Nerves whirled in her stomach. "Oh."

A ramp made of light appeared from the wide opening of his spaceship, and Kazstrom accelerated to go up. The bike came to a stop, and he got off to assist her.

Next, she gawked as metal parts from the motorcycle clanked as they connected and formed sections of a jaguar. A tail uncurled, and the headlights morphed into a pair of aqua feline eyes that met hers with keen interest.

She gasped, taking one step back, fearing the animal that was twice her size might view her as a snack.

"No need to fear Warcat. He won't bite." Kazstrom stroked the satin coat of the cat.

The interesting animal that was partially made of metal purred as it pranced off to the far corner of the spaceship, where it plopped down and yawned. Placing a hand on her chest to calm her drumming heart, she stared in disbelief at the fantastical transformation that just took place.

She'd wished for adventure. Perhaps God heard her and delivered this insane event. The adventure she had in mind didn't involve a threat to her life or aliens. Or shape-shifting jaguars. Or a spaceship.

Teegan ran her fingertips over the cool metal wall, then turned in a slow circle. The ship's interior was the size of a studio apartment she had when she was in college. On one side of the ship, several computer screens hummed alongside a desk with a lot of buttons. Virtual screens with abstract symbols and codes floated around. The ship didn't look like the examples on television, cramped with wires, machines, and computers. This spaceship was spacious, like it followed some feng shui decorating method to ensure good energy flow. She stood under a beam of warm light that tingled her skin, but not in a bad way. The atmosphere didn't make her feel cold or scared. There was a classy ambiance to it, including a lovely scent which reminded her of coffee.

The opposite side held a kitchenette and a lounge with velvety sofas in abstract shapes. On one sofa was a pile of books, folders, and opened boxes. She made out a jacket, some pants, and socks in a heap of clothes that sat beside a chair. The disorderly image reminded her of her brother, who needed a maid to help keep his home clean.

Metallic furniture lit up from the electrical currents of whatever was inside it. On a pole hung something that looked like an apron. Her attention swerved over to Kazstrom as he tapped a screen. She imagined this muscular alien cooking and pushed the idea away because she liked it too much.

On the coffee table beside the lounge, a strange plant with long leaves twirled inside a silver pot. As it danced, blue water spouted out from it like a fountain. She was lost in the wonder of the spaceship until her skin tingled from his closeness.

Turning, she met his eyes, and she swore she heard sparks crackle between them. He watched her with an intensity that held her in place. He mesmerized her with those golden eyes that looked like suns. Her fingers itched to touch the dark hair and blue skin. She didn't deny the attraction to this otherworldly being, but she wondered if it was because he had just saved her life. Because her cheeks burned, she forced herself to break the gaze.

"Are you okay?" he asked in a deep and exotic voice with a delicious accent that made him more magnetic.

"Yes, thank you for saving me." Her feet shifted as a slight movement told her the spaceship had lifted off the ground. It wasn't anything like the airplanes she had traveled in. There was hardly a sound. Her ears popped and relief settled in her as they moved away from danger.

His face twitched, and he hissed out an expression that was more obvious now.

Pain.

SEVEN

Kazstrom

PAIN SHOT down Kazstrom's back like lightning blades, forcing several curses out of his mouth. Malastrom! Battling with Artwell and Bartu had torn his injury wider.

"Are you hurt?" she asked, standing beside him as he programmed the ship to cruise while in cloaking mode.

Kazstrom looked at her, and genuine concern swam in her eyes.

His corra skipped again. "It's just a wound. I'll take care of it. What's your name?" He went to a cabinet, retrieved two painkillers, and swallowed them.

"Teegan Moore. Where's your wound? Do you need help with it? Did those rebels injure you?"

So many questions. So curious. So caring, so... damn attractive. She didn't even know him. Her opinion of him would change after he took back the Soulstar. That was the entire purpose of having her on his spaceship, wasn't it? Healing his wound was the main priority right now. The battle for the advancement was only a month away.

Because he didn't need any help, he didn't reply. He pointed to the chairs at the kitchenette. "You can have a seat anywhere, Teegan."

She wandered to a virtual screen. "Where are we going?"

"To Norak." He studied her as she touched the screen, zooming in and out. "I'll take you back to Earth when the threat's gone. I can drop you off right now if you don't want to go with me, but those Ensaab Rebels won't give up looking for the Soulstar."

Her eyebrows furrowed with worry. "Why do they want it? It's just a moonstone. There are a bunch of moonstones all over the world. Why this one?" Her shoulders slouched. "What if I just give it up? Will they leave me alone? I don't need any more problems on my plate."

Kazstrom heard the sadness in her voice, the kind that didn't just happen overnight. Who had hurt her?

"They'll still come after you." He eyed her as she twirled the pendant with adoration. "They'll assume you had a part in killing Artwell and Bartu. There's more to this story than you realize. Artwell and Bartu are rebel soldiers for the Ensaab Rebellion. Someone told them to retrieve the moonstone. I'm going to find out who hired them and why."

More importantly, how did they know the Aurora Matrix was damaged? That energetic bridge was his responsibility. He had kept it safe from harm all these solar cycles. Who would desecrate this sacred bridge in Norak? Too many. The energy from the Aurora Matrix fed out to all living things within Norak like a corra pumping blood to the body. Norak thrived when the Aurora Matrix emerged from the Norak Mountains thousands of solar cycles ago. It had been growing and extending ever since.

Kazstrom vowed to destroy whoever damaged it and sent a message to the Galactic Coalition of Truth, alerting them of Artwell and Bartu's crimes on Earth.

"What are those symbols on your face?" she asked.

He ran a hand down the side of his neck. "Cosmic codes." No one had ever asked him about them before, probably because they were found on many Norakians. "I guess you can say they're my birthmarks."

"They're interesting. It's like they tell a story with their abstract symbols. You know, like hieroglyphics."

The way she made sense of things fascinated him. "Yes, I can see that. But I believe mine are just codes, simple artwork gifted to me at birth."

Teegan didn't speak while she studied his cosmic codes like someone reading a compelling book. He didn't mind the attention at all, especially from her. Her eyes filled with intrigue with every touch, and she bit her bottom lip in deep concentration. He'd pay up all his credits to know what went on in her head as she examined him. He considered asking her, but he didn't want to intrude on her private moment.

Kazstrom let her trace the cosmic codes with her fingers, like an artist admiring a fine sculpture. Her touch sent a thrill down his spine, pooled at his groin, and desire swelled in him. Malastrom! That effect she had on him was quick and forceful, and he didn't even know her. Perhaps he was reacting as any male would to a beautiful female's touch.

She was torturing him. He preferred this kind of torture to the agony on his back.

Kazstrom cleared his throat. "Did you find a story on my neck?"

His words broke her concentration, and she gave him an embarrassed smile. "Sorry for my brazenness. I couldn't help it. They're so intricate."

"No need to apologize. I like your bluntness."

She ambled to a chair, sat down, and gave him an inquisitive look. "What were you doing on Earth? Do you want the moonstone too?"

Straight to the point. He had a weakness for intelligent females. She deserved the truth. "Yes, I want it. I *need* the Soulstar."

"Why?"

"To heal my wound."

Her eyebrows pulled in, revealing she was expecting an answer that was more elaborate, more fantastical.

"Show me your wound." She paused, about to say more, then closed her mouth.

"You have another question for me?"

"Why did you save me? You could've easily yanked the moonstone from my neck and left. But you didn't. Why?"

What do you want from me? That was the real question, he thought, and smiled at her diplomacy.

"Let's just say that since I don't like the Ensaab Rebels, I'd rather side with you. Though I tend to get what I want, I don't steal jewelry. Maybe I'm curious about your story, and about how the Soulstar came into your possession. Maybe I want to study a human female. You must have heard about alien abductions."

She gasped as terror filled her eyes and drained her face of color. "Why do you want to abduct us?"

Kazstrom shouldn't have scared her with that comment, but he needed her to keep her distance. Her questions made him acknowledge too much, and he didn't like it.

What *did* he want from her? Aside from the Soulstar, he wasn't sure. Perhaps it was the Norakian warrior principle to help those in need that made him want to keep her safe.

Guilt gnawed at him. "I don't abduct humans, but there are

some star races that do. I'm not sure why. Maybe they're interested in the human evolution. I have my own way of educating myself, and it doesn't involve abductions or anything cruel or barbaric."

Color returned to her cheeks as her keen eyes remained on him, probably weighing the truth of his words.

Kazstrom took his ship out of Earth's atmosphere and into the Milky Way. He waited for her objection, but something else came instead.

"I'll go with you. I have four reasons. One, I don't want to get killed by those rebels by staying on Earth. Two, I don't want to jeopardize my brother or my friends' lives by placing them in harm's way. Three, I've got a lot of bills to pay and not enough money to do so. This would be the perfect escape, even if it's temporary. And four, I'll consider this a mini vacation until it's time to go home." She paused, looking at the virtual space map. "I know you could very well kill me in Norak. If you do so, please let me enjoy my vacation first. I've had a rough year."

Teegan gave him one look and glanced back to the map, leaving him to think about her reasons and to wonder what had happened to her.

Unsure why he felt the need to explain, he said, "If I wanted to hurt you, I would have done so already. I wouldn't have saved you."

She gave him a warm smile. "I know. Thank you."

His corra skipped. Like the first time he saw her, the rhythm of his corra changed. He didn't want to admit it, but his attraction to her made him feel alive. When she had her arms wrapped around him on the ride back to the ship, her dynamic energy tantalized him, confirming that she was the feminine energy he had picked up on earlier.

Upon recognition, his corra hammered in a way he hadn't experienced before. It was like an internal festivity that both terrified and fascinated him. He couldn't remember the last time he was this attracted to a human, or any female, on this level. He had dated and mated with several females before. None had spoken to his corra this way.

None had made his groin react this quickly.

When she asked to see his wound, she was demanding he proved his truth. He admired her pragmatism and pulled up a chair beside her. "If you want to see my injury, then you need to tell me how you learned to speak my native language."

Teegan held up the pendant. "This moonstone. It changed everything for me today. It changed my life, my body, all of my senses. Right before those rebels entered the store, it told me to hide it. I sensed its urgency, and I listened."

Fascination spiked in him. "It talked to you?"

She nodded. "It had a soothing feminine voice."

The phenomenon baffled Kazstrom. Though he wasn't a sorcerer, he had never heard of anyone conversing with a magical stone. Glancing at the moonstone, he noted it suited her like it was made for her. The soft pink color complimented her skin and eyes.

He met her gaze, and a fierceness he hadn't seen from a distance emerged up close. He couldn't say why, but he was drawn to her eyes. They were like gateways that pulled him in. Purple flecks glittered within her brown irises like tiny stars. She lured him in without doing a damn thing. Sitting inches away, he inhaled her floral scent. Rose, with a hint of lilac. And something else. Something mysteriously seductive.

"There was ringing in my ears, and my body began heating up for no reason. I knew something strange was happening to me, but I couldn't explain it. The moonstone knew danger was coming, and it alerted me," she said, meeting his eyes. "I guess there's a fifth reason I'm going with you. The moonstone said you needed my help, that I should go with you. It made little sense then, but it does now. Maybe I'm supposed to help heal your wound. Something about it makes me trust it."

"That moonstone came from one of our three moons," he said. "And since you mentioned it had a feminine voice, my guess is that the Soulstar is from Farra. Farra has divine feminine energy, whereas Jarra is masculine, and Yarra is the balance of the two energies." He pulled over the virtual screen and showed her the moons.

"Wow, they're beautiful. I love the soft glows," she said.

He nodded. "They add magic to the night sky."

"I also felt something when I saw you—" She snapped her mouth closed and switched the topic. "The Soulstar almost burned my skin when you ushered me to get onto your motorcycle. I was trying to decide if I wanted to die by those aliens or take my chances with you."

Though Kazstrom heard her words, he was more interested in the unfinished sentence. "What did you feel when you saw me?"

Teegan shot him a glance of annoyance that soon changed to a challenge. "I felt like my life was in danger."

You're not a very good liar, Teegan.

Nothing would stop him from finding out the truth to her incomplete statement. For now, he wouldn't press on.

For some reason, Kazstrom had a feeling that retrieving the Soulstar from Teegan wouldn't be as easy as he had thought. The Soulstar had chosen her for a specific reason. It told her to help him. Did the moonstone know something he didn't? Or was it referring to his injury?

In Norak, the citizens prayed to the two Suns and the three Moons. They believed that these celestial bodies were Gateways to the Gods. If he took the moonstone from her, wouldn't that be going against the wishes of the three Moons?

Though he had stopped praying to them when he had been

orphaned, he still believed in a higher power, but he mostly believed in himself. Regardless, he kept an open mind, and the last thing he wanted was to bring darkness upon himself.

Malastrom! How was he supposed to heal his injury now? The poison was making him weak. His muscles were sore and tight, while his reflexes were slow. Not to mention the burning sensation that came and went. How was he going to prepare for the assessment?

How was he supposed to concentrate on his promotion when he was responsible for Teegan's life in Norak?

She fascinated him with her connection to the Soulstar. Perhaps the more he got to know her, an answer would come to help him.

"Now that we know you can speak and understand Norakian," Kazstrom said. "Let's experiment."

EIGHT

Teegan

TEEGAN FOLLOWED Kazstrom over to a circular table where he gestured to the chair covered in aqua velvet. She sat on the comfortable cushion as he pulled up a map in the air that portrayed a massive cluster of stars and galaxies.

She recognized the swirls of galaxies from the science books in her classroom. "That looks like the Milky Way."

"A little, but it's not. This is your galaxy." He pointed to the tiny dot and zoomed in. He moved to another image. "This is Alarus, our galaxy. It's close to the Andromeda galaxy, which is next to yours."

She'd heard of Andromeda before, but knew nothing about it.

"And this is our planet, Terrakado." It was beautiful, in shades of blues and purples. He flipped to a new image. "Norak is the largest region on Terrakado. The rebels you encountered were from the Ensaab region, right here. Then there's Yorri, another enemy region."

He showed her his allies and the entire geography of his planet. She was amazed, like a kid learning something for the first time. She learned that Norak was a regal and powerful area on the planet. Many wanted to overthrow the Norakians.

Kazstrom brought over a device with a speaker. He turned a knob, and a broken voice sounded. "Do you understand that?"

"No, it sounds like a garbage disposal."

He laughed, and her heart soared. "That's an excellent description of the rebels. That's the Ensaabs' native tongue."

"But I understood it in the bookstore," Teegan said.

"Hold on. We'll get to that." He tapped a few buttons. "What about this?"

This was high-pitched with a slight hissing sound. "Sounds like a bunch of snakes hissing or whistling."

His eyes beamed, but she couldn't tell if he was trying to stifle a laugh or was proud of her correct answer.

"Many of the Yorris are reptilian hybrids. I'm surprised you know so much, and at the same time, you don't."

Annoyed, she narrowed her eyes. "I didn't know aliens could insult and praise at the same time."

"I didn't mean it that way. Don't you see? You have a gift without knowing it. Now, let's try the universal language, which was what the rebels used in the bookstore."

"Welcome to Terrakado. I hope you enjoy this marvelous planet." Teegan's mind translated the sentences perfectly.

"With the universal language, you can communicate with everyone on Terrakado. The Soulstar has given you a precious gift." He turned off the device.

Teegan's brows pushed together in confusion. "Why me? I know it wants me to help you. I feel it. But why me? There could be a hundred people more qualified. Like astronomers or anyone who knows more about space and otherworldly things. Or even doctors who have medical training."

She couldn't explain the powerful connection to the Soul-star and Kazstrom. The whole scenario was too bizarre. She couldn't find any logic to it. Perhaps logic wasn't the answer.

With eyes set on hers, he was probably wondering the same thing. "We'll find out," he said. "I understand several human languages, but that's because I've been studying your kind for many solar cycles, which are years to you."

"You've been studying us?" The alien abduction concept popped back into her mind.

What appeared like guilt flashed across his face. "Not the way you're thinking. Like I said before, I don't abduct humans. I study humans through ancient texts and modern research from the Intergalactic Library. I admit my previous visits to Earth have been educational."

Teegan tried to imagine the library. "Your collection of books must be huge."

"It's not just books. It's a collection of artifacts and rare findings from all over the Cosmos in different dimensions. There are ancient rocks, crystals, fossils, plants, and so many other things. Basically, it's like a galactic museum. There are energetic codes embedded in everything that ever existed. This blueprint of energy teaches us about the history of that particular item. And the library offers this knowledge for curious star-beings like myself. I like to investigate things that interest me, Teegan."

Something in the way he spoke her name made her stomach tighten. "And human beings interest you?"

His eyes wandered over her face like an artist studying a masterpiece. "Only the fascinating ones."

Heat warmed her cheeks and traveled down to her neck, but she didn't shy away from this irresistible blue being who made her want decadent things.

A buzzing sounded on his computer.

"Malastrom!" He broke the gaze on her and went to pick up the call.

Teegan smiled for two reasons. Firstly, "malastrom" translated to "fuck" in her brain, and it sounded enticing in Norakian. Secondly, she couldn't stop the vision of his appealing lips kissing her. Both reasons carried the hint of adventure.

NINE

Kazstrom

KAZSTROM DIDN'T APPRECIATE the interruption to his flirtatious conversation with Teegan. The flashing name added to his annoyance. He deactivated the video for the call and only activated the voice.

"What do you want, Bannon?"

"Where are you?" Bannon's demanding tone irked Kazstrom.

Bannon was the assistant to General Moraku, who was Kazstrom's superior. Bannon wasn't an official Norakian warrior, but rather, a warrior who assisted the General with whatever he needed.

"Somewhere in the Cosmos," Kazstrom said, not wanting to give him any information. "Why do you want to know?"

"You can't just abandon your responsibilities and take off. Who's monitoring the Aurora Matrix? Who did you notify about your absence? Who—"

Frustration flared as Kazstrom tried his best to contain his temper.

"Did anyone ever tell you you're an irritating asshole?" Kazstrom asked in a calm voice. "Let me remind you, I don't report to you. I don't appreciate the condescending tone. I'm not irresponsible. What I do on my own time is none of your business. It's no one's business. Not even Moraku's. And if he has an issue with me, have him contact me. Better yet, I'll be in Norak shortly, so I'll come to see him." He let the anger show through his words.

Bannon needed to be pushed back into his lane. A smart individual would know when to back off. Bannon wasn't stupid, but he was a pompous ass who thought he was better than everyone else because of his family ties. His uncle was Elder Kai, one of the most prominent Elders within the Norakian government.

Kazstrom was no saint, but he knew his place. He knew how to perform his own investigation before making accusations. Bannon was overstepping his boundaries. What irritated Kazstrom more was that Moraku didn't seem to mind Bannon's attitude. Kazstrom didn't understand Moraku's disregard for Bannon's behavior.

General Atreyu, Kazstrom's mentor, would never have allowed such disrespect from anyone.

Bannon let out a laugh that sounded like two toads mating in his throat. Teegan winced and chuckled where she sat.

"Don't envy me because Moraku favors me," Bannon said. "If I were you, I'd be very careful, Kaz. One day, you might report to me."

Nobody called him Kaz except his close friends, and Bannon was no friend.

"Keep dreaming, Bannon. I'd rather resign than work for you. If you had checked on the Aurora Matrix, you would have known that Magnetti is monitoring it for me. If you had asked your questions respectfully, I would have told you the Elders already know I'm on a special errand." Kazstrom was grateful he had the video off. To see Bannon's face would only elevate his anger. "Do you not know that I was injured in a recent battle—two weeks ago to be exact—or do you not care, and just want to toss around accusations? In addition, Moraku should know what I'm up to. He was the one who suggested I go on this trip. So do your job and stop wasting my time."

Kazstrom ended the call before Bannon could reply. He sent his warrior brother, Magnetti, a message to triple-check on the Aurora Matrix and report back to him.

Teegan jutted her chin at his vambrace and rolled her eyes. "He sounds like a belching bully."

Kazstrom smiled at the perfect description. "More like a pregnant frog."

Warcat prowled over to Kazstrom. "You didn't refill my snacks."

Teegan gawked in amazement, pointing at Warcat. "He talks."

Warcat curled his tail and stared at her. "I do. So do you."

Teegan just nodded. "I don't know what to say. I've never spoken to an animal before."

Warcat wrinkled his nose. "Say hello. Kaz is right; I don't bite." The aqua eyes brightened. "Unless I have to."

Teegan widened her eyes as the animal circled her, stopped, and peered up like a big, lazy cat, begging for affection. Smiling, she tapped his nose and ran a finger over the metallic plates on the top of his head. "Well, hello to you."

Kazstrom crossed his arms. "It appears he doesn't need me anymore."

She scratched all four of Warcat's ears. "You're a handsome cat with a sense of humor."

Warcat purred. "Thank you." He whirled to Kazstrom. "I'll always need you, especially when I'm hungry."

Teegan let out a joyous laugh that warmed up the entire spaceship.

Kazstrom pulled out a bag of dried meat and dumped it into a large bowl on the floor. The motion aggravated his wound, making him grunt. He needed to clean his wound and reseal it.

"Your snacks are ready."

Warcat devoured his meal without comment.

Kazstrom went back to the lounge, where Teegan played with a small virtual screen. "I want you to understand something. There's going to be danger where we're heading. Like Earth, Norak is full of all kinds of individuals. I'll keep you safe, but I want you to know what you're getting into. I want you to be prepared."

Eventually, he knew the Ensaab Rebels would come to him for retribution regarding Bartu and Artwell. He'd deal with that later. As long as she stayed close to him, he could protect her.

"Danger lurks everywhere. The only danger-free place is Heaven. And we both know that only exists after death, right?" Teegan said. "I'm not really expecting anything. Well, maybe a little adventure."

He arched an eyebrow. "Adventure?"

She shrugged. "I've been living a very routine lifestyle where I work two jobs to pay my bills. That didn't really allow me the luxury to go places." Her face beamed, probably from the adventures playing out in her mind. "I want to try things I haven't done before. See things I haven't seen before. I want to feel alive, you know?"

Her honesty fell onto him, seeping into his veins, his corra. He wanted to make her wishes come true.

"I'll see what I can do." He went behind the kitchenette and poured two cups of coffee, offering one to her. "Consider this your first out-of-this-world delicacy."

Her smile stretched across her face, revealing perfect teeth. She took the cup and sniffed. "It smells good. What is it?"

"Neptunian coffee. It's magnificent, isn't it?"

"No way! Like from the planet?"

Kazstrom nodded. "That's the one."

"Wow. Coffee is every teacher's lifeline." She sipped and let out a delightful sigh that had him staring at her lips. "This is heaven on my lips. I teach second graders, and they have a way of draining your energy."

She sniffed, sipped, and sighed again.

"Really?"

"You didn't catch that in your research?"

He hadn't gotten to that part yet. "What else would I find if I dig *thoroughly*, Teegan?" He loved saying her name. His mouth just discovered a long-lost remembrance.

She gave him a shrug. "Nothing much. I'm boring."

There goes another lie.

There was nothing dull about her. But he'd keep that statement to himself.

"The students are lucky to have you," he said and meant it.

From his observation, she had a protector's energy. She had portrayed that when she stood up to Artwell in the shop. She was probably the kind of teacher who was tough, but also kind.

"Teachers make a difference that lasts a lifetime." He had teachers at the orphanage and General Atreyu to thank for that.

"I hope so." She sent him a glance filled with gratitude. "The rebels called you a Norakian warrior. What exactly do you do?"

She remembered details about him. What else was inside that interesting brain of hers?

"The Norakian warriors are like the CIA's special task force of your country. My warrior brothers and sisters carry out secret missions on top of our regular responsibilities. I'm tasked to protect the Aurora Matrix. My warrior brother, Hadano, used to assist me, but he works on Asteroid Icarus now. The Aurora Matrix is an energetic source for Norak. I make sure it's safe from invaders."

"There are female warriors?"

"Yes. We're not sexist." He leaned against the counter where he could study her features. She had a few freckles that dotted her face like beauty marks. "Every gender can train to be a warrior. Becoming a Norakian warrior isn't just based on fighting skills, war tactics, or strength. It requires a well-rounded education, hence my studies on humans. Knowledge is power. That's a universal statement."

"And it's an accurate statement," she said.

"Like Earth, Norak has its problems too. Just different problems."

"That's life everywhere, I suppose."

Kazstrom loved the casualness of their conversation. Like breathing, it flowed effortlessly. Teegan was a human who could speak his language, and he was a star-being warrior from a galaxy the people of her planet didn't know existed. And yet, their conversation seemed so normal.

So right.

"This is as close to Neptune as I'll ever get." She sipped again and purred. "It's like drinking magic. It's the best coffee I've ever had."

"You're welcome." He flinched as pain stabbed at his back.

"You need to take care of that wound, and you need to show it to me, remember?" she reminded him.

Kazstrom wanted to protect her from the horrifying sight. "It's not something you'd want to see. Once you see it, you can't unsee it."

"I'm a big girl," she said, placing down her cup of coffee. "If I didn't want to see it, I wouldn't have asked. Show me."

"Teegan..." The wound wasn't something he was proud of.

Worse, he didn't want her to see him this way. Not that he was vain or anything, but a warrior had pride in the body he'd worked hard to maintain. Now there was a huge blemish running across his back. He had done his best to seal up the wound prior to this trip, but he knew the battle with the Ensaabs had made it worse.

"I have an older brother who used to get into fights when he was younger. I've seen injuries." She got up from the chair and stood inches from him. "Don't be shy."

"I'm not," he said too quickly.

She angled her head. Her kind, brown eyes widened and waited.

"I need to clean it and add a new sealant. Maybe you can help with that." He wanted to see if she could stomach the gore.

"Okay," she agreed.

Kazstrom grabbed the care kit, offered her a pair of gloves to protect her hands, and performed a quick demonstration on his arm of how to clean and seal the wound. Next, he sat on a chair with his back to her. He removed his jacket and knit top, tossing them onto a chair. She gasped and traced his skin with her fingertips.

"You have so many scars." Her voice was low. Her fingers touched several old scars that no longer bothered him.

When she came to the current injury, she was extra careful. "It looks like someone carved a deadly weapon into your back. Who did this to you?"

Her gentle touch soothed and cooled the flaming cut.

"A Yorri commander who destroyed a village near our border. His sword was poisonous. The wound wasn't this big in the beginning. Now it's grown. I tore it open during my fight with Artwell and Bartu. The poison will eventually kill me before anything else."

Silence hung for the next few minutes. He watched her reflection in the mirror on the wall and took in all her features. The crease between her brows, the concentration in her eyes, and the softening of her face when she touched a sensitive area fascinated him. She cleaned the wound with such kindness and tenderness that, for a moment, he didn't mind the pain at all. If the wound had been left to him, he would have cleaned it quickly and with less gentleness.

The healing ointment began to cool his enflamed skin and Kazstrom sighed with relief.

Teegan sprayed a sealant over the wound, then she placed everything back into the kit, tossed the gloves into the trash, and faced him. "You do need the Soulstar."

"Yes."

She considered him for a while, as if she could see through the depths of him, through the dark and the dire. As if she witnessed something he didn't want anyone to know.

She pursed her lips and her eyes gleamed. "I have an idea."

"What is it?"

"I'll ask the Soulstar if she can heal you."

TEN

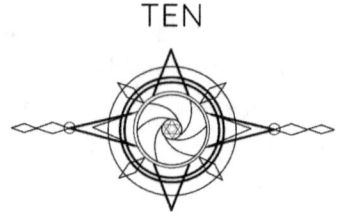

Teegan

WHEN TEEGAN HAD LOOKED into Kazstrom's eyes, she had recognized loneliness that made her want to embrace him. The loneliness was subtle, like the secrets of a summer's night that grabbed with curiosity and wonder. It made her want to know everything about him. In a strange way, she saw herself in him. A longing that couldn't be described in words.

She took off the necklace and held the moonstone pendant in her hand. It glowed, sending iridescent sparkles around her palm. Its energy warmed her skin just the way Kazstrom's presence warmed her body.

The pulsation of the Soulstar grew stronger. With her fingers, she rubbed the stone and asked in the English language. "Are you there?" She repeated the steps as she had done in the bookstore.

It didn't take long for the stone's reply. "Yes."

The Soulstar glowed brighter.

Hope surged in Teegan. "I have a friend who's injured. He needs your help. Can you heal him?"

Kazstrom pinched his eyebrows as his gaze darted from Teegan to the glowing moonstone.

"I can't hear her," he whispered.

The moonstone sent a burst of energy out, circulating the entire room. "He cannot hear me because my words are meant for you. I chose you for a reason. I cannot heal him because my powers are reserved for another purpose."

Teegan's heart sank.

Kazstrom probably saw the disappointment. "What did she say?" His tone remained calm and controlled.

Teegan placed her hand on his arm. "She can't heal you because she needs to save her powers for another purpose. You can't hear her because her words are meant for me."

What appeared to be discouragement and setback flashed in his eyes, but warmth replaced them quickly, like a leader who knew it was time to modify his plans to suit the situation.

Kazstrom covered his hand over hers, giving her a comforting nod. "I like her no-nonsense attitude."

Teegan should be the one comforting him, not the other way around. How was he going to survive? There had to be a way.

The Soulstar's response had her wondering what its initial message to her could mean. How did it want her to help him?

She turned back to the Soulstar. "If you can't assist him, is there another way to heal him?"

"He already knows who can help him. He was misguided." The Soulstar sent an extra burst of light into the room. "The Aurora Matrix is in danger. I need your help to find a door."

"A door? What door? Why me?"

Kazstrom grabbed her hand in a protective gesture. The contact of his hand over hers with the moonstone sent a powerful jolt through her body. The jolt sent them both stumbling apart. Kazstrom clutched her arm, stabilizing her.

With the moonstone still in her hand, Teegan asked, "What just happened?"

"Find the door. You will know what to do..." The voice faded.

"Where do I start?"

The Soulstar's luminescence disappeared, along with the pulsing energy.

Kazstrom looked at her. "What did she say to you?"

"She said the Aurora Matrix is in danger. She wants me to find some door."

His jaw tightened as concern swam in his eyes. That reaction was more prominent than when she told him the Soulstar couldn't heal him.

ELEVEN

Kazstrom

CONCERN SPIKED in Kazstrom for the Aurora Matrix. The energies from the two suns and three moons helped power the Aurora Matrix. There was a cosmic connection between the bridge and the moonstone. What the Soulstar revealed was sacred information. A warning.

The Aurora Matrix was the lifeline of Norak. The sacred energy that made up the bridge fed the entire Norak region with vitality. Norak was his home. The residence to many families who had come from all over the Cosmos when their sanctuaries were destroyed because of war or star explosions. He had a responsibility, a mission of loyalty, to protect this home at all costs.

Concern flashed across Teegan's face. "Are you all right?"

"Not really. If the divine bridge is in danger, so is everyone in Norak," Kazstrom said as questions circulated his mind.

This sacred moonstone didn't just pick a random human for

a task. It had chosen Teegan for a special reason. Whatever it was, it had to do with the Aurora Matrix.

"She said there's a door I need to find," Teegan said. "She made it sound like the door is connected to the bridge."

He let out a loud curse and sent Magnetti another message, asking him to look at every corner of the Aurora Matrix and perform a frequency reading for the entire bridge.

Whatever was happening to the bridge wouldn't be easy to discover. Kazstrom would have to investigate further when he returned.

When he was done directing Magnetti, he turned to Teegan. "It appears you have an important role here. The Soulstar chose you because she believes you can help the bridge. Are you willing to help me protect it? There are a lot of innocent lives at stake."

"I'll help." She didn't hesitate one iota.

"You might die."

"You *are* dying," she retorted, gesturing to his wound. "How are you tolerating the pain?"

"Battles, death, wounds, and pain are all part of being a warrior. Painkillers help the pain. I'm not used to revealing my weaknesses to those around me."

"You don't need to hide your pain from me. I'm not your enemy," she said as hope glimmered in her eyes. "Oh, the Soulstar said something else. She said that you know who can help you, and that you were misguided. What does that mean?"

Her excitement lifted his mood. Kazstrom knew someone who could assist him, but he didn't want to intrude on her busy schedule. Furthermore, he had thought his poisonous wound was beyond her treatment ability. He didn't know why he hadn't considered her first.

When he first acquired the wound, he had been in extreme

pain, and logic had run off somewhere when he was told the Soulstar was his only solution.

Kazstrom's nostrils flared at the notion of the misguided information. Could the Soulstar be wrong? Was it being intentionally misleading? Or was it a genuine mistake? He had a lot to think about before he confronted the star-being who had been adamant about the Soulstar being the only option for his survival.

Teegan waited for an answer, looking at him with her big brown eyes. He gave her the easy one. "There's a healer who might be able to help me. Her name is El Lara. She's a Priestess of the Elseon Grove."

"That's wonderful news! Any opportunity is better than no opportunity." Genuine relief sparked across her face, and he didn't know what to do about his fondness for her. He recalled the powerful jolt that had coursed through his body earlier. Their combined energy was so robust, he felt it at the roots of his hair. His skin hissed out a sound that hummed in his ear.

What the solar storm was that all about?!

Kazstrom didn't want, need, or have time for any distractions other than protecting the Aurora Matrix, obliterating the wound on his back, and attaining that promotion. But here he was thinking about Teegan, acknowledging the powerful urge to keep her safe. For a moment, the thought of her safety rose above all else. Surprised at that, he blinked and brought himself back from wherever his mind had meandered to.

She had no idea what was being asked of her. The Soulstar's request for her to find some damn door was no small feat.

"May I see the moonstone?" he asked.

"It went quiet after that weird power surge." She dropped it into his palm.

Kazstrom examined it, and she was right. He didn't sense any energy pulsing from it. Did he accidentally cut off its frequency? He had been concerned about Teegan, and he didn't think about the consequences of touching it.

"I hope we didn't damage its frequency." He placed the necklace over her neck, and pain raked down his back.

He tried not to show the discomfort even though he knew the poison was escalating.

"Is it the wound?"

Somehow, she knew. Nodding, Kazstrom tapped the button on the keyboard of the virtual screen. "Just a minor distress." That couldn't be further from the truth, but he could handle it. She had enough on her mind.

The dark shades that had concealed the panoramic windows on his spaceship cleared, revealing a cosmic landscape. The background was a dark canvas with splashes of colorful nebulae that took on abstract shapes. Within the sea of colors, stars twinkled. Beauty and peacefulness overwhelmed her, lifting her spirit. In that moment, the Universe bewildered her, making her insignificant in comparison to everything else in front of her.

She gasped. "Wow."

Rushing over, she sat down on the window seat. The wonder in her eyes reminded him of how he used to view the world before thieves killed his parents, how he had believed that anything was possible, that there was magic everywhere, that he was worthy of all that was good.

That had all changed in an instant. Now, he viewed the world for its many facets. As a warrior, he had to sharpen that skill to survive. Dark corners often lingered around that which was full of light.

Because Teegan was the light that came to assist him, he knew darkness would also want to suffocate that radiance.

TWELVE

Teegan

TEEGAN DIDN'T DARE BLINK, fearing she'd miss a shooting star or an asteroid with a squirrel-like animal riding it as it flew by.

"What are those things? What are they doing?"

Kazstrom stood beside her. "Bush Tails. They're daring—more like stupid—beings that love to asteroid-race."

"Asteroid-race? Is that a sport or form of entertainment?" She stared at a group of fast-moving asteroids in all shapes and sizes with various versions of Bush Tails on them. The way the asteroids flipped, turned and clashed made her think of drag racing.

"Both, I suppose. It's for those who desire wild adventures." He tossed her a sarcastic glance.

She rolled her eyes. "I want adventure, but not like that. I want all my limbs intact."

She leaned back against the metal wall, sank into the plush

velvet seat, and looked around, allowing the universe to charm her. Moments like these made her life and issues appear so trivial compared to all that was out there.

Even though she was sitting inside a sleek spaceship that belonged to the most attractive blue alien, while watching strange animals asteroid-race among a million twinkling stars, she still hadn't grasped the entirety of it all. Not yet, anyway.

There was so much to take in. She needed time.

In the distance, a cluster of bright blue stars twinkled. She'd seen their formation before. "What are those stars over there? They look familiar."

Crossing his arms, Kazstrom said, "That's the Pleiades, part of the Taurus constellation. We have friends there."

"What kinds of friends?"

"Star-beings like me. Or aliens, as humans like to call us."

She shouldn't be surprised, but she was. "Are there many of your kind out here?"

Kazstrom nodded. "Life exists everywhere."

"Do you prefer being addressed as a star-being, an alien, or super-man-beast?"

He let out a chuckle. "Most of us Norakians find the word 'star-being' more dignified."

She made a note of that.

A quiet moment passed as they watched the stars. Then he asked, "Are you scared?"

She had carried that terror with her from the moment the Ensaab Rebels entered her bookstore. But he wasn't asking about that.

"Yes, I am. You'd be, too, if you were heading to a new planet, a new world you know nothing about. Not to mention, not knowing anyone."

"You know me." His eyes seared into her with an intensity that warmed her blood. "I'll do my best to protect you. If what the Soulstar says is true, then you're agreeing to a dangerous mission."

"I know." Teegan kept her gaze on a pink nebula that looked as though a phoenix were emerging from it.

"I've been protecting the Aurora Matrix all these solar cycles with my warrior brothers and sisters. We've kept enemies away as best as we could. But as the bridge expands and grows stronger, power-hungry star races might find a way to take it."

Teegan tried to imagine how one could remove a bridge. "You mean like dismantling it?"

"They can't literally take the bridge from its location. It's an energetic bridge that's anchored into the Norak mountains. But they can try to take over Norak." His jaw steeled at those words. "I'll fight that to my last breath."

"Oh." She didn't like the picture that formed in her head. Though she hadn't lived through any wars, she saw enough on television to know that violence and death would come to the innocent. "What if I fail? What if I can't find that door?" She couldn't help the despair that snuck into her voice.

Kazstrom turned to her. "Then we find another way. You're not in this alone. You have me and my legion."

"I've asked myself many times, why me? I don't have any special skills or magic. I'm sure someone from your planet can assist the Soulstar better."

He sat down next to her and the cushions shifted. "I have questions too. But the answers aren't ready to be revealed yet. There are certain things in the Cosmos that none of us can understand. All we can do is trust the events that are thrown at us." He wrapped his fingers around her chin, shifting it from side to side. He examined her face like an inventor admiring a splendid creation. "Are you sure you're human, and not some goddess in disguise from a star system even I don't know about?"

She snorted a laugh that was unladylike. "I'm definitely not a goddess."

"I disagree."

His low voice sent a series of nerves tumbling inside her. His blue skin darkened and the abstract codes on his face glowed.

"You should have a talk with my ex-fiancé. He'll convince you otherwise," she said with a half laugh.

Something deadly sparked in his eyes. "Did he hurt you?"

"Not physically. But there are other ways to hurt those closest to you without raising a fist." She looked at him, trying to see why he was so curious about her personal life. All she saw was herself at the center of his amber irises. "He didn't love me the way I thought he did. He found another 'goddess' to love."

Kazstrom stared out at a green cluster of stars, probably processing her statements.

When he faced her, he said, "Some humans are just plain stupid. Your ex-fiancé was unaware of what he had. His loss."

Teegan's heart fluttered, the oddest combination of joy and anxiety. How could this star-being, this exceptional man who didn't even know her, say all the right things?

It was his turn to share. "What about you?"

"What about me?" He tried to play ignorant.

"I just shared a part of my personal life with you. It's only fair that I get to know something about you too. Besides, we'll be spending a lot of time together on this mission. So it's nice to know who I'm dealing with."

"Okay. I don't have an ex-fiancée. I'm not attached to any mate. I've been so dedicated to my duty and training that I haven't had time for female friends." A pause, then, "However, there's someone who's caught my interest." His eyes gleamed. "She's beautiful, smart, *very* curious, and has all the qualities of a goddess."

Her pulse quickened and heat rushed, pooling at her core. She didn't know how to respond, so she didn't.

The smirk remained on his face. "It would be best to think of this mission as an adventure. A challenge. I like challenges." He got up and returned to his computer screens. "I like to win."

"I imagine you do," she said. How many female hearts had he won?

Teegan's attraction to him increased the more she spoke to him. But he didn't need to know that. He had to focus on his health, and she had to focus on locating the elusive door for the Soulstar. More importantly, she wanted to know why she was chosen for this task. What was her connection to the moonstone?

About twenty minutes later, Kazstrom said, "We're approaching Terrakado."

On the virtual screen, Teegan zoomed in on a planet with large asteroids in the distance. Three moons floated nearby. From what she could speculate, the amount of land and water on Terrakado was about fifty-fifty. Earth had more water.

"It's a beautiful planet," she said. "I love the different shades of blues and purples. Is it the same size as Earth?"

"Terrakado is twice the size of your planet."

Teegan dropped into a state of amazement when the two suns beamed at her. They glowed brightly, like eyes watching over the planet. "Your suns are magnificent." One was slightly smaller than the other, but that could be because of the distance between them.

"They are one of many divine creations of the Cosmos. They help sustain life on our planet, just like your sun."

"Does your planet orbit both suns?"

"Yes, it has a wide circumbinary orbit."

Spectre Seven entered Terrakado's atmosphere and veered around some tall mountains. Teegan gasped at the magic of the sacred bridge. The Aurora Matrix stood out from everything else in the area. Its energy extended all the way up into the sky, like the aurora borealis, where colors of blues, greens, pinks, and purples blended into a magical ribbon that wound around the land.

From above, Norak was the most colorful region of all the regions she had passed. So much vibrancy, so much life, radiated from it. The Aurora Matrix was like an iridescent strip that came from an enormous mountain and ribboned around a city, and came to a sudden stop like it was unfinished.

"I see why foreign invaders would want Norak."

Kazstrom stood beside her. "It's mesmerizing, isn't it?" His shirt, blue leather jacket, and jeans were now replaced by what she assumed was the Norakian warrior armor.

In awe, Teegan rose from the velvet cushion and gave him a once over. He appeared so regal, so powerful—absolutely stunning. With the gleaming sword on his back, he portrayed a god with midnight hair. She loved the contrast of it against the blue skin. The gold metal plates tailored around his shoulders acted like protective shields that enhanced his already large biceps. The undershirt was chain mail, but a closer inspection showed that it was composed of some kind of high-performance textured fabric whose surface bounced back when she poked it. A pair of black pants with the same high-performance attribute as the undershirt made the muscles stand out on his thighs and butt.

She peeked at his behind and enjoyed the view.

Metal plates wrapped around his knees, while a pair of dark boots conformed around his calves and feet like weapons.

"May I?" She gestured toward the intricate forearm guard with flashing symbols that resembled a sacred language.

Though she understood the Norakian and the universal language orally, she didn't connect to these symbols.

Nodding, he lifted his arm for her examination. "This vambrace is made from the finest Norakian alloy for strength and durability. Would you like to try it on?"

She laughed. "God, no. I just want to touch it."

And touch you, she wanted to say.

She ran her fingers over his vambrace, traveling up to the exposed blue skin of his arm. The color reminded her of the sea. Powerful and filled with secrets. At the same time, wild and dangerous. The taut muscles that were twice the size of her palm begged to be touched. Without hesitation, she obliged and squeezed. The cosmic codes glowed on his arm. She continued to caress his skin, and the codes brightened even more.

She stole a glance at him, and his eyes pinned on her. So much intensity, so much desire stirred in them.

Color flushed her cheeks. "Sorry. Did I squeeze too hard?" She dropped her hand.

"Not at all. I like the way you examine me. Is this how you examine your men and their clothing?"

She laughed. "No. You're the first." She should stop talking.

"Is it because you're attracted to me?" He should stop asking questions.

A flirtatious look glittered in his eyes. With that kind of confidence and audacity, her resistance to him weakened.

Admitting her attraction to him would be stepping into unstable territory, one she had promised to stay away from. She wasn't ready for a relationship. More importantly, she wasn't ready to open her heart again. If things didn't go well, she didn't know if she could handle another heartache. She didn't want to complicate matters. She had to keep her distance to make things easier when it was time for her to go back home.

"Are you always this confident?" she asked. His eyes were like windows that showed her possibilities.

He didn't answer. Instead, he gripped her chin with his thumb and finger. "May I?"

He had allowed her to explore him when she had asked. Although she agreed to his request, she couldn't move a muscle, and no words came from her mouth.

THIRTEEN

Kazstrom

KAZSTROM GRINNED when he sensed her racing corra. He loved her reaction to him. All nerves and vulnerability with a dash of excitement. Her eyes brightened, and her mouth was slightly open, but no sounds came.

He considered himself a confident male. A confident warrior who won battles. He knew what he wanted. And right now, he wanted a taste of her.

When she didn't reply, he asked again, "May I?"

He hoped she'd say yes because a "no" would devastate his curiosity.

As soon as she muttered a soft yes, he lowered his lips to hers. The softness of her made him think of the Venusian clouds with their lovely colors and grace. Her hands braced against his broad chest. His mouth moved over her lips, teasing and seducing until she moaned. He slid his tongue between her lips and matched her eagerness.

She tasted like a long-forgotten dream tucked away on some

unknown planet. Another exploration revealed an irresistible sweetness that made him crave more.

Teegan responded to him with the same passion. Heat exploded and throbbed between them. He broke the kiss to wander over her cheek and settled at the junction of her neck and shoulder where he claimed it with several more kisses.

"Kaz." Her breathing heightened as she sighed his name.

Kazstrom loved the way it sounded from her lips. He lifted his head to look at her. "I'm going to enjoy getting to know you. I love how you say my name."

With her lips a little swollen from the assault of his, distress appeared in her eyes. "I don't know what to do about you."

"Think of me as the bonus to your 'adventure.' You get to decide what you want. I won't push you. Most of all, I won't hurt you." Because he knew about her past, he understood the caution. "I'll be honest with you. I thought a taste of you would satisfy me after just one kiss. I was wrong. I want more, Teegan. Whenever you're ready for it."

"You don't know me."

"But I will." He brushed the loose strand of hair away from her face. "For the moment, I know enough."

Things could get tricky between them, but he couldn't help this yearning to be close to her. Not when his corra was beating like a storm. Not when the shared energy between them gave him an inexplicable boost to his cellular structure. His muscles tightened and relaxed in response to this newness.

He didn't forget his wound, his responsibility to the Aurora Matrix, and his opportunity to get promoted. He hadn't wanted any distraction that would deter him from achieving his goals, but Teegan wasn't a distraction; she was the calm within the chaos, the silence in space. There was more to her, and he wanted to find out everything about her.

He went back to his computer and prepared to land. "Let's get ready. You're about to step on foreign soil."

"Where are we heading?" she asked.

"We're going to visit my friend, El Lara." What would the Priestess think of Teegan? Would El Lara be able to heal his wound as the Soulstar had suggested?

FOURTEEN

Teegan

THEY FLEW past a village and landed in an open field.

Before exiting the spaceship, Teegan turned to Kazstrom. "Do I need to wear something to help me move and breathe? A spacesuit? A mask? Is there enough oxygen here? Is it the same kind of oxygen that's on Earth?"

She probably sounded like an idiot, but she didn't care.

"You should be fine. Yes, it's the same oxygen, just on a higher frequency. Take slow breaths to help you acclimate."

Teegan got off *Spectre Seven* and inhaled a deep breath, closing her eyes to concentrate on her body's reaction. Energy coursed through her lungs, reminding her of a soothing yoga session where she could breathe easily. Opening her eyes, she stood on the flat, asphalt-like ground and checked her equilibrium. She didn't wobble or feel dizzy. Her heart rate calmed, like a normal day.

Satisfied that her body had adjusted well, she glanced around. Spaceships in all shapes, sizes, and metallic colors docked in an organized sequence. She imagined invisible lines marking their spots to regulate all the incoming and outgoing traffic to maintain safety within the spaceship hub.

In the distance, giant mountains stood like protective gods with pink, blue, and purple trees accentuating the landscape. A few green trees squeezed into the mix.

"Welcome to Norak's largest city, Nouridan. This is one of our many Aero Terminals," Kazstrom said, with Warcat right beside him.

Warcat's coat of black and gold deepened. This planet's energy probably gave him an automatic color boost.

Large ships with three or four levels flashed in, while some flashed out like magic, making her blink to ensure she actually saw what she thought she saw.

"How can they flash like that?" She pointed to the massive spaceships.

"It's their cloaking modality. It's to keep them invisible if they don't want to be seen."

The advanced technology baffled and intrigued her. *Earth has a lot of catching up to do.*

A group of humanoid citizens and animals in various colors with multiple eyes, legs, tails, and heads strode by. A few robotic humanoids also crossed their path and paid no attention to them. She didn't see any humans.

A sleek car that resembled a long fish with dark windows flew above her. Several more automobiles that looked like abstract animals flew by. One longship that resembled a centipede, carrying several star-beings, floated by with its many legs. Could that be their version of public transportation?

Despite the busy atmosphere, there wasn't a lot of noise. The air traffic didn't produce a lot of exhaust as she had expected. She inhaled a breath, and her lungs rejoiced the way they did when she went hiking in the woods. She didn't have any trouble adjusting to the atmosphere here. The clean air energized her body. As on Earth, the sky was blue, but the clouds had more texture. The soil was brown, and the rocks came in all colors. There were more shades of blue and purple, which was probably why the planet appeared bluish purple from space.

"Am I the first human here?" Teegan asked.

"No, there have been a small number of humans that have passed through Norak. My warrior brother, Hadano, fell in love with a human psychiatrist about five solar cycles ago. They live on Asteroid Icarus now. I haven't met her yet."

If she wasn't the first, then there shouldn't be a need to keep her presence hidden, right? "Then it should be okay for me to roam without trouble?"

"Norak is an open and welcoming region, kind of like your country. We have many star-immigrants from all over the Cosmos living in Norak. But there are some individuals who might cause trouble, especially when they know you're new to the area. It's better to be safe than sorry."

Teegan's eyes followed two blue humanoids with yellow ponytails walking across the road, each holding a colorful drink as they chatted. The happy image tightened her chest as she missed her friends.

"Ready? Hop on." Kazstrom was already seated on Warcat.

She had been so in awe of her surroundings, she hadn't noticed Warcat had transformed into the motorcycle. She would need new clothing if her regular mode of transportation was going to be a motorcycle. A knee-length dress wasn't appropriate attire, not to mention that she needed to blend in with normal Norakian fashion.

Once she was situated, Kazstrom took off on a road that had glowing signals embedded in the cement.

A monowheel that hovered about a foot above the cement slowed beside them.

A purple star-being with flappy ears smiled. "Greetings, Kazstrom. Thank you for your donation to the Cosmic Corra Orphanage. Will you be stopping by soon? The kids miss their warrior."

"You're welcome, Fen," Kazstrom said. "I'll stop by as soon as I can."

Lifting one flappy ear, the purple being eyed her and smiled. She smiled back.

"That would be nice. The children would like that." He nodded to Kazstrom and spiraled away.

The geometric-shaped homes or buildings came in various sizes and heights. Some were brick, while others were metal. Some were anchored to the land, while some were elevated like floating homes. The entire scenery was so magical. She couldn't stop admiring the wonder of it all.

"We're taking the minor roads to avoid speculation and explanation." Kazstrom turned onto a small dirt road with mostly gray and white rocks. "The fewer people know about a human visitor, the better. Curiosity sometimes leads to trouble."

Agreeing, she tightened her arms around his waist and remembered the kiss they had shared. She didn't know where their relationship would go from here. Her heart told her to let it be and not analyze. Something deep within her core told her to trust him.

Kaz was right. This could be the perfect adventure with the perfect love affair. She never liked the word "affair" because it had a negative connotation, indicating that the relationship was only temporary. But perhaps that suited her current situation. Eventually, she had to go back. Maverick and Steffani would be looking for her soon.

But for now, she could enjoy this temporary romance from

another world. *What happens in Norak stays in Norak.* She pressed her cheek against his back and listened to his heartbeat. Her chest tightened a bit—nothing uncomfortable, just different. Each time his heart thumped, hers responded. This connection made her feel close to him in some strange way.

About twenty minutes later, they came to a wide fissure that separated two landmasses. On the opposite side, a curtain of energy draped down from the sky, creating a barrier that kept out intruders. A single bridge allowed passage between the two terrains.

Kazstrom sped up onto the bridge. Up close, she noted the bridge was made of moving rocks held together by something unseen. Below the bridge was a body of water. She estimated the bridge covered about two to three miles.

As they drove off the bridge and continued on a dirt path, Teegan turned back and noticed the bridge fading. Five minutes later, the motorcycle slowed as they entered a woody area where lush vegetation grew. Trees with pink and purple leaves brightened the area. Blue and purple bamboo swayed behind white rocks. Green shrubberies with large leaves and fragrant flowers welcomed them. A pink bloom that was twice the size of her hand drooped beside her. Music sprang from it. When she glanced inside, a bug with several eyes and hands banged on a set of drum-like instruments. She smelled rain and rivers—all the things that assisted life.

Teegan and Kazstrom got off of the motorcycle. Warcat shifted into his jaguar form and accompanied them as they made their way through the path that belonged in a fantasyland. Enormous creatures loomed, with long necks, long legs, and narrow arms that drifted as they rearranged the vines and tree limbs that had fallen too low.

An automobile made from leaves, twigs, and metal roared over, with a slim plant-being with large eyes sitting in the driver's seat. The creature turned to Kazstrom. "Would you like a ride?" The plant-mobile had seating ample enough for four individuals.

"We're good, Plantiss. But thank you. I'm showing our new friend, Teegan, around Elseon Grove."

Plantiss nodded to her and smiled. She returned the same gesture.

Kazstrom placed his hand on her back as she stepped over a log filled with adorable creatures gazing at them.

"I feel like I'm in a magical world," she said.

"El Lara is an amazing priestess. This place flourishes because of her, and this Grove is the reason Norak is a gem to Terrakado."

Teegan gasped when an island floating in the sky appeared. "Oh, my goodness! What is that?"

"El Lara's home."

"I've never seen an island in the air before." Mesmerized, Teegan gazed up at the white stone house, tree, and waterfall that dripped sparkling water to the pool below it. Roots covered in flowers dangled, swaying back and forth as birds and butterflies played with them.

"The Elseon Grove is different from the hustle and bustle of Nouridan. The energy of the Aurora Matrix feeds the grove too. The grove is closed off to the public."

A growl sounded somewhere, and Warcat darted after it.

"How come you get to come here?"

"I'm a Norakian warrior. I have access to everything." He smiled. "And now you can benefit from it because you're with me."

You're with me. Those words did something to her insides and had her placing a hand over her stomach to soothe the quivering.

"What brings you here, Kazstrom?" A beautiful blue being

emerged from the woods on the back of a purple parrot that was three times her size. She had long white hair with purple high-lights and wore a light green gown. An intricate star glowed on her forehead. On either side of the parrot's body were straw baskets overflowing with plants.

The parrot dipped its head to allow the female star-being to jump off, landing in front of them.

"El Lara." Kazstrom tapped his right fist to his chest and gave her a slight nod. "This is my new friend, Teegan."

Warcat returned, circled the priestess, and purred, earning him a loving scratch on the head.

El Lara repeated the fist-to-heart gesture and glanced at Teegan. She was even more beautiful up close, with her purple eyes. Slim and graceful, she was about five inches taller than Teegan's average height. A small green snake that blended with the Priestess's dress slithered around her wrist like a bracelet.

"We have an unknown visitor, Sizzler," El Lara spoke to her snake.

"Hello, very nice to meet you both." Teegan waved, feeling awkward. But she didn't want to get bitten by the snake. Also, a handshake would appear strange. It would take her time to understand the proper greeting etiquette, if there was any.

The Priestess also possessed the cosmic codes on her fore-head and the sides of her face, but they weren't as many or as prominent as Kazstrom's.

El Lara's eyebrows pinched together. "You know our language."

It wasn't a question. With a stern face, El Lara examined Teegan, rattling her nerves.

"The Soulstar from Farra gifted her that ability. It's one reason we're here today." Kazstrom stepped closer to Teegan.

"Really?" El Lara turned toward her parrot and detached one of the baskets, handing it over to Teegan.

The weight of it was more than Teegan had expected. She should've spent more time at the gym. Pride had her using both arms to lift the basket. She turned to the side to avoid the overflowing plants from poking her eyes out.

"Make yourself useful." El Lara tossed the second basket.

Kazstrom caught it with one arm. *Showoff.*

He reached over to take the one from Teegan, but El Lara said, "We all have to carry our own weight in this Grove. If the Soulstar chose her, then she'll be fine." She whipped Kazstrom a sharp look. "Let's drop these off, and then you can tell me what you want."

They dumped the baskets inside a massive greenhouse, where a floating ball of energy orbited the room like a mini sun, giving light to the plants. Two plant-beings with roots and leaves coming out of their heads greeted them from the greenhouse.

Kazstrom and Teegan followed El Lara into the office area. In the room, an abundance of books and artifacts graced several walls and bookshelves. From the wide window, she saw Warcat prancing around with a white jaguar with long ears.

They sat on stone stools at a round table, and a droid that was half cactus and half robot offered them blue drinks. Another winged droid flew down, placing a platter of green cupcakes and other delicious pastries before them.

Teegan's stomach growled, but she didn't want to be the first to grab a piece.

Kazstrom placed two pastries onto Teegan's plate, one on his and one on El Lara's.

"Thank you," Teegan said.

El Lara's purple eyes glinted. "Why are you here, Kazstrom?"

"I need your help with a nasty wound. I was told you could help me. I know you're busy with the Grove, so I hope I'm not interrupting."

El Lara's eyebrows arched. "You're injured? When? And who told you I could help?"

"The Soulstar told me," Teegan interjected. "The injury on his back is expanding."

"It told you?" The Priestess's voice hinted of disbelief. "We'll get back to that topic. I want to see his injury." She got up from her seat and went over to Kazstrom's back. "There's a time for interrupting me, Kaz. Norak needs you. I live in Norak, and that means I need you alive too. Let's have a look."

Kazstrom stripped his armor and undershirt and placed them on the side table.

El Lara hissed. "Why didn't you come to me as soon as you got injured? This will leave a scar now."

"I have a collection of them, so one more won't mean anything. Can you heal me?"

The Priestess angled her head. "How many times have I healed the Norakian warriors? Too many."

A weight Teegan didn't know she had been carrying slid off her shoulders.

"This Yorri poison can be eliminated with ease if it's treated immediately. But it's been sitting here, eating at your flesh. The poison is now in your bloodstream. Why didn't you come to me first?"

El Lara went to a storage cabinet and pulled out a tray. She placed utensils, jars filled with liquids, empty jars, and ointments on the tray and brought them back to the table.

Teegan rose from her seat and watched El Lara cleanse his wound.

Kazstrom let out a sigh. "I was busy on the hunt for the Soulstar because I thought its energy could heal me."

"It probably could," the Priestess said. "But that's a rare stone. What if you didn't find it?"

Jaw set and eyes deep in thoughts, Kazstrom said nothing

for a while. Then, "I was tricked into believing that the Soulstar was the only option for my survival. He looked at my injury."

El Lara placed down a jar. "Who?"

"Moraku," Kazstrom said. "He was adamant that I needed the Soulstar."

"Why would he say that?" El Lara picked up the jar again.

"I'm going to find out as soon as you heal me."

"Your healing will not be instantaneous. You must bathe in the Star Lagoon and rest a while. I don't want you ripping the wound wider." El Lara opened the jar, pulled out a small bug with a long green body and too many legs. She placed it on Kazstrom's wound.

Teegan gasped when the bug grew until it covered a third of his back. With its wide mouth, the bug moved around, sucking out the dark purple blood, which darkened its body. Transfixed by the healing method, she couldn't look away.

When the bug was done, El Lara picked it up and placed in a larger container where it spat out the dark blood.

El Lara sealed the wound with the sealant Teegan had used on Kazstrom's spaceship and turned to Teegan. "You don't find this repulsive?"

"As a teacher of young children, I've seen my fair share of injuries," Teegan said. "And I have a brother who's gotten hurt before. Besides, I think when you face the dark in all its nastiness, you see it for what it is. You don't need to fear it anymore. It's easier to move on from that point."

As Teegan spoke, her list of issues and bills flashed across her mind. They were all out in the open for her to see.

El Lara stared at Teegan and considered her words. The Priestess's stern face softened and her eyes warmed.

"Those are wise words. I like how you look at things." She washed her hands from a bowl of glistening water, dried them on a lush towel, and sat down. "So, tell me, what did the Soul-star say to you?"

Teegan pulled out the pendant and showed it to her as she explained what had happened and how she had agreed to help find the secret door. "Do you know where it is?"

El Lara went to the wide window and stared out. "No, I don't. The Aurora Matrix has provided the life source for this Grove and all of its inhabitants for thousands of solar cycles." She faced Kazstrom. "We can't let anything happen to it."

"I know, and I won't."

The Priestess looked at Teegan. "Thank you for agreeing to help us. I don't trust outsiders easily. Kazstrom knows this. He knows he shouldn't be bringing foreigners to Elseon Grove without notifying me first." Sizzler poked its head out. "He didn't notify me about you. You're the first human to enter here. And to be honest, it annoyed me." There was no unpleasant undertone to her voice this time.

"I'm sorry. With the excruciating pain and what the Soul-star has stirred up, it slipped my mind," Kazstrom said as his vambrace flashed a message. He typed something on the screen and glanced up. "Moraku asked if I've found the Soulstar. He wants to see it."

"Navigate him with caution. There's more to this picture than what we're seeing." The star on El Lara's forehead beamed. "Are you still vying for the General position?"

"I am. I need my strength back so I can continue the train-ing. I have to defeat Moraku to obtain that position."

"There's no one else more capable, more deserving than you. However, you must not forget that the Aurora Matrix is our priority right now."

Kazstrom tapped a fist to his heart and looked at El Lara. "*Nona faiya, nona lux. Coma faiya, coma vita.* I've never given up on what matters to me. It's the Norakian way."

No faith, no light. With faith, all life.

The words snuggled into Teegan's heart and made themselves at home. The energy reverberated down her spine, as if awakening a prayer she had forgotten.

"Something is happening in Norak. I don't know what it is. But I've been feeling it, especially in the last few days," El Lara said. "A very dark energy is growing, or rather, has been growing. I felt it strongly today, and when you brought Teegan here, it made sense. The Soulstar is here to help us. Perhaps our moon, Farra, knew it and recruited the necessary help." She tossed Teegan a warm smile.

"Where is this darkness coming from?" Irritation infused Kazstrom's words, making the veins on his neck pulse. "What galaxy? What planet?"

"It's coming from here, right here in Norak. But it's distorted. I can't see anything." The star on El Lara's forehead twinkled. "I'll see what I can find out and let you know."

Like a mother, El Lara had a gentle yet fierce protectiveness toward him, even though she didn't look old enough to have an adult son. Teegan admired their exchange of mutual respect and trust.

Kazstrom turned and placed a gentle hand on Teegan's back. "We should get going. We need to go see Moraku, my superior."

"Did he ask you about your injury?" Teegan asked.

Kazstrom and El Lara exchanged a curious glance.

He raised an eyebrow. "No, why?"

"That negligence shows me what kind of character he is. Star-beings aren't that different to humans. We're prone to the same emotions: greed, power, all that stuff," Teegan reasoned. "He wants the moonstone, which means he knows more about it than he's letting on. He might know where the elusive door is." A smile formed on her lips. "I'm going to tell Moraku he can't have my Soulstar. That's when his true colors will show."

Amusement and pride sparked in Kazstrom's eyes.

El Lara let out a chuckle. "I suppose I know why the Soulstar chose you. I don't have to worry about Kaz now. He has you watching his back." She gathered all the jars back onto the tray. "Don't stay out too long. You need to return for the complete healing."

FIFTEEN

Kazstrom

KAZSTROM AND TEEGAN rode on Warcat to the Norakian Palace, which was composed of three majestic triangles and a Ribbon Tower. Together, the architecture stood like a powerful beacon at the center of Nouridan.

He parked Warcat in the public lot and took Teegan inside the pyramid that held several offices, including his. Conversations from the crowds in the area boomed around them. They sat on a two-seater circulator, which was a large transparent ball with cushioned seating that took them to the tenth level of the building. In the hallway, with a gorgeous view of the Norakian Palace, Teegan glanced at the massive triangles. "They're larger than the Egyptian pyramids."

"Five times larger." Kazstrom remembered that fact from the Intergalactic Library.

"What's the spiral sculpture?" Teegan pointed to the tall building that looked like several ribbons twisting together.

"That's the Ribbon Tower. The Elders have many cosmic conferences there."

"You have innovative architecture here," she said as she fell into step with him.

Kazstrom and Teegan waited for Moraku in the newly renovated conference room. Why had Moraku updated his office furniture from the previous simple decor? Now, exquisite furniture enhanced the room, giving it more style, more superiority.

The interior set up drew the eyes to the tall windows with a magnificent view of Nouridan. A long table made from Norakian Purple Pine sat at the center of the room, surrounded by ten metal chairs with long backs. Artistic sculptures that moved like flowing water graced the walls.

"These giant chairs look like they can swallow me." Teegan tapped the backing and glanced around it. "This isn't going to shape-shift on me, right?"

"No."

"Good." She appeared so small when placed in a chair made for warriors. "Is there a government in Norak? What's it like? I know Moraku is a General. Where does that put him on the political ladder?"

He admired the spark in her mind. It showed that she had a desire for learning and understanding. Curiosity was how he had excelled in school.

"We have seven Elders, who are at the top of Norak," Kazstrom said. "They have innate wisdom, powers, and connection to the Cosmos. Next are the Masters, then the Ambassadors, the Generals and the Captain of the Norakian warriors, then the warriors themselves. El Lara is a Priestess, and she ranks with the General. It can get confusing, so we joined the Masters and the Ambassadors into one group, called the Officials."

"It is confusing, but that's like the government for my country too. You call them Elders; how old are they?"

"Some of them are a thousand solar cycles old."

Teegan's mouth dropped. "How old are you?"

"Three hundred solar cycles," Kazstrom said. "We live on a higher frequency, so our life spans are longer. Earth has a lower frequency and a lot of density, which makes it hard for your bodies to adjust to a longer life."

"What about El Lara?"

"She's two hundred solar cycles older than me," he said.

Teegan sucked in a breath. "Wow, she doesn't look it at all. She looks like she's only a few years older than me, and I'm only twenty-seven."

"But you have wisdom and knowledge that are centuries old." He loved the way her eyes lit up with gratification.

"Thanks." She chuckled, and the serious inquisitiveness returned. "Do you have planetary laws? You know, something similar to our international laws? How do you interact with all the adjacent regions and other planets? I mean, is there anything preventing all the 'bad' star-beings from coming to Earth and abducting or killing humans?"

He leaned into the table and studied her. "You've been thinking about this."

She lifted a shoulder. "Now that I'm on a secret mission, sitting in a conference room on an unfamiliar planet, it makes sense to know how things work."

He finished her thought for her. "You want to know what you've gotten yourself into."

She pursed those irresistible lips. "Wouldn't you? Details matter."

If he was anywhere else, he'd have pulled her to him and devoured that tantalizing mouth. "There's the Galactic Coalition of Truth, or GCOT. Something close to your United

Nations, but this is a thousand times more powerful, more effective. It is respected by all the Cosmos."

"Who's part of it?" Teegan asked.

"Each region from various galaxies has one or several members on that board. They make sure that those who defy the cosmic laws will pay," Kazstrom said. "They deal mostly with major cosmic problems. We normally notify them of regional issues, but it's our responsibility to resolve them. Unless we need their assistance." He leaned back in the chair. "We don't allow star-beings to go to other planets and wreak havoc. Regulations are set up to help achieve peace. But as you know, there are those who will always break the laws. Even here in Norak, we've fought off wars with other star races who believe that regulations don't apply to them. The battle between Light and Dark is constant. Does that answer your question?"

She stared at the table and nodded. "Yes. I guess it's the same everywhere."

Moraku entered the room with Bannon beside him like a pet.

Only fifty solar cycles older than Kazstrom, Moraku was a light-blue-skinned warrior with an angular face and blue eyes. He had red hair, worn back in a tail by a strip of leather. He wore an armor with one large gold plate of fortisium on his right shoulder, followed by smaller overlapping plates that covered his entire arm. The rest of the attire was gunmetal gray, composed of the smart-tech fabric. The visible muscles showed that he had been training. A lot.

Bannon was a few inches shorter than Moraku, which meant he was also shorter than Kazstrom, though his character often gave him the impression that he was bigger and above everyone else. Bannon had long dark eyes on a narrow face covered with unattractive bumps that also reached his bald head. Black metal armor covered his body except for areas where his orange, scaly skin was exposed.

Bannon's eyes landed on Teegan. Irritation surged in Kazstrom. Kazstrom should get her new clothes so she could blend in. He got up from his seat and greeted Moraku with a fist to his chest. Moraku and Bannon returned the greeting.

Following him, Teegan rose, gave them both a nod, and sat down again.

Moraku and Bannon took seats across from Kazstrom and Teegan. Bannon spoke first, "I see you've made it back to Norak."

Ignoring him, Kazstrom introduced Teegan to Moraku. "Teegan is the owner of the Soulstar. She was kind enough to accompany me all the way from Earth."

"Oh, it's a pleasure to meet you." Bannon smiled, revealing sharp fangs. "What did my friend, Kaz, offer you in exchange for your company?"

We are not friends. Kazstrom met his gaze with an arched eyebrow.

"He needed my help. I enjoy helping people, so we bargained. My help for a free trip to another planet. I'm always open to free vacations," Teegan said with a seriousness that had Bannon staring at her in disbelief. "Plus, his wound is getting worse." She placed a hand to her corra. "I didn't have the heart to say no."

Teegan came into the meeting knowing there were individuals who didn't have good intentions for him. The way she played the game with innocence and diplomacy earned his admiration.

"You speak Norakian. How?" Bannon asked.

"I also speak the universal language. It's a long story," Teegan said. "Perhaps we can discuss it another time."

Moraku met Kazstrom's gaze. "You're still injured? The

Soulstar didn't heal you?" His concern appeared authentic, but it was that authenticity that had Kazstrom believing him in the first place. Kazstrom hadn't had any reason to suspect anything.

But he had learned his lesson and was extra cautious now. The muscle on his back contracted, reminding him he needed to return to El Lara for the full treatment. The painkillers he took earlier had probably worn off. "No, it can't."

"That's strange. It's a powerful moonstone. It should have been able to. Where is it?" Moraku asked.

Teegan pulled out her necklace. "Right here. This was a gift from my best friend. It's beautiful, isn't it? What's so special about it? It's just a gemstone, right?"

Bannon scoffed. "It's not just any gemstone. Its powers can—"

"May I see it?" Moraku walked around the table to Teegan.

Kazstrom pushed his seat back, arriving beside her. She let Moraku hold the stone, while the chain still hung around her neck. No lights pulsed from it the way they did before. Kazstrom's vambrace vibrated, and he took a quick glance at the message from Magnetti before setting it aside for now.

"It's a magnificent moonstone," Moraku said, turning it from side to side. "Do you mind if I borrow it for examination? I promise I'll return it."

Teegan grabbed the Soulstar back. "I mind. I'm very attached to it. You see, I'm millions of light-years away from my home. This is the only thing I have that reminds me of home. It helps me adjust to Norak. Besides, I want to study it myself. I need to help Kazstrom heal, remember?"

Bannon jutted his pointy chin at the Soulstar. "But you don't know how it works."

"Do you?" Teegan asked.

"We have machines that can dissect it."

"My moonstone is not some dead animal, and I don't want it dissected in any way." Teegan glared at him.

Bannon shook his head. "Humans know nothing."

Teegan cocked her head. "I *know* when a bully is trying to frighten someone half his size. I know bullies have major insecurity issues. I know bullies exist on every planet, even here. Do you know what I'm talking about?" Her voice rose like a storm, which left Bannon blinking.

Kazstrom stifled a smile.

"That's enough, Bannon. Teegan is Kazstrom's guest. That means she's our guest," Moraku said. "Kazstrom's health is most important. Let's hope she discovers a way to heal him."

Bannon turned to Kazstrom. "Get well and prepare yourself. I'm also competing for General Atreyu's replacement."

"Prepare yourself to lose," Kazstrom replied.

Was this the reason Moraku had misled Kazstrom into believing his wound was more drastic than it really was? Kazstrom had left his injury untreated while searching for the Soulstar. Did Moraku want to make sure Kazstrom would lose to Bannon?

It would be more difficult for Kazstrom to win the competition now. Moraku would no doubt give Bannon the advantage. Bannon's uncle, Elder Kai, had significant influence. What was Moraku after?

SIXTEEN

Teegan

"HOW DO YOU DEAL WITH THEM?" Teegan asked as they left the Norakian Palace. "Everything they say means something else."

She followed Kazstrom up a wide spiral staircase made of energy. The swirling colors made it difficult to see if the steps were solid. She hesitated to step on, fearing she'd fall right through. With her foot, she tapped on a step, and to her surprise, touched a solid surface. Relief settled, and she continued moving up. Her body tingled from the pulsation. As she concentrated on the colorful lights circling her legs and body in slow motion, she relaxed.

"It's politics." Kazstrom strode to the center of the bridge. Waves of energy swirled around him and Warcat.

"It's bullshit," she huffed out a breath, trying not to let the negative energy from that conference suffocate her. "Politics is bullshit most of the time. It's like that on Earth too. Drives me nuts. Moraku is supposed to be your superior, but he's not acting like one. What's his agenda?"

Kazstrom took her hand and pulled her close to him. "You surprised them. You held your ground with subtlety."

"I didn't like the way they spoke to you. Especially Bannon." She loved how her small hand felt safe in his rough palm. "I can't wait for you to kick his butt and win the competition."

Kazstrom's eyes darkened. "I didn't like the way he looked at you."

Teegan couldn't remember anything about Bannon except his bald head and his aggressive attitude toward the Soulstar. "How did he look at me?"

"Like you were dessert. Like you were his." Kazstrom lifted her hand and kissed it. "I don't share."

"I'm not his," she said and had him smirking. "And I don't share, either." Her skin still tingled from the kiss long after he released her hand.

"This is the Aurora Matrix." Kazstrom gestured to the wide area. "It provides energy such as electricity, among other things, to Norak. It nourishes the plants, animals, all the living inhabitants in Norak. It energizes the air quality."

Teegan glanced at the multiple layers of iridescent lights that made up the bridge. When she stared at one spot, abstract shapes connected to each other. "What are those transparent things?"

"Sacred geometry. They're all over the Cosmos, even on Earth. You can't see them because of their high vibrations."

Being able to see the geometric shapes connecting and forming beautiful patterns mesmerized her. She pinched herself, and the pain confirmed she wasn't dreaming.

Warcat roamed further down the bridge, which curved around the city and beyond. Teegan recalled the extraordinary sight of the bridge from above when she was inside his space-ship. Standing on the massive bridge, she felt tiny.

The energy of the bridge caressed her body, soothing the nerves she had picked up from Moraku and Bannon. Heat swirled around her palms. "Are you allowed to use the bridge?" Teegan asked, staring up at some monowheels, air-bikes, and autoships that flew in the sky.

"Only a few get to use it, and only when we're scouring it for any foreign energies that don't belong here. We keep it as pure as possible."

"The Soulstar said it's in danger. What do you think she means?" Teegan strode to where the bridge curved around several giant trees. In the distance, the bridge entered the side of a mountain with a gray and white surface. "Does it go through the mountain?"

"No, it doesn't. It's a mystery how it emerged from the side of the mountain and started expanding."

An idea excited Teegan. "Maybe the door is inside the mountain."

"The bridge stops at the mountainside. We can't enter the mountain. There's no opening, unless we create one. But I'd rather not disrupt the landmass." Kazstrom glanced at his vambrace. "Where is Magnetti?"

Warcat stalked back from wherever he had gone. "There's a foreign scent here."

She hadn't heard him speak for a while, so she almost forgot he could. It would take her time to adjust to all the fantastical things before her. She scratched his head, and he leaned in for more affection.

"Where?" Kazstrom asked.

A flap of wings had them turning toward the sky. A giant bird that resembled an eagle descended with a blue star-being dressed in warrior armor similar to Kazstrom's. Behind him was a beautiful, dark-skinned warrior with white hair and purple highlights.

Teegan moved closer to Kazstrom as the giant bird landed. It was roughly the size of an elephant, probably bigger with the wing extension. When it cocked its head at her, she noted the size of its beak could swallow her like a worm.

"Be nice, Amenti," said the warrior with spiky, blond hair, who was decked out in silver and black armor.

He ran a hand across the blue and orange feathers of his bird. Instantly, the bird shrank in size and perched on his shoulder like a pet finch. "Sorry, she's curious about new visitors. I'm Magnetti, Kazstrom's warrior brother."

He held a fist to his chest, tapped two times, and nodded.

Nodding, she smiled. "Nice to meet you."

"I'm Aleeya, Kazstrom's warrior sister." She gave the same fist-to-heart greeting.

Up close, Aleeya was even more appealing with her bright brown eyes. Toned muscles gave her an athletic appearance. She wore purple and gold armor, and the boots that came just below her knees completed the spectacular look. *Aleeya could kick ass.* Both Aleeya and Magnetti had cosmic birthmarks like Kazstrom, but they were all different symbols.

"Glad you're back, Captain." Magnetti placed a hand on Kazstrom's shoulder. He stood a few inches taller than Kazstrom, but that could be because of his spiky hair. "The damaged area is over here."

Amenti, still miniaturized, flew down and perched on the back of Warcat. It squawked and conversed with the jaguar. Warcat didn't reply to her. Maybe they understood each other differently. With what she had witnessed ever since she stepped foot onto Norak, she wouldn't be surprised.

Magnetti led them to a group of large trees with circular blue leaves. "The shade from the trees hid it well, but then I noticed a few dried leaves falling from the tree. Aleeya and I scanned every inch of the Aurora Matrix. The frequency here is weak." He pulled out a screen from his silver vambrace and showed Kazstrom.

"Send me a copy of the reading and everything else you've got." Kazstrom crouched and placed a hand at the edge of the bridge. "Someone stole an energetic section from here. The energy is dull and weak."

Aleeya lowered beside Kazstrom. "They knew what they were doing. The bridge has been trying to remedy itself, but it's having a hard time. Based on the reading, this happened weeks ago."

Warcat stalked over with Amenti now on his head. "There are two foreign energies. One is Ensaab filth. I can't pick up the other."

The muscle in Kazstrom's eyebrow twitched. "Catalog the scent. We need a record of it."

"Already done," the cat growled.

Kazstrom winced as he stroked Warcat's smooth coat. "We have to heal the bridge back to its thriving frequency. We'll search for whoever is responsible."

"I can help with that." Aleeya got up and gestured to Kazstrom's back. "How's your injury?"

"I need to get back to El Lara soon. Muscle spasms aren't fun." Kazstrom shared his story about the Soulstar while he reviewed another area on the bridge.

"You have a lot on your plate," Magnetti said. "Just let us know how we can help."

"I'm back now, so I can resume watching over the bridge. I would appreciate any help you can offer regarding this investigation. Keep me posted on what you find out. I'll do the same. Let's keep this quiet for now. I'll update Moraku when it's appropriate. I don't want Bannon in my business."

"I heard he's competing for the promotion," Magnetti said.

"You're going to kick his ass with ease," Aleeya said. "*I* can kick his ass."

"You certainly can," Teegan agreed and grinned.

"I really like her." Aleeya gave Teegan a one-arm hug. "I've got to go. Take care of stubborn Kaz for me."

Kazstrom made a disapproving sound. "I am not stubborn."

"Says every stubborn star-being that ever existed." Aleeya winked at Teegan.

Magnetti laughed. "It was nice to meet you, Teegan. See you soon."

Amenti shifted to her full beast size and flew off with Magnetti and Aleeya on her back.

"I like your brother and sister." Teegan stared after them. Unlike the vibes she got from Moraku and Bannon, Magnetti and Aleeya were like family.

"Based on what just occurred, I have to reconsider my opinion of them," Kazstrom said. "Let's get back to Elseon. The wound is killing me."

SEVENTEEN

Teegan

PREPARING for their transportation to the guest cabin on El Lara's floating island, Teegan and Kazstrom stood next to the purple parrot, Mimic.

"You can stay in the cabin up there. There are two bedrooms, two baths, and an office for you to work in if you need to." El Lara looked at Kazstrom. "But I suggest you use this time to heal." Her attention swiveled to Teegan. "I hope the food serves you well. If there's anything you need, let me know. Or you can ask Mimic, and she'll let me know."

Marveled at all the fantastical creatures she'd met, Teegan stroked the soft purple feathers on Mimic's neck, and the bird cocked its head with approval. "At your service."

Compared to Amenti, Magnetti's battle-bird, Mimic appeared more approachable.

"She's not annoying like the others." El Lara made some kissing sounds when she approached Mimic.

The parrot dipped her head in affection. Warcat flew across the courtyard with a white jaguar.

"He can stay here and play with Nari. Or you can have him accompany you."

"I'll stay here." Warcat perked his four ears and chased Nari.

At Teegan's chuckle, Kazstrom shrugged. "Is there anything special I'm supposed to do in the Star Lagoon to speed up the healing?"

"Just swim in it. Submerse yourself for as long as you can. It's a healing pool, so it'll do what it needs to do. It'll push the poison out of you and transmute that dark energy into something better."

"Thank you. We're ready," he told Mimic.

Nerves tumbled inside Teegan as she glanced up at the large bird and imagined the many ways she could die. A simple fall would crack her bones and smash her brain.

"You'll be safe with me," Kazstrom said.

Teegan sat in front of Kazstrom on a saddle-like thing with a backing. He held her close. There was no harness, only two small handles on the sides of the saddle for her to grip. That didn't settle her nerves. She was grateful for Kazstrom's presence. When the parrot flew up to the floating island, her heart pounded, and her stomach turned at the visceral sensation of fear, reminding her of a roller coaster experience. The flight wasn't smooth, like his spaceship.

"Are you okay?" Kazstrom asked as he jumped off when Mimic lowered her body.

Teegan tensed at the landing. "That was interesting. Thank you for the flight."

"You're welcome," Mimic replied in her high-pitched voice. "If you need anything, I'll be over there." She gestured to a floating tree with large limbs stretched out in many directions and roots that looked like a long beard. "Enjoy your evening."

With her feet on the light purple grass, Teegan absorbed her environment. She noted the island was rich with vibrant vegetation, including patches of green among the purple. Floral trees gave off a lovely fragrance to the area. An adorable cabin made of stone stood at the center.

Teegan gawked at the guesthouse. "This isn't a guest cabin. This looks more like a fancy lake house."

She pushed open the wooden doors and stepped on crystal flooring. She wandered around the elegant living room that belonged on some luxurious television show. Couches, chairs, and curtains were designed in soft colors that drew you in like an embrace. A small kitchen with high-tech equipment looked like it could probably create top-notch meals. Her eyes went to the scenic view beyond the set of glass doors.

Kazstrom palmed a screen on the wall, and Teegan watched as the island floated elsewhere.

"Where are we going?"

"Just further out so we can see the entire sky." He pressed something, and lights brightened around the interior and exterior of the house.

When the island came to a stop, Teegan went to the window and sucked in a breath at how high they had gone above the Elseon Grove. They had the sky to themselves. Her heart soared from the beauty and peace, erasing the nerves that had clung to her from the bird flight.

Kazstrom pointed to the sparkling lights in the backyard. "That must be the Star Lagoon."

Outside, Teegan stood beside the most beautiful lagoon she'd ever seen. It was like one of those vacation advertisements for Hawaii or some other tropical place. A mini waterfall hung from the air, pouring down liquid stars that illuminated the pool. Where did the body of water come from? How could it be suspended like that?

She had too many questions and reminded herself that she was now on a different planet, in a different galaxy, where technology and magical things were on a whole new level. The Star Lagoon twinkled with various stars of gold, white, and pink. A variety of plants, rocks, and white sand landscaped the area with perfection. The atmosphere was private, yet open to a sky that appeared like someone had tossed a jar of glitter at it.

She kicked off her sandals, sat down, and let the purple grass tickle her soles.

Kazstrom went to the edge of the lagoon, faced her, and began to undress. The armor and sword clanked to the ground, followed by the boots. She should turn away to give him privacy, but she couldn't move her eyes.

Smiling, he asked, "What are you thinking?" His smart-tech shirt came off, followed by his belt adorned with knives and a sleek, silver gun.

About how your muscles would feel against me. The cosmic codes on his body winked at her.

She lifted her gaze to meet his. "Do you want me to give you privacy?"

"Stay." His voice came out slow and controlled. "I want you here with me. I want you to see everything you've been curious about."

The confidence in his words sent a thrill through her body.

When his vambraces, pants, and everything thudded to the ground, she gasped at the magnificent sight of him. Firm muscles padded a gorgeous physique made to arouse females. Her eyes wandered and landed on the spectacular creation that held her attention: his size. Cosmic codes illuminated down the length of him, making him the most alluring man she'd ever seen.

Heat inflamed her blood, but she kept on staring.

Kaz gave her an inviting look. "You should join me in the pool."

The intensity of his eyes tightened her loins.

Somehow, she found a sliver of logic and said, "You need to heal yourself first." Still sitting, she fisted her hands into the grass to stabilize herself. "Take care of that wound."

Chuckling, he turned and stepped into the pool. His behind was just as glorious.

EIGHTEEN

Kazstrom

THE WARM WATER of the Star Lagoon welcomed Kazstrom, allowing him to see all the issues clearly. He had to heal his injury, figure out who had damaged the Aurora Matrix, and make sure he was equipped to defeat Bannon in next month's trial. Not only that, he wanted to know why Moraku had deceived him into believing the Soulstar was the only thing that could've cured him. Even if Moraku wanted Bannon to win, how did that connect to the Soulstar?

Despite the complications, Kazstrom couldn't stop thinking about Teegan. The magnetism between them increased every minute he was with her. Her energy fed his, and he couldn't break the addiction. There was an odd connection to her that he didn't understand. It wasn't just physical attraction he felt with her. It was something more. Something deep within his soul.

His body hummed with passion whenever she was near. He didn't know how much longer he could refrain from touching her.

Teegan was threatening his self-control. The way she looked at him and took in every inch of his body, had him reacting with an impressive hard-on that should have embarrassed him. But he reveled in being the center of her universe.

When Kazstrom heard water splash behind him, he turned around and found Teegan half-submerged in the pool water. All his issues vanished, leaving only her in his vision.

She wore nothing except the Soulstar necklace. Sparkles danced around her. "I accepted your invitation."

Smiling, he pulled her close. Her breasts kissed his chest. Her hands cupped the star-filled water, emptying them onto him. She swiveled him around so she had access to his back. "Let me help you bathe." She splashed water onto the wound, easing the discomfort. She dragged him to an area where they sat on smooth rocks layered like stairs. "Submerge your entire back," she told him, "and I'll reward you."

Laughing and eager to find out what she meant, Kazstrom flipped back, dipped the wound into the water, and his skin sighed from the massage. Energy nibbled his back, sending waves of sensations to his muscles. He stayed in that position for a while. When he sat up, he watched her swim a few laps.

Teegan swam back to the rocks and straddled him. On his lap, starry water dripped down between the valley of her breasts like liquid gems. The gorgeous globes begged to be touched. Or rather, a part of him pleaded to claim them. He obliged, and she sighed against his hands.

"Is this the adventure you wanted, Ms. Moore?" His fingers teased and taunted her nipples.

"Yes," she moaned. When her fingers found him, her lips curved in a seductive smile. She stroked and watched him glow underwater. "You're beautiful," she murmured.

"You're killing me," he panted.

She let out a laugh. "I wouldn't want that. I need you

healthy and strong. I need you to show me the kind of skills a General like you would have when passion takes over."

Her glorious words penetrated his corra. He captured her lips with his and devoured her. The tantalizing strokes of her tongue inflamed him, sending shock waves down his body. She tasted like the best and worst decision he'd ever made. On one hand, he nibbled on a flavor he didn't know existed. Something sweet, cosmic, and challenging all at once. On the other hand, he knew this one taste would never be enough.

His roughness surrendered to her softness. His loneliness welcomed her affection. She was exactly what he needed. She intensified the kiss, and a low growl escaped him. They broke free, panting for breath. He whispered things he wanted to do to her, and she stroked him faster. He kissed down the column of her neck and ravaged her breasts like they were his last meal. She moaned and watched him adore her.

"You have no idea what your touch is doing to me," he said between clenched teeth. His corra pounded like he was in battle.

"I'm a schoolteacher with an exceptional lesson plan." With her free hand, she traced the codes that glowed for her. His body responded to her demands.

Kazstrom didn't know a single hand could pleasure him like that, could make him so vulnerable.

"Malastrom!" He yanked her face to him and saw his desperation in her eyes. "I've never met someone with your skills. Dangerous skills that could slice a warrior with a simple touch. Malastrom!"

"You're going to need a punishment for that potty mouth." She smiled, released her grip of him, and gave his mouth one passionate kiss to remember. "But not tonight," she whispered against his lips. "Tonight, you need to rest. Doctor's orders."

Malastrom the stars and beyond!

She laughed at the obvious disappointment on his face. The tease and taunt tortured him to no end. He was hot, bothered, and glowing like an ancient scripture of codes. He didn't move as sparkling water dripped from her lovely figure as she got out of the pool and wrapped herself up with one of the robes on the side bench.

"This feels more like a punishment than a reward," he called after her. "I can't wait for the lesson, Ms. Moore."

Chuckling, she tossed him a mischievous look and entered the cabin.

Kazstrom spent a few more minutes in the pool so his body could calm down. He floated on the surface of the water so his wound could benefit from the healing energies.

When he got into the bathroom, he glanced at his injury in the mirror. Energetic threads had stitched up the wound. There was only a slim line that hinted at the injury. Amazing, he thought.

That night, Kazstrom let Teegan take the bedroom with the wide windows, and he took the other. She wanted to gaze at the stars while he worked. He wanted to further his investigation and see all the updates from Magnetti and Aleeya. When his eyes couldn't take it anymore, he went to bed and fell into a dream.

Kazstrom is a warrior fighting beside his love, Teegan. The surroundings place them on some world from a lifetime ago. They are star-beings from a different race with pink, scaly skin. They are lovers, and she is a warrior. A variety of emotions stir in him as he fights off enemies, trying to protect her. He's assisting her on a mission, but they're outnumbered. A sword slices through his arm and leg. In the process of helping her escape, he kills five enemies but breaks a few ribs.

She runs with a large stone secured in her arms. She's protecting it from the dark army that pours down from the hills.

Because of his wounds, he can't get to her fast enough. He recalls his promise to keep her safe and love her till the end of time. That pledge gives him the strength to kill several more soldiers even as he sustains more injuries.

Out of nowhere, an arrow penetrates her back and exits through her chest. He screams for her, but nothing comes out as blood floods his mouth.

Thirty feet away, she falls to the ground, and the stone breaks in half. The light that glows from the stone is the same light as the Soulstar. Its energy pulses and pounds. A second later, a colossal explosion devours the entire area.

Kazstrom woke up drenched in sweat with a hand reaching for his love, who was not there. She was sleeping in the other room. He gasped for air and waited for his corra to calm. He finally understood his connection to Teegan.

KAZSTROM OPENED his eyes to the quiet of dawn and couldn't fall back asleep. He lowered the floating island close to the ground and left a message on the wall screen, informing Teegan of where he'd be when she woke.

Last night's dream had changed things for Kazstrom. He understood why he was led to her, why the Soulstar had chosen her. Nothing was a coincidence. The Cosmos was always working in mysterious ways. Sometimes the answers came in dreams. He'd share the dream with Teegan later.

Right now, the need to train coursed through him, and he went to El Lara's exercise studio. His muscles had weakened, and so had his stamina. When he looked at his wound this morning, there was only a faint scar left. Hope surged in him. He would regain his strength soon enough, and he'd kick Bannon's ass for the advancement. It would be the perfect opportunity to defeat him in public. Bannon wanted notoriety, and Kazstrom would be happy to deliver that.

Kazstrom stretched his arms out, twisted, and bent forward and backward, testing out his flexibility. Satisfied that there was no discomfort in his back, he entered a cardio booth, chose a lovely scenic view for a virtual run and obstacle course, and began sweating. An hour later, he entered a battle booth, where he fought off several warriors. He added some weights to his workout and ended the exercise with a stretch on the large spider-web machine.

After a quick shower, Kazstrom got dressed in a fresh pair of dark pants and new smart-tech shirt.

"Kazstrom?"

Teegan's call caught his attention. Fear coated her words and had him rushing out to the main hall. She was still wearing the silk robe El Lara had offered from the night before, but she was trembling.

Kazstrom was by her side in seconds. "What's wrong?"

Her face paled as she shoved her right hand forward, revealing a dark bruise bubbling from her palm. When the bubble shrank, a worm began moving under her skin. "What is that? It hurts."

"It's an Ensaab worm. A poisonous parasite."

NINETEEN

Teegan

TEEGAN COULDN'T BELIEVE what she was hearing. "A parasite? How did it get into me?" She envisioned a gross worm invading her body, squirming around and contaminating her. The image twisted her stomach in knots.

Fire burned in Kazstrom's eyes as he gripped her wrist, studying the nasty image. "Did the Ensaab Rebels touch you at all? Anywhere?"

Teegan flipped through her memory. "No, I don't think so." They had come into the shop, browsed, and harassed Steffani...

Shit.

"Wait a second. I felt a pinch when Artwell grabbed my hand and squeezed it. I dismissed it because it didn't last long."

"It only takes a second for an Ensaab parasite to break through the skin's surface. I'm surprised it took this long to show itself. The good news is that it's contained. Let's go find El Lara."

Teegan's heart kicked as she imagined how this parasite

could infect her. Would she develop an otherworldly illness? Would her immune system be able to fight off this foreign thing?

A few minutes later, they sat in a healing room filled with medical supplies lined up like a doctor's office, but the room didn't have the sterile smell or the cold, white walls that Teegan was used to. This room welcomed her with pastel colors, chairs, and many plants. Even the sheets covering the exam table were pink and soft as satin. The comfortable atmosphere eased her distress. Every time the worm moved, her palm ached.

El Lara pulled on gloves while Kazstrom stood beside her, eyeing the worm that had now broken through Teegan's skin, revealing two heads. She bit back the pain as blood oozed from her palm. The gross image churned her stomach, but she didn't move her gaze. She wanted to see what nasty thing had invaded her.

She glanced at Kazstrom, and the tension dug deep lines into his forehead. His frustration told her he'd chop the worm up, like a sausage.

She had almost forgotten about her dream last night. That powerful dream where she was his lover from another time. Another world. She had been running away from an enemy who wanted her gemstone. Though they had looked different, she recognized her soul. And his. She had been injured and died trying to deliver the stone somewhere. The persuasive part was that she knew the stone was the Soulstar.

"Why don't you have a seat over there?" El Lara told Kazstrom, pointing to a chair against the wall. "She'll be fine."

The Priestess's words pulled Teegan out of her reverie.

"I want to watch," he said in a tone that told El Lara he wasn't going anywhere. El Lara arched an eyebrow, which had him sighing. "I need to see it, please."

"Suit yourself. It's not a pretty process when I have to cut her skin wider, remove this parasite, kill it, and stitch her up."

"I've seen nasty wounds. This isn't new to me." He picked up a sharp tool from her collection and twirled it between his fingers. "But the death of this worm will be a pretty sight."

El Lara held up a jar of green ointment to Teegan. "This will numb you in a second. Your skin will absorb it." She rubbed it on Teegan's palm, avoiding the worm. Her skin prickled as it absorbed the ointment and numbed her hand.

"Do you want to watch like this crazy male over here?" El Lara gestured an elbow toward Kazstrom.

"Yes." Teegan glared at the wiggly thing on her palm. "I want to see what it looks like."

"The perfect match," El Lara muttered.

A scalpel with a blade of energy cut into Teegan's skin. She winced from the sight of blood oozing from her palm more than the sensation of the cut, or the extraction of the worm. The two-headed creature measured about four inches in length and had the color of rotting eggplant. El Lara dropped it into a container and cleaned up the wound.

The two heads of the worm let out a loud cry that gave her goosebumps. The awful sound carried an echo that went on and on.

Kazstrom cursed, stabbed the worm, and sliced it into pieces. The rancid smell burned her nose, and she turned away for breath.

"She's in danger," Kazstrom said calmly.

El Lara finished up the stitching on Teegan's palm, added a different ointment onto it, and sealed the wound with a spray. "Be extra careful now."

"What do you mean?" Teegan asked.

El Lara gathered the dead worm, tossed it into a machine, removed her gloves, and washed her hands.

Kazstrom tucked his hands into his pockets and walked to the window. "I should have scanned your body for parasites before letting you off my spaceship. I could've stopped that worm from wreaking havoc on your body." He pounded a fist on the wall, rattling a hanging plant. "That would've stopped the Ensaab from coming after you."

Understanding now, she said, "They were after me from the beginning."

"Before, they were after you for the Soulstar. Now, they're after you for the deaths of their comrades: Bartu and Artwell."

"But I didn't kill them."

He faced her. "It doesn't matter. That worm just told them you did. The wails carry the worm's energy and yours to the Ensaabs."

Teegan stared at the machine that was chopping up the worm, sounding like her food blender. It was absurdly amusing that a small worm could give her so much trouble.

"They won't believe me even if I admit to killing the rebels," Kazstrom said. "But they will believe their parasite."

Teegan angled her head in disbelief. "It says a lot about their kind if they believe the garbled sounds of a fricking dying worm. A worm that probably doesn't even have a brain!" She tapped her head. "We have a saying on Earth that goes something like this: You can't fix stupid. That feels appropriate right now."

El Lara smiled. "I like how you make sense of things. I wish it was that simple. Take this herbal drink." She offered a cup of mint green liquids. "It'll help your body remove any residual toxins. The bruise will disappear in a few days."

Teegan gulped down the drink that tasted like bitter tea. "Thank you. I guess we'll deal with them when they come." An idea popped into her mind. "Do you think the Star Lagoon pushed the worm out of me? Otherwise, it would've taken its time desecrating my body?"

El Lara considered Teegan's comment. "That's a strong possibility."

"The Soulstar also radiated beautifully when it was submerged in the water."

"The water of the lagoon is blessed with magic and potent energy. It empowers everything it touches."

Contemplating if the moonstone, in conjunction with the waters from the lagoon had saved her, Teegan's mind wandered back to her dream. "I dreamed about you last night."

He shot her an inquisitive glance. "I did too."

"If you don't mind, I'd like to hear it," El Lara said. "Let's get comfortable in the common area. This room is for surgeries and medical treatments."

Teegan looked over to Kazstrom for his opinion. When he nodded, she replied, "I'd love your interpretation."

For the next few minutes, Kazstrom and Teegan sat in the lounge chairs and shared the same dream from different perspectives.

"I've never experienced the same dream with anyone before." Teegan tried to wrap her head around the incredible experience.

"Same goes for me," Kazstrom added. "But I know what the dream means."

El Lara intertwined her elegant fingers. "I'm sure you do."

Teegan was the only one without a clue. "What does it mean?"

"It means that we have a deep connection that spans time and space. It means that you were my lover, my mate from a life-time ago," Kazstrom said. "It means that we're meeting again to work toward another mission. We're fated to be lovers once again. We're starmates."

Teegan didn't know how to respond. A deep part of her comprehended his explanation. That would explain the imme-diate attraction to him and the way his energy caressed hers when they were close. She felt at home with him, as if she knew him from a different time.

"It makes sense," Teegan said. "In the dream, I was trying to deliver the Soulstar somewhere, but I never made it. And now, I'm given that opportunity again." She met Kazstrom's gaze. "Are starmates the same as soulmates?"

El Lara nodded. "Similar. This is a rare phenomenon that the Cosmos planned for both of you. You loved each other at one point in time. That affection was powerful enough to continue here and now."

Teegan's heart hammered in her chest, celebrating a truth that had been spoken out loud. A part of her feared this truth, while another part thrilled at the beauty of it.

"But, I don't know what to do with the Soulstar." Teegan ran a hand through her messy hair. She needed to wash up and change out of the silk robe. "I don't know where that 'door' is. Am I supposed to open it?"

"I'll help you. May I borrow the Soulstar for a day or two?" El Lara asked. "I want to study it with my other crystals."

Teegan trusted the Priestess, unlike Moraku or Bannon. She pulled off the necklace and offered it to El Lara. "There has been no communication with it since I left Kaz's spaceship."

"The moonstone is intelligent," El Lara said. "Perhaps it sensed danger and went into hiding. Perhaps it's conserving energy."

Teegan hadn't considered that. There were too many things beyond her scope of understanding. She reviewed the mental list that had been on her mind.

One, she agreed to help a star-being and a moonstone on a strange mission in another galaxy. That alone should have told her she was embarking on an extraordinary journey. Two, she was intimate with a male she'd just met. This wasn't her style at all, but it felt *right* in an inexplicable way. Not only that, she *wanted* more of it. She felt powerful, knowing what she could do to him. A teacher who could bring a warrior to his knees. That made her smile.

Three—the most important of all—was the way her heart responded to him. It was uncontrollable. The barriers she had built up after her last relationship failed against him. She had no protection. That made her vulnerable, and it scared the shit out of her. And now, this truth about them being starmates escalated her vulnerability even more.

She watched as Kazstrom and the Priestess discussed the moonstone. Teegan wasn't sure if her heart could withstand another heartache.

Stop worrying, Teegan. Stop analyzing.

Teegan had thought she could have fun with him in a no-strings-attached kind of relationship. But she feared that wouldn't be possible given this recent information. Besides, did he feel the same way about her? What if he only wanted temporary fun and wasn't a genuine believer in starmates?

She'd find out soon enough.

"I'll see you both later." El Lara held up the Soulstar. "I've got some work to take care of."

"Thank you for taking care of me." Teegan got up and embraced El Lara. "I appreciate it."

"You're welcome. A healer's job is to heal." The Priestess strode off.

Teegan looked at Kazstrom. "I have two requests."

"What are your requests?" Kazstrom rose from the chair and brushed a knuckle down her cheek.

"One, I'd like more of that Neptunian coffee. Two, I need new clothes that would help me fit in. I don't want to stand out, especially now, when the Ensaabs are after me."

Kazstrom's face hardened at those words. She rubbed away the tension between his brows.

"Okay, to both requests," he said.

"Actually, I have two more."

The laugh lines deepened around his lips. "How can I help?"

"The third request is I need to learn some self-defense skills to protect myself."

"I can protect you," Kazstrom said with conviction.

"I know you can. But what if you're not around? I want to make sure I can at least escape my enemies."

He considered her statement. "Okay. I can teach you."

"The fourth request is very important. I'll die if you don't agree."

The seriousness on his face had her grinning. "What is it?"

"I'm starving. You need to feed me." Her stomach growled. She hadn't eaten anything since the pastries El Lara provided when they arrived at Elseon Grove.

Relief settled in his eyes. "I can make that happen. I'll take care of my starmate."

He kissed her forehead, cheek, and lips. The tenderness swelled her heart, and she knew he believed in the message of that dream.

Back at the guest cabin, Kazstrom offered her a platter of Norakian delicacies. She went for the Neptunian coffee over the high-vibe neon drink. She struggled between an herbal medley muffin and the floral honey roll before deciding on the blue fruit tart that taunted her nose with its sweetness. As she indulged in her breakfast, an idea percolated in her mind, sending her sense of adventure to maximum height.

She couldn't wait to take the initiative and put the idea into motion.

TWENTY

Kazstrom

THE NEXT DAY, El Lara returned the Soulstar to Teegan. The stone didn't speak to the Priestess, nor did it activate. Teegan frowned and placed the necklace over her neck. With slumped shoulders, she entered Kazstrom's spaceship.

"We'll find it." Kazstrom steered toward a crowded section of the city.

"Searching for this ambiguous door is more difficult than looking for a needle in a haystack." She stared out the panoramic window. "At least with the needle, I have a haystack to start with. With the Soulstar, it could be anywhere." She let out a heavy breath. "I'm ready to go shopping. It has always helped clear my mind."

Kazstrom landed his spaceship in a public dock and took Teegan to the Shopping Plaza of Nouridan. Unlike the calm and quietness of Elseon, the shopping area was busy in the air and on the ground. The Shopping Plaza comprised of a large ground level building in a geometric shape that connected to several smaller buildings in the sky. The connection was through glass tubes where customers could travel to the various outlets using energetic escalators or the circulators.

He hadn't spent a lot of time in this area due to his travels. But he wanted to show Teegan his city, the place that held so much of him.

On the sidewalk, Teegan glanced up at the active traffic. "Do the spaceships, flying cars, and air-bikes ever get into accidents?"

"Sometimes, but not too many. Their ships have sensors, and they have sky markers visible on their screens."

"I'm still trying to absorb all of this wonder," Teegan said. El Lara had given her a blue cloak to wear that cinched at the waist.

Kazstrom didn't need her to stand out. That Ensaab worm had made her a target. Though this was Norak, he still glanced around, making sure there were no Ensaabs in the area. Enemies had a way of disguising themselves when entering other territories to get the deed done. He had done it several times in the past.

They strode by the Cosmic Corra Orphanage, where children played in the yard. A group of children trained on an obstacle course that was fun but also tested their strength and endurance. It was how he had trained when he lived there. He loved the challenge, loved the opportunity to prove to himself that he could achieve whatever he wanted.

Elliat, a ten solar cycle-old boy with antlers and brown fur, spotted Kazstrom, waved, and rushed over.

"Kaz! Are you coming to visit us? We miss you!" Elliat beamed at him and stared at Teegan.

"I'll stop by soon. I'm showing my friend, Teegan, around. She needs to buy a few things. This is Elliat."

Teegan waved at Elliat, and he returned the gesture.

"I've advanced to sword training. Will you come to demonstrate again?" Elliat pretended to swing an invisible sword.

"I'd be happy to. Are you doing well with your other studies?"

"Yes! I've scored high on all of them!" Elliat's ears perked with delight.

"Go back to your training before your teachers wonder where you are." Kazstrom jerked his chin back to the yard. "Say hello to everyone for me."

Elliat gave him a tight hug and smiled at Teegan. "I'm studying about humans right now. Your kind is very interesting." Then he rushed off.

"Is this where you grew up?" The tenderness in her voice matched her eyes.

"Yes. My parents were killed during my tenth solar cycle. I was an only child. This place took me in, fed me, educated me, and trained me." He paused, reliving the memories. "I owe my life to them."

"They're lucky to have you."

He faced her. "I'm lucky to have them."

Kazstrom's gaze swiveled to the five-story building that housed orphans from all over the planet. Two separate buildings, connected to the main one, served as the housing and training facilities. "My warrior brothers and sisters grew up here as well. This was family to me."

Family. A precious word with a meaning he'd lost when his parents died. But he'd found that meaning again at the orphanage. There, he discovered his foundation, and the drive to become the best he could be. He would never forget that feeling of helplessness that overwhelmed him for years after their deaths. If only he'd had the skills and the power, he would've been able to stop the thieves. Been able to *do* something. It was that unforgettable emotion that had pushed—and continued to push—him to be his best version of himself so he could protect those he loved.

"They saved your life," Teegan said. "You survived that difficult time. You made something of yourself."

He treasured how she discerned life's intricacies. "They gave me the support I needed to succeed."

"Elliat loves and respects you. He looks up to you."

"We're all driven by someone, something." Kazstrom adjusted the metallic plate on his chest uniform and met her eyes. Brown glistened with purple flecks. "Or some dream."

"A warrior needs a dream to defend." Teegan brushed a gentle hand on his cheek. "What is your dream?"

"To have the power to protect what is mine." He clutched the hand on his face.

"That's a wonderful dream." She gave him a warm smile and browsed the selection of shops from the enormous directory that hovered in the sky.

The strong desire to keep her safe surged through him. They were gifted with an incredible connection that spanned lifetimes. She was his from beyond this life, and he was hers. He let the truth of it sink into the well of him until it settled into a permanent spot. They were cosmic starmates; inseparable and devoted. They came together by a power beyond the stars.

In the dream, he recalled his love, honor, and allegiance to her. His purpose had been to assist her to deliver the stone into a well. He had failed then, but he would not fail this time. Absentmindedly, his hand went to the constriction around his chest. With Teegan, he was learning to adjust to many new emotions.

Kazstrom led Teegan to the Outdoor Emporium near the sidewalk, where shops were set up in tents. "The pleasant weather brings out these vendors. They have fresh fruits and vegetables grown from gardens inside their homes."

"I'm overwhelmed with amazement. This is a fabulous farmer's market." Teegan pointed to the floating pot with a tree. "How's that plant floating? And what are these interesting triangle-shaped things?" Her hands touched the fruits, dangling in bunches.

"The answer to your first question is magnetism. It's a powerful force that you can't see, but it's there. In high-frequency worlds, we can manipulate it easily. And yes, that's also how the islands float, in case you're wondering." Her eyes sparkled with curiosity, and he continued, "The answer to your second question is pink Norakian apples." He gestured to the vendor to pack up a few for him. "You can try them. They're sweet and sour with a nice crunch."

"Thank you." She paused, and another question arose. "Does that mean Earth is a lower frequency? Can you explain that a little more? This whole frequency thing fascinates me."

"There are many dimensions within the Cosmos. Earth is a third-dimensional matrix field. It's very dense there, lots of heavy energies. Terrakado vibrates on an eighth-dimensional matrix field. So, the higher the dimension, the higher the frequency." He paused, trying to find the best way to explain the complexity of the Cosmos to her. "It means we think from a higher perspective, a different consciousness. We're not constricted with certain belief systems. Creativity and possibilities are limitless here, hence the advanced technology, floating islands, and so on."

"It sounds impressive." Her eyes sparkled, begging for more.

Captivated by her absorption of knowledge, he continued, "Possibilities are limitless on Earth too, but to achieve that takes longer on your planet. In higher dimensional fields, forms of thought create energetic alignments that synchronize with the trinity waves. These waves manifest realities—existences that may appear impossible to worlds with lower frequencies. Does that make sense?"

Teegan nodded slowly. "I think so. On Earth, to get to your dreams is like trying to navigate through the thick mud. You'll get there eventually, but it's going to take patience, perseverance, and conviction. And most humans don't have that all the time." She tapped her temple. "Seems like the power is here."

He loved her practicality. "Yes, but that's only a small portion of it. The largest power is here, in your heart. It emits powerful magnetic frequencies that are multiple times stronger than your mind. We call it corra here. Corra is the sacred center of the soul."

She placed a hand to her chest and smiled. "I love that word, that definition. Corra, the sacred soul-heart. My 'corra' is beating with excitement at all of this wonderful merchandise." And just like that, she charmed his corra and started shopping.

Kazstrom watched her delighted face as she browsed various items like a kid in wonder. He wanted to offer her the leisure to shop and get to know the area.

He gave her his universal badge of credits. "You can use this to buy anything you like."

Teegan eyed him. "Are you sure?"

"Yes, I'm sure. I'll hang outside the shop. You have fun." Kazstrom wanted to keep an eye on her, but he also wanted to give her the freedom to explore.

"All right. Don't worry about me. I won't have any trouble using your credits."

Kazstrom glanced at the several boutiques in front of him. "Just don't buy the entire plaza."

She gave him a mischievous look. "Would you be angry if I bought ten *large* bags full of clothes with your badge?" She stretched out her arms for emphasis.

Kazstrom widened his eyes, trying to understand why

females loved clothing. His warrior sisters had a wide selection of warrior armor, whereas he only had five to switch off for different days. Even then, they all looked similar. "I wouldn't be angry. I'd be worried. My home doesn't have a large closet for that many clothes."

"Your place?" She flicked him an inquisitive gaze. "We're going to your place? When?"

They couldn't stay at El Lara's guest cabin forever. She had done enough for them. He had forgotten to mention it to Teegan. "We can't keep intruding on El Lara. Plus, I don't want the Ensaabs coming near Elseon. That's Norak's sacred grove. I figure you can stay with me while we figure out the next step regarding the Soulstar. Sorry, I forgot to mention it to you."

"Great idea. I'd love to see your home. I was just joking about the ten bags. Is this shopping spree considered payment for my assistance here in Norak? I hope so because I don't have any currency to pay you back."

Kazstrom didn't want her currency. He wanted to give her everything. But he didn't know how to say it without sounding silly. So he settled with a simple answer. "Sure. Consider that your payment. I'd like to give my appreciation to those who help me."

"In that case, I'm aiming for two *enormous* bags. I'll see you soon." She laughed and entered the beauty product shop.

Kazstrom stood on the sidewalk and placed an order of fruits and snacks for the children, flowers for the female teachers, and dried meat for the male instructors. He ordered a droid to deliver the food to the Cosmic Corra Orphanage and left a message he'd visit soon.

As he wandered along the front of the beauty product shop, he browsed a stand that sold random trinkets and realized he had never given his badge of credits to any female before.

TWENTY-ONE

Teegan

TEEGAN COULD STILL SEE Kazstrom's shock when she announced her shopping intentions. Goodness, she had only been kidding. The surprise in his eyes brought a smile to her face. A part of her wanted to fill up two enormous bags just to see his reaction. Though she loved shopping—what girl didn't? —she couldn't take advantage of him like that. She appreciated his generosity, but she preferred paying for her own things. There was a satisfaction to that, even though she didn't mind getting spoiled once in a while from her significant other.

Josh had never been this generous toward her. She couldn't remember the last time he bought her anything. It was true what people said about having comparisons. They helped you see things. Kazstrom was the opposite of Josh. Josh couldn't measure up to Kaz's kindness. She had witnessed his good heart in the way he interacted with Elliat from the orphanage.

Kazstrom's background had given him empathy for those who were in his position. Her heart ached for him; for the child who lost so much, so young. She had no doubt his upbringing had shaped him into the warrior he was now. He cared for his people.

Teegan admired his inner drive. She could relate to the pain of grief. It stabbed you in different ways. She understood how that loss had propelled him forward. She had been blessed with loving parents until her early twenties. He had only been a child, lonely and frightened. Perhaps his way of dealing with loss was to prove to others—and to himself—that he was worthy of his accomplishments despite his past.

She could empathize with that. Didn't she want to prove to Josh and to herself that she could survive on her own? That she could pay her bills, mend herself, and achieve her dreams with no one's help? That despite the financial mess she had gotten herself into, she was managing. Well, that was before she went off to another planet. Her bills would be late now. She'd deal with them when she returned.

When would she return? The thought brought on a sadness deep within her soul.

She didn't want to think about the cosmic starmate connection with him. Nerves rattled every time she thought about it. Perhaps she wasn't ready to face that truth. She'd think about it sooner or later. Later, she decided.

For now, she had some shopping to do. Teegan browsed and discovered many high-tech beauty tools that would make women celebrate on Earth. She saw a quick demonstration of the boob-lifter, butt-toner, and skin pore-reducer. The innovative technology astounded her. When the male salesclerk asked if she wanted to see other tools that could enhance the male body parts, Teegan declined and left.

She glanced at the selection of stores and spotted a boutique with an interesting selection of female fashion. She waved a hand, inviting Kazstrom to join her. He looked at the boutique, shook his head, and went to a sidewalk vendor with a display of gadgets. His reaction was exactly what she had expected. Smiling, she entered the shop and grabbed a handful of shirts, pants, dresses, and undergarments in a variety of fabrics and styles. She also tried on some shoes, socks, and a few fun accessories. She smirked when she found a rack of provocative lingerie.

This had been the adventure that burst in her mind.

She held up a few delectable lingerie pieces and imagined what Kazstrom would think. Just imagining herself in them made her feel seductive and beautiful. When was the last time she felt like that? She couldn't recall.

Teegan had worn nothing so tiny in her life. These sexy pieces seduced and weren't meant to be worn for long durations.

She placed the three lingerie sets on the counter and grinned at the female salesclerk with the long pink braid. "I'll take these. I'm going to try the others on."

The gills on the side of the clerk's neck fanned out when she replied, "Wonderful. You can go behind the curtain. I'll wrap these up for you."

After trying them on in the back room, Teegan purchased all of them, which fit into one large bag. While she was leaving, a table with baskets of colorful accessories stopped her.

Someone wearing a brown hooded cloak stood beside her. "Those would look lovely on you."

When a male's graveled voice sounded next to her, she turned. Before she got a glimpse, a bubble of smoke blasted into her face. She inhaled for breath and her body stiffened.

Terror surged as numbness overcame her. She couldn't move and was trapped in an in-between place where she knew something was wrong with her, but she couldn't reach her mind to decipher it. She couldn't control her body; her hands dropped the bag of clothing. She tried calling for Kazstrom, but her throat tightened, and her tongue froze. He wrapped an arm around her, and her head collapsed onto his shoulder. He led her away from the accessory table. She tried to stop him, but her feet didn't listen as the cloaked person took her out the back door.

He brought her somewhere quiet and asked questions she couldn't hear. She was transported somewhere else while her physical body remained.

He yanked the necklace from her neck. She tried reaching for it, but her hands didn't respond. Then Teegan dropped to the ground, and her mind went blank.

TWENTY-TWO

Kazstrom

WHEN TERROR SHUDDERED through Kazstrom's body, he knew something was wrong. He rushed into the fashion boutique and didn't see Teegan.

"Where is the human female?" he asked the salesclerk, who was busy folding something on the counter.

"She left with the male dressed in a cloak. She didn't look well, so I assumed he took her home. They left through the back door. She dropped her shopping bag." The clerk pointed to a large bag beside the counter.

"I'll take that." Kazstrom fled toward the back, but knew whoever had taken her was long gone.

He ran outside, scoured the area, and spotted nothing. His corra pounded as fear rose in him.

He stopped to take a breath to clear his mind. Then he alerted any Norakian foot soldiers within the vicinity to look for a human female. He also contacted his own soldiers to do the same.

Malastrom! He shouldn't have left her alone.

Kazstrom returned to the boutique to look for clues.

The salesclerk took one look at his face and asked, "Is something wrong?"

"Someone abducted her. What did the male look like?" Kazstrom walked around the store and noticed the camera in the corner. "Is that working?"

The clerk pulled a virtual screen, showing Teegan browsing a table of accessories with a cloaked being beside her. A puff of smoke blasted into her face and she collapsed onto his shoulder.

Kazstrom clenched his fists as concern and anger boiled inside him. Who was this star-being? Was it an Ensaab? He tapped his vambrace, made a copy of the video, and sent it to himself.

An alert popped on his vambrace from his soldier. "A body has been located in the back of the Emporium. Two males are in custody."

Fear skewered his gut.

Within minutes, Kazstrom arrived at the scene about two miles away from the shopping area. Three Norakian soldiers were asking two star-beings questions, while medics had Teegan on a cot inside the emergency autobus.

"Is she okay?" Her face was drained of color, and he vowed to destroy the individual who did this to her. He glanced at her bare neck. Where was the necklace? Was this a simple thievery or something more?

Nodding, the three-eyed medic said, "She appears fine. No scratches or bruises. Seems like she inhaled some toxic fumes. She should wake soon."

Relieved, Kazstrom went back to the soldiers who stood with the two Norakian citizens with dark blue skin and pointy heads.

"These males claimed they found her and were taking her back home. They said she was a friend."

Kazstrom was not in the mood for deception. He was in the mood to break something. He glared at the criminals and grabbed the closest one to him with the crooked nose. "You know her? How?"

The one with the crooked nose took one glance at Kazstrom, and the lie that had wanted to come out of his mouth changed. "N-N-No, I was wrong... We don't know her. We just found her on the ground."

"But, we had fun plans for her." The male with the narrow face expressed a sleazy smile, revealing rotten teeth. "Look at her, she looks delicious. And she's human." He licked his mouth, not understanding the magnitude of the crime he wanted to pursue.

Kazstrom's fist landed into his face. Four teeth flew out of his mouth while his body thudded to the ground. "No atrocious intentions should ever be bestowed on anyone, especially in Norak. If we find out any of you are committing heinous crimes, you will be sent to Asteroid Karma immediately. Understand?"

Kazstrom didn't want to imagine what would've happened to Teegan if the soldiers hadn't spotted these idiots.

The criminals both nodded. Kazstrom whirled to the soldiers. "Book them, catalog their DNA, and then let them stay in the city prison for one night."

The emergency autobus took Teegan back to Kazstrom's place. After he tucked her into his bed, he went out to the living room and activated his computer screens. He retrieved the file from the clothing store. As he replayed the video repeatedly, he made a mental list of who it could be. Who had wanted the Soulstar that desperately?

This individual knew she would be at the Shopping Plaza with him. The cloaked being was about Kazstrom's height. It was hard to tell his build since the cloak hid the actual physique. He must have followed Kazstrom and Teegan and waited for her to be alone.

Cursing, Kazstrom wished he hadn't left her. What if this individual had done something worse? Did those idiots scare off the cloaked being before he could do anything else? Huffing out a frustrated breath, Kazstrom ran a hand through his hair and closed his eyes.

TWENTY-THREE

Teegan

WHEN TEEGAN WOKE, she had a pounding headache. She wobbled from the imbalanced equilibrium, and braced a hand to the wall for stability as she wandered out to look for Kazstrom. She found him working at a desk, jaw set with eyes focused on the computer screen. His face strained with frustration, probably because of her.

When terror had paralyzed her, she had called for him in her mind, but forming that thought had been difficult. All she could do was hold his image in her vision and pray.

The star-being didn't hurt her. At least, she didn't remember feeling anything. But he took the Soulstar. Bastard. She wished she'd had the energy to push away that hood so she could see his face.

Bracing against the wall, Teegan reviewed Kazstrom's home. The comfortable and luxurious feel from his spaceship carried over here. Two large navy couches that could be beds sat against soft gray walls that wrapped up the living space like an elegant present. A beautiful shaggy rug splashed across marbled flooring and gave the room a nice pop of teal. The coffee table, side table, and dining table shared the same dark purple wood she had seen in Moraku's conference room.

What also carried over from his spaceship was the clutter. Kazstrom had piles of books, files, and boxes all over the living room. Clothes covered those boxes. She couldn't tell if they were dirty laundry or washed clothing that needed to be put away. His messy habit sprinkled itself over the elegance of his home. Overall, his home wasn't that bad for someone who lived by himself.

Did he live here alone?

When Kazstrom met her gaze, he strode over to assist her. "How are you feeling? What are you doing up?"

"I need something for my headache. Do you have some painkillers?" Teegan sank into the comfy couch with lots of pillows.

Kazstrom offered two round squishy pill things and a glass of aqua water.

Teegan popped them into her mouth, chewed, swallowed, and placed the glass down on the coffee table. "Thank you. Your painkillers taste like candies."

Kazstrom sat down beside her. "I only get the best kind." He brushed some tangles from her hair. "Did you recognize the individual who did this to you? I'm sorry I left you alone. I'm going to find him."

And I'm going to kill him, was what his eyes portrayed.

"You do this a lot when you're stressed or pissed off." She reached up and rubbed the pinched space between his brows. She moved her fingers down to his tight jaw. "I'm not a child who needs monitoring. And I appreciate you trusting me to shop on my own."

The scowl faded from his face. He took her hand and kissed

the top of it. "I could tear him apart for what he did. Paralyzing you and leaving you out in the empty field like that. Anything could've happened to you." Their fingers intertwined. "That moment took a few solar cycles from me. You see those wrinkles near my eyes? They exist because of you."

She laughed at the tease. "They're wisdom whiskers. They make you look very attractive." She kissed them and drew back.

"Tell me what you remember from the event." His eyes tensed, serious and stern. "Start from the beginning. Don't leave any details out."

She told him nothing stood out until the cloaked person came up beside her. "Before I could see him, a puff of smoke went into my face and paralyzed me to some extent."

"You inhaled some toxic fumes. Your body will regain its strength by tomorrow. Did you notice anything about him? Skin color, facial features? Any tails? Horns? How about the voice?"

"His voice was low and sounded like gravel breaking against each other. Just a strange odor, but that could've been the fumes."

"A voice synthesizer can modify voices."

Teegan studied her small hand secured in his protectiveness. She loved the look of it, the feel of it. With that simple gesture, he made her feel safe, wanted, and loved. Wasn't this her dream? To be loved and cherished? She had found what she'd been looking for by going outside of the Milky Way. That acknowledgment both baffled and amused her.

Not in a million years did she ever think she would experience life on another planet outside of her galaxy. As she sat beside this stunning blue male who made her feel cherished, she realized that her heart believed in love again. That second chances existed. That she was worthy of this beautiful man.

She arrived on this planet with two hot suns, but it was this blue warrior who burned away all her doubts.

"We have to find the Soulstar. I've been thinking of ways to connect to it. Perhaps when we find the moonstone, and when the three moons are full, I can bring it outside to absorb the moons' energies. What if our shared dream was a clue to something? In the dream, I remembered seeing a stone wall, or was it a mountainside? Perhaps we're supposed to look at those angles?"

"Perhaps. Rest a couple of days, and we'll sit down and figure out a plan."

Feeling filthy from the entire ordeal, Teegan wanted a shower. She remembered her bag of clothes and slapped a hand to her head. "My clothes. I left my bag at the shop."

Kazstrom got up from the couch, strode over to a closet, and pulled out the bag. "This huge thing? Did you buy half of the shop?"

Teegan jumped up and ran over to look at her purchases. "Yes!" She chuckled. "I mean yes, that's my bag. And no, I only bought a small portion. I was being good." She dug into the bag for a small purse she had bought. She pulled out his universal badge and handed it over. "Thank you."

"Keep it. You might need to purchase more things later on. I have another one I can use."

She narrowed her eyes at him. "Are you crazy? You're going to trust me with this badge after you saw what I did with it?"

"You have self-control. I see it. I trust you." He peeked into the bag. "Are you going to show me what you purchased?"

She pulled the bag away from him. "No. I'm going to shower and try on the soft pajamas. Where can I hang my stuff? Do you have a guest room?"

He eyed her. "I do. But I think you should share my room. I have a massive bed."

She pursed her lips in consideration. "That you do. It's very comfortable. But I don't want to intrude. I need space for my own things." She could imagine herself in bed with him. That image thrilled her, but she wanted privacy to think about certain things. About him. It would be hard to think with Kaz distracting her. Besides, she wanted a private area so she could connect to the Soulstar.

Smiling, he led her down the hall to a room with a bed smaller than his, but it was still big. "Would this do?" The closet was twice as large as the one she had at home.

"Wow. I *should* have bought the entire store." Teegan strode around the room, touching the pale pink curtains. A long elegant vase stood on the windowsill. Two air plants floated above the side table with a crescent moon lamp. "This room has a female touch. Whose room is this?" She pushed down the jealousy that nibbled at her.

Kazstrom didn't reply. Instead, he leaned against the wall with his hands inside his pants pockets, his feet crossed at the ankles, and considered her. Amusement swam in those golden eyes.

She crossed her arms. "What?"

"I like that you're jealous."

"I'm not jealous," she said too quickly. Too defensively.

"Okay," he said, still wearing that smug look. "You're right, this room has a female flair. But that's because my warrior brothers and sisters have stayed here before. The sisters found the room dull, so they asked if they could change it up. I said yes. Do you like it?"

The tangled nerves untangled inside of her. "They did a superb job. It's very welcoming."

"I'll let Aleeya, Andara, and Zori know."

As she walked past him back to the closet, he cupped a hand under her elbow and pulled her to him. "Tell me, were you jealous?" His warm breath brushed her lips, sending a thrill down her body. "I want to hear exactly what you were thinking."

His chest rose and fell. When she looked into his eyes, all that came out was the truth. "Yes, I was."

Then he kissed her like he hadn't seen her in weeks. He broke the kiss to nibble at her ear. "That's what I wanted to hear. When you're ready, I'll have you in my bed."

Teegan was too distracted to make any coherent statement. "I'm... going to shower now."

Pleasure glittered in his eyes. "Is that an invitation?"

"No!" Her cheeks burned. Though the idea excited her, she just wanted a quick shower so she could rest.

Enjoying himself, he said, "I'll have dinner ready for you. I'm an excellent cook."

She remembered the kitchen on his spaceship. "You can really cook? Not like heating a meal kind of thing?"

"I enjoy it when there's time, when I have a reason to. I'll make something for you."

Glancing at the simple décor of the bathroom, she assumed his warrior sisters had helped him with the interior decorations as well.

From a virtual screen, Teegan chose the kind of shower she wanted. She decided on a short one, added a massage, and an energy blast. It didn't take long for her to shower with the five water sprays that cleansed her in every direction. The fragrant shampoo that came from the potted plant on the shelf didn't require any conditioner. Not only did the shower wash her, it also massaged her aching muscles. When she was done, she felt invigorated.

The white cotton pajama top and matching shorts made her body sigh. In one minute, her hair dried from the air blaster attached to the wall. Lotion secreted from an aloe-like plant made her skin smooth as silk.

When Teegan arrived in the kitchen, Kazstrom wore an apron and stood in front of a metallic stove. The counter needed a good cleaning. "Do you have someone who cleans for you?"

He let out a breath. "Yes, I have a housemaid. I haven't had time to schedule her yet. She does a good job in *Spectre Seven* and here. I can be a slob when I'm too busy with other things."

Teegan chuckled.

Something sizzled on a floating pan with a lid that hovered just an inch above it. She admired the innovative design that prevented oil splatter. The stove had a flat surface with a screen that glowed with options. On the marbled counter, vegetables spun around inside a large bowl. A small whirlpool of water was being sucked into the jar beside it.

She took a seat on the stool at the counter. "What are you using the excess water for?"

"To water the houseplants." He pointed to the rectangular vase near the window where several plants bloomed.

"I like your recycling approach." Her stomach growled. "Smells delicious, Chef Kaz. What are you making?"

He laughed. "Don't call me that. I don't cook that often, and I don't want my legion expecting this kind of treatment whenever they're over. We're having salad and seared fowless thighs."

"Fair enough. You can just cook for me." She got up from the stool and went to look. "What's a fowless?" The seared skin reminded her of chicken.

"Where's my food?" Warcat emerged from a room outside of the living room and nuzzled against Teegan's leg.

Teegan scratched his ears. "Hey there, did you enjoy your time with your friend, Nari?"

Warcat purred. "When are we going back to El Lara's?"

Kazstrom pulled out a bowl and dumped some food into it. "Not anytime soon. We have a lot of work to do. I should've taken you with me to the Shopping Plaza. You would've been able to track Teegan's scent quicker."

Warcat curled his tail around her leg. "I'm sorry that I wasn't there. Are you okay?"

"I'm fine." She bent down and whispered. "I prefer you spend time with your beautiful friend."

Warcat growled with glee, stalked over to his meal, and dove in. "Thank you for the meal."

A while after the delicious dinner, Kazstrom prepared to train in the lower level, where he had a gym. "I'll show you some defensive moves tomorrow. You should rest tonight, though. Give your body a full day to remove all the toxins."

He read her mind, she thought. She was just going to ask him. "Sounds good to me. Thank you."

In bed, Teegan's mind wandered back to the cloaked male. What did he want with the Soulstar? She sat up in bed, concentrating on the moonstone. Perhaps she could connect to it.

"Where are you? Can you hear me?"

The sound of static crackled. Hope bloomed inside her as she pushed on. "Where are you?"

"We will reunite soon." More static sounded, followed by silence.

Why didn't the Soulstar answer her question? Why did it give her a statement that pushed her to ask more questions?

Too exhausted to concentrate further, Teegan lowered to the bed and envisioned the defensive skills Kazstrom had planned for her. She definitely needed something to protect herself.

TWENTY-FOUR

Kazstrom

THE NEXT MORNING, Kazstrom took Teegan outside in his backyard. He had a day planned to teach her some basic self-defense moves with the humanoid droid.

He programmed the droid to the beginner's level, where the movements were easy. "Punch and kick him like this. He'll block you but keep at it. This will train your reflexes and muscle memory."

Kazstrom pulled back an arm and swung at the droid's face. The droid blocked, and Kazstrom swung the other arm. "Your turn."

It took Teegan several attempts to get the hang of it. After thirty minutes, he let her learn another skill.

Kazstrom gave her some plastic balls the size of cherries. "Watch me."

He held the plastic ball between his index and middle finger. He positioned himself and whipped it toward a target board that was attached to a fat tree trunk that sat at the far end of the yard, about thirty feet away. "Hold, aim, and pitch it forward. Try to aim at that tree. The more you practice, the more you attain muscle memory. When you achieve that, I'll let you try the actual stuff."

Teegan pitched one ball to the target and missed. She tried again and came closer. "What's the actual stuff?"

"Fire-cherries. They're small bombs," he said. "You'll hurt yourself with them right now."

His vambrace buzzed with an urgent message from Magnetti. Kazstrom unlocked the video. "What's going on?"

"There's a dead body near the Aurora Matrix. It's infected with Ensaab parasites."

"Contain the area," Kazstrom said. "Keep everyone away. I'll be right there."

He turned to Teegan. "Sorry, I've got to take care of this. I don't want anyone getting infected."

"Don't worry about me. I'll spend the day honing my skills. Besides, it's safer for me to stay home. I don't want to be near any Ensaab parasites."

"I agree. Take your time practicing," he said. "If you need anything, you can reach me from the communication-monitor on the living room wall. There's also one in the kitchen."

"I will, thanks." She jerked her chin toward his back. "How's your wound?"

He demonstrated by stretching out his arms, bending his back forward and sideways. "A lot better. My guess is I'm about ninety-five-percent healed."

Kazstrom took Warcat and met Magnetti two miles from the Aurora Matrix. Magnetti had sectioned off the small street near a family complex. The Crime Division Investigators had secured the body in a protective foam that prevented further contamination.

Kazstrom nodded to the three CDIs as they snapped images and took samples from the body and the dead worms.

He greeted Magnetti with a fist to the chest. "How did you discover this body?"

Magnetti returned the gesture. "I was heading to the gym with Amenti." He pointed to his battle bird, who was perched on the roof of a nearby building, watching over them. "I heard someone scream, and we descended and found him."

Kazstrom walked up to the crime scene but maintained an eight-foot distance. The foul odor, rotting flesh, and dead worms told him the male had been dead for days, possibly a week.

"Who stumbled on him?" Kazstrom asked.

"An older female who was chasing after her pet. She almost fainted when she recognized the dead male," Magnetti said. "She said he's a wanderer. She'd seen him around the local shelters."

How did a wanderer get infected by Ensaab parasites? Did he encounter an enemy that had ended his life? Or was it pure, bad luck that had killed him?

Magnetti glanced at his vambrace. "You got this? I want to get in a workout before my appointment."

"Go. I'll take over. Thank you for alerting me." Kazstrom needed exercise too. "I'll probably join you after I wrap this up."

Two hours later, before the CDIs left, he asked them to send him a copy of the evidence. Normally, he'd let the Crime Division take care of the small city crimes, but he was interested in this one because it was so close to the Aurora Matrix and because of those Ensaab worms.

How many Ensaab Rebels were in Norak? What were they doing? There was a connection somewhere. He just needed to find it. An excellent exercise session would clear his mind.

Teegan's beautiful face popped into his vision and sent a jolt to his body, speeding up his corra. He couldn't wait to see her, to touch her, but standing around dead Ensaab worms had made his body filthy. Energy could pulse beyond an eight-foot distance, and negative energy was no exception. A good sweat and shower to wash off Ensaab filth was what he needed before he returned home.

Kazstrom arrived at the training facilities inside the Norakian Palace and headed to his locker. He changed into a stretched-tech top and shorts that allowed his skin to breathe with ease while he sweated up a storm.

Last night, he had sent out an alert to the citizens, asking them for any recordings they might have taken around the vicinity of the Shopping Plaza. He was requesting the public's help to solve a crime. The citizens enjoyed contributing, especially when they could do it anonymously. Someone could have recorded something on their vambraces, wristbands, earrings, belts, eyeglasses, and many other electronics. There were so many options available now that Kazstrom couldn't keep up with them all. He preferred his simple vambrace to do all his communication and recordings.

Now, he just had to wait for the information to come in.

He found Magnetti working with the strength-training robot. "Everything went well?"

Kazstrom nodded. "The CDIs are efficient."

"We're already receiving some recordings into the system about the Shopping Plaza," Magnetti said. "I can help narrow them for you. The last thing we need is a long list of pet recordings."

That was true. They've had strange videos and tips come in before. "Thank you. I'd appreciate the assistance." Kazstrom chose a robotic opponent and began dueling.

"How's Teegan? Was she hurt?" Magnetti wiped sweat from his forehead.

"She's fine now." The image brought out the rage in

Kazstrom. He used it on his enemy. Heat fired him up, causing him to remove his shirt.

Kazstrom spent thirty minutes dueling with the robot, another thirty minutes with a scaly droid, an hour of weight training, followed by twenty minutes battling with Magnetti before he took off for his appointment.

Kazstrom had to regain his endurance, not to mention practice wielding his sword. He wasn't going to give Bannon any chance to steal that promotion from him.

He cursed under his breath when Bannon entered the gym with two of his soldiers, who were also bald. The soldiers went about their own workouts while Bannon approached Kazstrom.

"Look who's here. I see your injuries are better." Bannon walked around Kazstrom as he worked on the leg machine. Bannon had a slight slant to his shoulder, courtesy of Kazstrom, from a duel several solar cycles ago when Bannon had fallen and cracked some bones that never healed appropriately.

Kazstrom believed Bannon's body matched his character: flawed inside and out.

"If I didn't already know you have a female mate, I'd say you're interested in me." Kazstrom's lips stretched into a wide smile. "Sorry, I'm not available."

One of Bannon's soldiers was in earshot and laughed. With one glare from Bannon, the amusement on his face disappeared. "You won't defeat me. I'll bet you on it. I've been training for months. What have you been doing? Chasing after moonstones and human females?"

"I'm too busy protecting Norak and doing my job to make senseless bets. Why don't you get a proper job and do something meaningful for your region instead of standing around, admiring my body? Anyway, we all know what happened the last time we dueled." Kazstrom gestured to Bannon's shoulder. "And that was just for fun."

Bannon flared his nostrils. "Let me remind you of what I do. I'm Moraku's assistant."

"I know what you are." Kazstrom stopped the leg machine and got off. "You're his pet. What exactly do you do for him? File away all the closed cases that the Norakian warriors worked on? Make conference appointments? Count his weapons?"

"I'm no secretary! Moraku knows where I stand." Bannon came up close to Kazstrom. "We're partners. We're a team. And if you know what's beneficial to you, I suggest you mind your tongue. Give respect where it's needed, and you might maintain your position when I become your superior."

Kazstrom snorted. "Those who deserve respect never ask for it. Like I said before, I'd resign the minute you became my superior. Enjoy your workout. I've got work to do."

As he walked away, leaving Bannon furious with anger, he bumped into Moraku. Strands of sweat-drenched hair escaped from the leather tie and fell over his angular face, a contrast of red lightning bolts slashing over his blue skin.

"Kazstrom, I heard there was an incident at the Shopping Plaza yesterday. How's Teegan?"

"She's fine, thank you. But the culprit stole her Soulstar," Kazstrom said, studying his reaction.

A shocked expression overcame Moraku. "What? We must get it back. That powerful stone is too dangerous in the wrong hands." He waved Bannon over. "Can you help Kazstrom investigate who has stolen Teegan's moonstone? Do what you can to assist."

"She lost it?" Bannon asked in disbelief.

"Someone stole it from her," Kazstrom corrected. "I've got the investigation under control. If you want to help me, perhaps you can help find out who's been contaminating the Aurora Matrix. That infection has been there for a while. It's clandestinely hidden, and that shows intention. This damage was no accident."

Bannon looked at Moraku. "Seems like Kazstrom has been slacking at his responsibility."

Kazstrom wasn't bothered by Bannon's attack. "I just want to remind you that the Aurora Matrix is the lifeline of Norak. It is everybody's responsibility to ensure its safety. Keeping it safe is one of my many jobs. And since you have so much time on your hands, Bannon, you can help gather information instead of pointing blame. Do you see me blaming you for doing nothing? Do you see me pointing fingers at you for not contributing to the welfare or safety of Norak?"

Bannon spat out, "You watch your mouth. You know nothing about my capabilities."

"You opened the door for criticism. My point is we're all on the same side, or are we not?" Kazstrom whirled to Moraku for confirmation.

Moraku placed a hand on Bannon's shoulders. "We're on the same side. Bannon's been a brilliant assistant to me. He knows what he's supposed to do."

"Have a great workout." With that, Kazstrom strode off, leaving Bannon stewing.

After the shower, Kazstrom got dressed in his warrior armor and went into his office, hoping some work would eradicate Bannon's irritation. Kazstrom had a wide corner space which allowed wonderful light to enter from the two large windows. The room had white walls, a large metal desk, and several computer screens. A few boxes containing evidence of closed cases and other miscellaneous items he'd forgotten to toss or file away sat in the corner, collecting dust.

A map of Norak spread against one wall. On the other wall was a side project he worked on when he had time. His plan was to expand the Cosmic Corra Orphanage and develop ways to provide for more support to this place that was so important to kids who had nowhere to go. Being General could give him leverage with the Elders. He could ask for funds easily.

But for now, he focused on the incident at the Shopping Plaza and the Aurora Matrix. He wanted to review any tips that came in from the public. He also created a workout plan that prepared his body for combat with Bannon. Kazstrom had less than a month. He had to make up for the time he had lost.

Kazstrom made a quick stop to inspect the Aurora Matrix. He wanted to make sure the death of that infested male wasn't a sign that something else was wrong with the sacred bridge.

TWENTY-FIVE

Teegan

IN THE MORNING, Teegan spent an hour punching and kicking the droid. After an hour of battle, she practiced whipping the plastic balls for a few more hours, then she took a break for lunch and began to tidy up the home. She sorted out the pile of clothes for Kazstrom and started a load of laundry in his Mighty-Washer-Dryer machine. After a few minutes of admiring the solar energy cleanse and dry his clothes, she resumed her routine. Though her arms and shoulders ached, she didn't give up. She even tried vaulting with her left hand, but it wasn't as successful as she'd hoped.

After another ten minutes of practice, she jumped for joy when she landed a few on the target on the ground. She gave her muscles some time to rest while she retrieved the scattered balls from the yard. After so many hours of practice, her fingers, hands, and arms had adapted to the movement.

Discipline helped people achieve their goals. She never took her brother's advice about taking self-defense courses; she never thought she would ever need it. What was Maverick up to now? Was he looking for her? Or did he give up thinking she was no longer alive? It had only been days since she left Earth. Maybe there was a way she could send him a message. Would that make things worse? How would he reach her? The current technology available on Earth didn't allow for a quick space rescue.

How was Steffani doing? Was it busy at the bookstore?

How long would it take her to help find the secret door for the Soulstar? Would she return to Earth and resume her job as a teacher? The school board would probably start interviewing for her replacement when she misses her status meeting tomorrow. At least she didn't have to worry about paying back the loan her ex-fiancé had bestowed upon her. But then again, she didn't have any money to her name in Norak either.

She had nothing here. Despite that, she felt free and not trapped by any means. How could she feel so liberated in a place so foreign to her?

Kazstrom popped into her mind, and her heart thudded. He made her feel loved, the kind of love no amount of money could ever buy. She sat down on the lounge chair and pondered on their fate. She was his from before, and he was hers. The idea sounded sweet and magical, like stories from fairytales. She knew he cared for her; she saw it in his eyes. Could he see the same in hers?

Any handsome man who looked like him and could also cook a delicious meal was a keeper.

Teegan used some time to focus on the Soulstar. Closing her eyes, she envisioned a bubble of energy protecting her, keeping all distractions outside, and concentrated on the image of the moonstone.

Where are you, Soulstar? Let me find you. Guide me to the secret door.

An image of rugged gray rocks flashed across her mind's eye. Another flash revealed a dark path.

Something sounded close by and Teegan opened her eyes. It was too early for Kazstrom to come back. Perhaps he wanted to surprise her. The nerves in her body told her differently.

With caution, she got up, tiptoed toward the house where she could peek inside. Two Ensaabs who looked like Artwell walked passed the front window. Teegan rushed back to the yard, hid inside the storage shed that housed outdoor furniture, and closed the door. She moved between the cushions and chairs, positioning herself so she could see out the small window on the door.

Loud footsteps reached the back, and her heart hammered when she recognized the purple diamond-shaped tattoos on their skin.

The Ensaab Rebels stood at the back door and glanced around. "Where is she?"

Teegan clamped a hand over her mouth as they stepped into the yard. Her body shuddered when they passed the storage shed, searching for her. Nerves piled in her stomach, and sweat dampened her hands. She took slow breaths, praying they would leave.

"Where is she? She should be here." The rebel with two mouths walked back toward the house. "Look everywhere. The stone is here somewhere."

"We need to hurry. They could be back anytime." The one with a huge wart kicked a chair. "Let's make it interesting for the Norakian warrior to come home to."

Their laughs sounded like they were choking on their own tongues. She wished they did.

She didn't dare leave the storage shed. What would they do if they discovered her? Where would they take her?

She had thought they were looking for her for retribution,

but based on their comments, it appeared their mission was the Soulstar. Perhaps it was both. Were they involved with the cloaked man who had taken her moonstone? If so, this invasion made little sense.

She couldn't access the communication-monitors in the living room and kitchen to contact Kazstrom, so Teegan found a metal stick leaning against the wall and clutched it in preparation. Her body trembled, but she dug for courage and gripped the stick tighter. Her life depended on it.

Crashing noises boomed in the house. What seemed like hours passed until all was silent.

With caution, Teegan opened the storage door, went into the house, and glared at the mess. The two couches were overturned, with cushions strewn everywhere. The rebels had knocked items from the kitchen counter onto the floor. She avoided the broken plates, jars, glasses as she made her way toward the bedrooms. The mattresses were toppled and drawers were empty of clothes.

Teegan leaned against a wall and calmed her racing heart. Was this the norm until she found the Soulstar and completed her mission? She knew the danger that accompanied the moonstone; she had accepted it when she agreed to help. But she couldn't fathom what would happen next time.

Would she ever be safe here in Norak? She'd never experienced this much terror in her life before. Was this all worth it? She was in Norak because of her inexplicable bond and desire for Kazstrom, and because of her incredible connection with the Soulstar. Everything inside her told her to stay with him, to see this through. But at what cost? Did he feel strongly about her the same way she felt for him? Fear raked a memory over her heart like nails over a chalkboard, making her cringe.

Would he get bored with her the way Josh did?

That realization was what she feared most. She shook her

head, removing this ordeal from her mind. It wanted her to succumb to fear. It wanted her to surrender.

Panic looked at her, and she looked back. No, she would not surrender. She had surrendered once when Josh had betrayed her, and that led her into a deep, dark hole that took a long time to crawl out of. She refused to allow that to happen ever again.

Teegan inhaled a breath, straightened her spine, and looked at the mess in the house. She'd deal with this. She'd deal with the Ensaab Rebels. Anger had a way of eliciting courage, and courage was exactly what she needed.

Would the Ensaab Rebels catch her off guard somewhere again? What if they brought an army here and demanded she pay for their comrades' deaths? The more she thought about it, the more it angered her. What right did they have to demand such things? Their rebels were the ones who came to Earth and caused trouble. She had every right to defend herself. What they did should be considered a crime, according to the Galactic Coalition of Truth, shouldn't it? She'd ask Kazstrom about that. Perhaps those rebels knew and didn't care.

She glanced around the room and her practical mind went to work. Because she didn't want to see Kazstrom infuriated, she cleaned. Then she'd contact him and let him know.

TWENTY-SIX

Kazstrom

ON THE AURORA MATRIX, Kazstrom and Warcat inspected the damaged area. He wanted to see if any changes had occurred since the last time he was there. As soon as he neared the area, he sensed the stagnant energy and knew the bridge had gotten worse. Where other areas illuminated vibrant colors, the corrupted section gave off a dull palette.

Warcat prowled around, sniffing. "They were here recently. The scent is stronger. But this time, it's not an Ensaab stench."

From the infested dead body, Kazstrom was certain Ensaab Rebels had been here. Perhaps they were working with someone else.

"What can you tell?" Kazstrom asked.

"It's masked."

Kazstrom pulled out a screen from his vambrace. Something told him to check the ley lines of Norak. Sure enough, this exact location was a potent intersection of the energetic meridian that ran throughout Norak. Through all of Terrakado. He went to a section of the bridge that dipped low, jumped down to the ground level, and wandered over to a dark spot hidden by shrubbery. He pulled up another screen that scanned the energy frequency. What he saw infuriated him.

Energy was being siphoned into a hole in the ground. From there, he could only imagine where it went. Someone was collecting it. But who? And why?

At least he knew how the Aurora Matrix was being damaged. Now he had to figure out how to stop the siphoning. Kazstrom walked around the location with Warcat. "Let me know where the energy drainage weakens. I need to create a perimeter so we can contain this, disturbing nothing else."

Warcat's sensory ability was a hundred times better than Kazstrom's. In a few minutes, Kazstrom and Warcat had marked the area on rocks and shrubberies. He made sure the markings were simple and wouldn't stand out if the individuals responsible returned before he could cut off the suction.

An idea sparked in his mind as he prepared to cover up the hole with the shrubbery. He reached behind and drew his sword. With his intention, the energetic blade of the sword extended, making it longer than when it was tucked inside the scabbard on his back. White light surrounded by a violet flame brightened the area. He swung the blade back and forth, slicing the energetic chords running from the bridge down the hole. The portal pulsed as a reaction to his sword's interference. Damn it all to void!

That experiment confirmed that he couldn't shove his entire blade into the damn pocket. He had wanted to. But instinct told him it would be too obvious a disruption. Kazstrom wanted the funneling to end, but he also wanted those responsible to pay. He had to maneuver with care.

What he needed was a powerful crystal grid that could cut off the energy flow into the portal slowly, allowing the Aurora

Matrix to recalibrate and heal. A sudden disruption could be a total shock to the system.

An uncomfortable feeling bloomed in Kazstrom's gut. Was Teegan all right? He had sensed her terror at the Shopping Plaza. She hadn't contacted him about anything today, so he assumed everything was fine. He covered the opening the way he had found it and hurried home.

The thought of Teegan waiting for him at home delighted him. He'd never had anyone wait for him before. He could get used to this joyful feeling.

At home, Warcat transformed back into his feline self and let out an unpleasant growl. "Ensaab stench."

In one second, Kazstrom was through the door. He found the couches overturned and Teegan cleaning up the mess in the kitchen.

Fury inflamed his blood as he rushed over to her. "What happened? Are you okay?"

Teegan fell into his embrace. Though her face portrayed courage, her body trembled. "I'm not hurt."

Those words soothed his anger a little.

Kazstrom pushed over the couch and sat down with her where she told him the story of what she had seen and where she had stayed hidden.

His fingers curled into fists as he listened and imagined the fear she had experienced. He had sensed it in his gut. "We don't know for sure if they came for retribution or just the Soulstar," he said. "If they came for the Soulstar, then they weren't the ones who kidnapped you."

"We have more enemies than we thought." She leaned into him.

He cupped her chin. "You're my curious corra, always thinking. I love that you can think practically, even when you're scared."

"There's more anger in me than fear. They have no right to come after me. So what if I killed those rebels—which I didn't. They came to Earth and wreaked havoc. I had a right to defend myself. They're the ones who should be punished by the Galactic Coalition of Truth. Right?"

She remembered what he had told her about the cosmic laws. Pride filled his chest. "You're right. I've already submitted Artwell and Bartu's crimes to the GCOT. And the Coalition has confirmed that they've notified and directed the Ensaab government to leave you alone. But as we can see, someone didn't listen. I need to make a special trip to see an old friend."

Warcat came to nuzzle Teegan's leg. "I'll rip off their legs for you."

She laughed and scratched his ear. "No, I don't want their stench on your paws."

The rebels had come for her because of that damn worm. No one was going to take her from him. Kazstrom had to stop this.

TWENTY-SEVEN

Kazstrom

THE NEXT DAY, Kazstrom left Teegan at home with Warcat. Warcat could keep her safe while he dealt with things. In addition, Kazstrom had sent two of his soldiers to guard the area around his home. As Captain of the Norakian warriors, he could command soldiers for whatever tasks he needed. However, he preferred not to use them for personal reasons. Despite that, he couldn't put Teegan in that frightening situation again.

He considered taking her along on his trips, but she would probably find it boring. His concentration would be split, worrying about her needs. Furthermore, he was entering Ensaab territory. Bringing her would appear like an offering. And he was not offering them anything.

Kazstrom contacted Magnetti on his vambrace. "It's Kaz. When you have a spare moment, can you swing by my home to make sure all is well? Warcat is with Teegan, but I'd feel better knowing you stopped by."

"Done. No problem," Magnetti said.

Satisfied with one task down, Kazstrom checked the images from the two droids he had activated around his home. The images they provided were from ground and aerial view. He should have done this a while ago, but he'd never had a reason to. This was his home, his private sanctuary. It had never been attacked before.

When Teegan had tried to hide her terror from him last night, he wanted to kill every single Ensaab Rebel for what she had endured. The thought of returning her to Earth crossed his mind. She'd be safe there now. The GCOT had ordered all Ensaabs to leave her alone. The Soulstar was now in Norak, so those who were interested in it wouldn't need to go to Earth.

Most of all, he feared this new terrifying event would make her want to leave Norak, leave him. Any sane female would run and stay away from all the danger. Doubts about their relationship had inundated him last night. Did she still have feelings for her ex-fiancé? It was a sensitive topic, and difficult to ask, so he never asked.

He cared for her too much, and if she wanted to leave, he'd understand. Even if that meant his corra would crack into stardust.

Kazstrom forced himself to stop thinking about it and concentrated on what he had to do. He took *Spectre Seven* to El Lara. He found her in the garden, pruning plants. Her assistant, Plantiss, had a cart full of lively seedlings that made adorable noises.

El Lara met his eyes and wiped her hands on her apron. "What brings you here today?"

"What if I said I missed you?"

She snorted. "Then I'll say there's a third sun in our galaxy, and it's called Fake News."

He laughed. "That's why I love visiting you." His expression turned serious. "I'm here because I need your help."

"I can tell. What can I do?" El Lara cleaned her hands from a small plant-being that dumped water out of its tubular head.

Kazstrom told her about his discovery under the bridge. "I know you've performed crystal grids before. I think your crystal grid can help cut off the source that's corrupting the Aurora Matrix. Maybe your grid can start the healing process."

"Give me the coordinates, and I'll make a clandestine visit. I need to see and feel the energy. I need to know what I'm dealing with before I can tailor a crystal grid for that purpose." She gestured to the cart of seedlings. "Norak always needs new trees and shrubberies to increase the air quality. I'll make sure no one will pay attention to my landscapers and me. It's what I do, anyway."

Nodding, Kazstrom said, "I tried to disturb the energy with my sword. The sword worked, but I didn't continue. I didn't want to alert whoever was behind this to figure out we've located the affected area."

"Good. I'm glad you left it alone. The healing shouldn't be too disruptive or intrusive. I want to know who's responsible. He or she will pay." El Lara looked at Kazstrom. "How's Teegan? Why isn't she with you?"

Kazstrom walked over to a fire-cherry bush. "Yesterday, two Ensaab Rebels came and wrecked my home while I was out. Teegan was home alone."

"What?" The star on her forehead brightened. "Is she all right?"

Kazstrom told her the story and where he was going after her place. "We're still looking into who kidnapped her. There could be different enemies wanting the moonstone. I don't know yet."

El Lara wrinkled her eyebrows. "The moonstone is intelligent. It won't fall into the wrong hands easily. Even if it's in the wrong hands, it'll know what to do. We just have to trust that."

"I know this may sound strange, but I have a weird feeling that the Soulstar is safe." Kazstrom knew someone had taken it, but somehow, he wasn't concerned. "I can't explain it."

"I understand. Maybe it's sending you a message. Let's not worry too much about it. If Teegan is worried, let her know your thoughts. The two of you are connected beyond explanation."

Kazstrom knew that too. "I need another favor. I'll need a supply of fire-cherries. I'll be teaching Teegan how to use them."

"Not a problem," El Lara said. "I'll prepare a supply for you soon. I can have it dropped off via flying droid."

"Great, thank you. I'll send an alert to my security system, so it knows your droids might be in the vicinity. When do you plan on visiting the bridge?"

"This is something that can't wait." Removing her apron, she headed into the office. "I need to make some arrangements so I can go today."

"Excellent. I was hoping you would." Kazstrom could always count on her efficiency. "Please keep me updated. Let me know what you see. Or if you need my assistance."

The Priestess whirled around and crossed her arms. "How long have we worked together? I may not always explain every detail of my methods with you, but they always align with what's best for Norak," she said. "I know how you work, and you know how I work. When was the last time I missed giving an update about something important?"

Kazstrom held his hands up. "Sorry, I didn't mean to offend. It was just a statement I make to everyone."

"I like that you're driven and always on top of things, but that kind of management skill doesn't work for everyone. Especially for people who don't work *for* you. I work *with* you." El

Lara huffed out a breath and smiled. "I've been wanting to say that for a long time."

Kazstrom knew he could be bossy and egotistical, but he was used to it. It got the job done, and he'd stepped on a few toes. For those who didn't see the end goal like he did, they should move out of the way and not hinder the mission. This was one reason he wanted to be General. He could bypass certain rules and regulations and make executive decisions that normally required many approvals. Being General gave him the power to do more for his region and those he cared about.

Like General Atreyu, El Lara was like a mentor to him. He respected her words and guidance. "Thank you for always working *with* me." He placed a fist to his corra and tapped.

"You always know what to say to get what you want." She pointed a finger at him. "That's a different kind of danger. I hope Teegan knows how to deal with you."

Teegan had her own way of making him weak and willing, but he wasn't going to share that with the Priestess. "Anyway, Captain Brixx from the Ensaab region should be expecting me soon. I sent him a meeting request last night. He replied promptly. I look forward to the fire-cherries." Kazstrom headed out to the garden, then stopped and looked at her. "Teegan was shocked when I told her your age. She said you're beautiful."

"She's a smart female. I'll thank her when I see her." The words put the glow back onto El Lara's face.

After informing the Ensaab guards that he was approaching to see Captain Brixx, Kazstrom landed *Spectre Seven*. Entering another region required clearance from the guard posts, whether it was through the air or on the ground. The same was required for those entering Norak as well. Though the regulations were known to all, there were always certain individuals who sneaked through in other ways.

Kazstrom strode into a two-story brick building. The guard took one look at him, nodded, and spoke into his tablet.

A minute later, Brixx opened a door and waved Kazstrom into a white room with a round table and several virtual screens. Brixx had shaved his green hair into abstract shapes that matched his twisty goatee. He wore a shiny black top that showed off his broad build. Textured pants highlighted an array of weapons on his belt. Unlike the rebels, Brixx didn't have the purple, diamond-shaped emblem tattooed on his chest. At least, Kazstrom couldn't see any on the gray skin that wasn't covered up with uniform.

"Welcome, Kazstrom." Brixx gestured to a chair across from him. "It's been a while since we've seen each other."

Kazstrom sat down. "It's probably a good thing. Every time we meet, it's usually because we have an issue to discuss."

Brixx released a short laugh. "You're right about that. What will we discuss today?"

Good diplomacy ensured a great relationship between regions. Brixx was one of the few Ensaabs Kazstrom didn't mind talking to. Like any skilled leader, Brixx listened, and he wanted the best for his home region.

"As you probably know from the Ensaab worm, two of your rebels were killed recently," Kazstrom said and explained about his encounter with them on Earth. That it was he who had killed Bartu and Artwell, but that they had infected Teegan when they brought trouble into her bookstore.

"I understand the situation, and I don't blame anyone for their deaths. The GCOT has already alerted us. We got their message, and that's why we haven't sent anyone after the human female."

Kazstrom leaned onto the table and considered Brixx. Brixx had no reason to lie. He had orders from the GCOT. Kazstrom couldn't imagine Brixx would waste time going after someone for killing rebels that had probably created too many issues for him.

"Two Ensaabs came to my home yesterday and turned it upside down, looking for Teegan." Kazstrom studied Brixx's reaction.

His green eyebrows pushed together. "They weren't sent by me or any Ensaabs in our government. Time is valuable for all of us. We wouldn't waste our energy on something that was already resolved in our eyes." He pushed away from his chair and activated a virtual screen with a long list of crimes.

Images of Bartu and Artwell splashed onto the list.

"You've done us a favor by ridding us of those rebels," Brixx said. "Yes, they were Ensaabs, and we don't appreciate another kind killing ours. But when it's justified, that case is closed. In addition, those Ensaab parasites aren't trustworthy. They love feeding off of rebel energies. They've created more complications than anything else."

Kazstrom chuckled and made a mental note to let Teegan know that not all Ensaabs adore their worms. He rose and stood beside Brixx, looking at the screen. "I'm glad to hear that. I'm going to find out who broke into my home, and they will pay."

Brixx pursed his lips. "Before you go, I want to mention something. Though we're from separate regions, we both serve our citizens with dignity and integrity. Those are qualities I admire in a leader. Not all Norakians are like that." He looked at Kazstrom, and there was something in his eyes that said he had important information to share. "I understand you're vying for General Atreyu's position. He was an outstanding leader."

"One of the best." Kazstrom eyed him. Where was this conversation going? He had a feeling it had nothing to do with the original Ensaab topic.

"You'd make a great replacement," Brixx said. "You need to watch your back, Kazstrom. I'd like to offer you some information. I don't need or want anything for it. Let's just say, I appreciate an ethical warrior. I'd rather collaborate with you than anyone else."

"I always appreciate useful information." Kazstrom flipped through the files in his mind on what Brixx could reveal. "What is it?"

"Atreyu didn't die from natural causes. I received this information while I was investigating something else. This data is indifferent to me. But it is not to you. That's all I know."

Kazstrom stood for a moment to process this new insight. Emotion whirled in him as he contemplated Brixx's words. If Atreyu didn't die from a natural corra attack as the doctor had concluded, what caused his death? More importantly, *who* caused it?

General Atreyu had been his mentor from when he was still in the orphanage. Kazstrom had learned his way because of this good man, an individual who was like a father to him. Anger, sadness, and vengeance all exploded into each other. He knew he needed time to calm the fire before he made any moves.

Kazstrom thanked Brixx for his time and information, dropped into the seat of his spaceship, and faced the cauldron of emotions that stirred within him.

TWENTY-EIGHT

Kazstrom

INSIDE *SPECTRE SEVEN*, Kazstrom activated the hovering mode while he worked at his desk. He stared out at clouds and mountains, a peaceful view that helped clear his mind. He needed clarity to think, to feel.

Who had killed General Atreyu? As a General, he had several enemies. But from those enemies, who would take the time to kill him in a slow and undetectable way?

A disruption to the corra took time and effort. It required patience. This wasn't a death that happened spontaneously. This was calculation.

In time, the pieces would fall into place.

For now, Kazstrom informed Magnetti and Aleeya about the recent development. He'd contact the other Norakian warriors at a later time.

"Can you get me his death record and any files he worked on prior to his death?" Kazstrom asked Magnetti and Aleeya. "Go back a full solar cycle."

Magnetti's shocked expression on the virtual screen was probably what Kazstrom had looked like earlier in Brixx's conference room. "Did Brixx tell you anything else?"

"No," Kazstrom said. "I've dealt with Brixx before. There's no reason for him to lie to me. He gains nothing."

"We've got this, Kaz," Aleeya said. "Let us know what you need us to do. General Atreyu was our mentor too."

"Getting justice for him is the responsibility of all Norakian warriors," Magnetti added.

"It is," Kazstrom agreed. "But I need both of you to keep this quiet for now. This development is too sensitive. We'll alert our brothers and sisters once we know more details. I don't want to deter them from their duties."

Understanding, Magnetti and Aleeya both nodded.

Satisfied with one completed task, Kazstrom leaned back in his chair, needing something to soothe him. Teegan's face emerged in his vision. Did she get enough rest? Was she having interesting conversations with Warcat?

Was she thinking about him?

He missed her more than he realized. Thoughts about Teegan always gave his mind the break it needed to recharge.

Kazstrom was about to contact El Lara, when the Priestess reached him first. He pulled up a screen with her face. "Good timing," he said. "I was wondering about your updates."

"I figured you would. I was going to hold off for another hour to torture you, but I'm a kind soul."

He laughed. "Thank you for your consideration. What do you have for me?"

"Watch this and ask questions later." El Lara sent him a video of the crystal grids.

One grid had various crystals floating in the air, creating a sacred geometric shape that resembled the Flower of Life. On the ground, another floral-shaped grid was formed by various moonstones and sunstones, alongside protective stones such as obsidian and black tourmaline. From what he understood, each crystal carried its own powerful code and activated the energy of the one near it. Together, they created a potency that was subtle, yet effective.

"Do you need to plug up the portal?" Kazstrom asked.

"No, we leave it as is. Let's not give out any clues that anything was done here. The crystal energy will seal it when it's time. The grids will disappear in a few minutes as their energies fuse with that of the Aurora Matrix. I can already sense the healing taking place," El Lara said. "It'll take a while for the bridge to heal itself and remove all the toxic energy. At least we located the infected area. Now you can focus on finding out who did this."

"The Soulstar was right from the beginning about the Aurora Matrix."

"Divinity works in magical ways that we can't explain. Nor should we try to. Just take it as it comes. Anyway, that's all I've got for you," El Lara said. "I didn't have time to gather the fire-cherries for you yet. The grids took me longer than I thought. I had to test out the appropriate crystals that resonated with the bridge. I'll get the fire-cherries to you later."

"Don't worry about it. Tomorrow is fine. Teegan is still exercising her muscles with what I gave her. She needs to ace that before I'll give her fire-cherries."

When that task was complete, the weight on his shoulders slid off a little. Kazstrom checked the time and decided he could look into the Shopping Plaza incident. He flew toward his office inside the Norakian Palace and landed *Spectre Seven* in the dock reserved for Norakian warriors. The dock gave an aerial view of Nouridan and provided private entry to the palace via a large platform composed of interlacing energy and neutronic beads.

He strode across the platform into the palace lobby and ambled into his office. He sat down at his desk and pulled up all the files that had been received from the public. Magnetti and Aleeya had reduced the list dramatically.

Kazstrom flipped through images and videos of passengers on autobuses, monowheels, air-bikes, spaceships, shoppers on foot, and those sitting around eating. He categorized them into three folders: no, maybe, and yes. Halfway through, his eyes blurred. The biggest list belonged to the "no" category, followed by "maybe." He stopped working and rubbed his tired eyes.

He went to the bathroom and splashed cold water onto his face to give him another dose of clarity. He returned to his desk and was about to turn off all the screens, when he caught a glimpse of two videos from a small virtual screen hidden behind a big one.

Both videos showed an image of a cloaked person around the shopping vicinity. The different angles allowed Kazstrom to form a clear vision of the individual's movement. He recognized a particular gesture that most would disregard. It was easier for him to pick it up because he had dealt with this individual before. Kazstrom replayed it again and again and couldn't take his eyes away from the slight unevenness of the culprit's shoulders. It wasn't an obvious flaw. But it was one Kazstrom was used to.

His hands clenched as his mind put together a strategy to deal with Bannon. Kazstrom spent the next hour formulating a plan to destroy him. Bannon had wanted Teegan's Soulstar from the first meeting. Did Moraku know about Bannon's action? Kazstrom's encounter with them in the training facilities portrayed they knew nothing about the incident.

He had a web of information to sort out.

If Bannon already had the Soulstar, he wouldn't send the Ensaab Rebels to look for it at Kazstrom's home. It just didn't make any sense. Unless he did it on purpose to throw the suspicion away from him. Could Bannon hire the Ensaab Rebels to do his dirty work? What else was he doing behind the wall of Moraku's protection? What were these two up to?

Kazstrom wasn't ready to share this new discovery with anyone. He saved the crucial files to a safe drive and sent a copy to himself. He had to make a solid case before he revealed this to the Elders. Bannon would be punished, and Kazstrom needed to make sure there was no opportunity for him to wheedle his way out. It mattered little who Bannon's family was; every citizen who committed a crime had to pay.

Before he knew it, the evening sky had come, and he was spent. He couldn't get another brain cell to work. He wanted to go home to Teegan. He missed her face, her scent, the softness of her skin, and so much more.

Kazstrom needed skin-to-skin contact. He needed something to remove the anxiety building in him.

He wanted her tonight.

KAZSTROM ENTERED HIS HOME, and something savory started his stomach growling. He kicked off his boots, removed his weapon and armor and set them aside as he followed the aroma to the dining table where a large pizza sat like a gorgeous centerpiece.

Wearing his apron, which looked like a long dress on her, Teegan set down two plates and grinned. "Welcome home."

Seeing her in his home, wearing his apron, and cooking him a meal changed something for him. He wrapped his arms around her and just held on. No words exchanged between them. Embracing her was embracing comfort.

She drew away and looked at him. "Are you okay?"

"I'm fine now." He smiled. "You've been busy. So, what did you make for dinner?"

"Warcat was kind enough to take me grocery shopping. You didn't have any dough, and I wanted to make pizza. Have a seat and let me know what you think." She removed the apron and hung it back onto the hook.

Kazstrom sat down, enjoying this experience more than he realized. "I've never had a pizza from the human world before."

She filled his cup with aqua water. "It's human-inspired pizza with Norakian ingredients. There are a lot of vegetables and herbs from your home garden. I didn't know you had a special cheese that tastes good but also helps remove fat. Where have you been all my life?" She placed the water pitcher down and pinched his cheeks playfully, like he was a kid. "That's the kind of invention that makes every human happy. Especially this one right here." She pointed to herself and sat across from him.

Kazstrom couldn't remember the last time he appreciated a meal this much. Not a single thought of anxiety or worry popped into his mind. All he could think about was her delight in a simple fat-removing cheese. He wanted to touch the lovely light brown hair that hung in loose waves, framing her face perfectly.

When he complimented her pizza, saying it was the best he'd ever eaten, her eyes sparkled, making the evening more special.

Did she know she was perfect for him? Did she know how much her presence affected him? She had transformed his life. Though he hadn't known her long, his soul knew her from eons ago. That placed her on his pedestal.

After he helped her wash the plates and put everything away, he pulled her to him. "Thank you for an unforgettable evening."

She gave him a light kiss on the lips. "It's not over yet, warrior." Her eyes gleamed with adventure. "This teacher has a lesson planned for you."

"Oh," was all he could say, even though his mind exploded with wild imagination. "I guess I should leave you alone more often. Look at all the surprises you serve up."

"I thought about you all day," she said seductively.

He tipped up her chin. "Is that so? What exactly did you think about?"

She blushed. "Everything."

Heat flared in his blood, but practicality had him slowing down. He needed a quick shower to wash away all the negative residue he had collected throughout the day. "Give me five minutes. I'm all sweaty from running around today."

"You're a man with admirable self-control. I like that." She leaned in and sniffed him. "I don't mind. Your scent is very male."

Chuckling, he said, "I mind. I don't want dirt and negative energy touching you." He brushed a knuckle down her cheek.

"Okay then, class starts in thirty minutes. Don't be late."

He laughed.

TWENTY-NINE

Teegan

TEEGAN BLAMED Kazstrom for the spike in hormones, needs, desires, and bravery. She had planned a special evening where she could teach him about conduct. He had to be reprimanded for giving her wild cravings. She bit her lip as a sexy image of him formed in her mind. She smiled at her adventurous spirit. This was unfamiliar territory for her. It thrilled her that he could provoke this courageous playfulness from her.

Thinking a nice ambiance would set the mood, she went to the music box on the wall and chose a soft rhythm. The box opened, releasing two robotic bugs the size of her thumb with iridescent wings. As they flew around, lovely melodies and sparkles sprang from the wings and filled the room.

Satisfied with the atmosphere, she stared at the lingerie sets she had purchased. She decided it was time to unleash the adventurous Teegan Moore. She chose the black floral lace that portrayed ultimate seduction. She put it on and looked at herself in the mirror. The scalloped edges exposed half of her breasts, leaving the rest to the imagination. The soft fabric stretched across her skin and modified itself around her curves and dips, enhancing her features beautifully.

Teegan put the other lingerie back into the drawer. Strong arms circled her waist, and she leaned into the scent of male and adventure. "That was fast."

"I didn't want to be late." Kazstrom's lips caressed her neck.

She closed her eyes and allowed him to adore her with kisses along her neck and shoulder. His hands wandered over her body, energizing her skin and nerves. With each kiss, her heart trembled and surrendered to something it didn't quite understand.

"I didn't want to get punished for my misconduct."

She laughed and turned to face the magnificent blue male with amber eyes that often turned gold. His black hair had a wild look from the quick dry of the towel. He wore only a towel around his waist. Her core tightened at the sight, and her mind painted a wicked reminder of what his manhood looked like. She bit her bottom lip, couldn't help it.

Kazstrom's eyes darkened with pleasure. "Do you want to see something, Teegan?" The way he said her name sounded like a secret that slid out from the deepest part of him.

Sexual need consumed her. Decadent intentions filled her mind as she flicked him a gaze. She yanked away the towel, revealing the marvel of him all ready for her. Like the rest of his body, it glowed with cosmic codes.

Kazstrom grabbed her face and kissed her. "I'm having you in my bed tonight." He clamped his teeth on her ear, whispering wicked intentions to her. Intentions that aroused every cell in her body. His warm breath and his explorative touch sent her pulse thundering.

He scooped her up, and she wrapped her legs around his waist, her arms around his neck. She captured his mouth, and their tongues did the tango. He couldn't get enough of her and angled his mouth, deepening the kiss. Passion roared between them, and he ushered her back against the wall.

"They're beautiful, but they're in my way." He tore off the underwear and his hands roamed freely. He glanced at her breasts as the mounds rose and fell with her breath. With his mouth, he traced the scalloped edge of her bra and used his teeth to pull away the fabric. Her nipple sprang free, and he claimed it with his mouth.

Teegan let out a moan as he adored one breast, then the other. She arched forward, offering him whatever he wanted. She fisted her hand in his hair, anchoring him where she wanted him. "Your behavior is outstanding," she moaned.

Desire filled his gaze as he unclasped her bra and tossed it to the floor. "I'll show you where I want to rank." He feasted on her in a way that made her feel like a queen.

Pleasure spiked in Teegan and she found herself in a dreamy state. He carried her in his arms and dropped her down onto his bed. Her skin sighed from the silky ivory sheets. The lights had dimmed, and the walls and ceiling reflected the night sky. She was at the center of the universe.

Kazstrom stood watching her, while the symbols on his body faded in and out like they were also breathing. She opened her arms to him.

Half of his body covered hers. "You're my corra, Teegan. Now and forever." He didn't give her a chance to reply as his tongue tangled with hers.

Energies mated and sent them both vibrating with desire. A low growl escaped his throat as she explored his body, learning the curves, the firmness, and where the scars had been. All those muscles. All for her. When his mouth left hers, she took in the sea of stars watching their lovemaking.

She gasped when his hand found her wet center. "It seems

like you're misbehaving, Ms. Moore." With that, he pushed in a finger and had her crying out his name.

She gripped the bed sheet, trying to stabilize the wild energy that wanted to burst. "I need you, now."

Kazstrom only gave her a wicked smile. "I love it when you beg. But not yet, my corra."

THIRTY

Kazstrom

KAZSTROM WASN'T DONE with her. He wanted to show her all the ways he could love her. He loved the way she responded to his every touch. She trembled when his lips possessed her skin, begging him for more. He was addicted to her moans and how she cried out his name.

He loved knowing he was the one who caused that desperation in her.

He gripped her hips and met her gaze. "I'm going to have an intimate study of your body."

Kazstrom gave her petals a gentle kiss, and her body quivered, inspiring him even more. Her scent intoxicated him, urging him on. He couldn't contain himself. He set his lips to the straining core of her. Her sweet taste filled his soul. She was a flavor he had savored long ago and was only now remembering.

Teegan moaned and twisted with pleasure as her back arched, offering everything to him. She was glorious.

She was his.

"I want you. I *need* you inside me," Teegan begged. Purple flecks in her irises twinkled from the dim light.

Her words were commands to his corra. He crawled on top of her and looked into her eyes. "So demanding." He reached into the side drawer, pulling out his Safe-Sex Spray.

With keen interest, Teegan watched him spray a clear liquid over the length of him. The liquid turned to a textured surface that covered him completely. She brushed a finger over the transparent surface and tested the stretchiness. "Oh... interesting."

He grinned. "It's extremely responsive. It has high-performance properties. The surface alters according to motion. We can try the other options next time."

"You aced the exam for creativity." Smiling, she dragged him down for a passionate kiss.

It wasn't his creation per se, but he was innovative in other areas she'd soon find out. "I've always been top of my class." He positioned himself where the length of him, the size of him, provoked her. She welcomed him. He entered her slowly, and energy sang between them. As he drove in further, the union sizzled and crackled like a celebration. "Are you all right?"

She placed a hand on his cheek. "I've never been better. Show me your talent, and I'll give you extra credit."

How could anyone resist her taunt and tease?

Kazstrom plunged into her, and pleasure roared in him. Energy swirled around them in sparks and waves of light. Sensations heightened, and he swore he could feel every cell, every muscle in his body vibrate. Her body matched his rhythm.

Slick skin slapped against skin. Breath against breath, their bodies trembled as they neared the edge. He gripped her face. "Look at me. I want to see you."

Her gaze never left his as they reached the pinnacle and

flew together. A delightful scream escaped her. He captured her mouth and muffled the cry that was his name.

Kazstrom collapsed beside her, gathering her up. He let his corra calm as his body absorbed her softness, her scent, her warmth, and the delectable experience. Together, they watched the residue of gold light that had formed from their combined energies.

"We did that? We created that beautiful aura?" Teegan asked in amazement.

"We did. That has never happened to me before."

"We're starmates, so maybe that's the reason."

"It's more than that. We're fated starmates from eons ago. Not just lovers meant for this lifetime. We're meant for many lifetimes."

Brushing strands of hair away from her beautiful face, he studied the blush that charmed her cheeks, the elegant slope of her jawline, the lovely dip of her chin, and the power of her eyes. The depths of her woke something in him. For the first time in his life, he knew what true liberation felt like. That a whisper of love was more potent than the boom of thunder.

Teegan held a power that could break him. She had no idea what she possessed. She was a divine orbit around the suns, a sacred formation of a new constellation, a ride on a dragon through space.

He was vulnerable with her. If he had to fall apart, it would be for her. And only her.

In a move that surprised and enchanted him, Teegan rolled on top of him, pushing him down with both hands. Her long hair brushed his face like soft kisses that both tickled and tantalized.

"You deserve the extra credit." She dropped kisses on his face, neck, chest, and went lower and lower, waking up nerves that were just settling from minutes ago. "I love how I make you illuminate. Even down here. Especially down here." Her eyes gleamed with mischief and passion as she watched the Safe-Sex protection dissolve from him like magic.

Kazstrom gasped when her hand wrapped around him and gave him the most galactic reward of a lifetime. He thought he knew how to mate, but a schoolteacher just showed him an incredible lesson he'd never forget.

After Teegan fell asleep, Kazstrom tucked her in. He took in the image of her sprawled on his bed and loved it. He pulled on a pair of soft pants and strode out to the kitchen for a glass of water. A realization occurred to him tonight. One that would require him to change his course of action. He was in love with her, and he didn't know what to do about it. Love was something that wasn't on his list of goals and accomplishments. Becoming General had always been his primary goal.

He'd never been in love before. Infatuation and lust were different. They could be dealt with easily. But what he felt for Teegan, and how his corra reacted to her, could not be resolved by a quick release of sexual energy.

What was he supposed to do? He was Captain of the Norakian warriors, so he always had plans and strategies. His feet had always been firmly planted on the ground. But Teegan had uprooted him, making him unstable in so many ways.

After tonight, his desire for Teegan increased. He wanted more of her. One night didn't satisfy him at all. Perhaps it was the energy they created together that inspired and motivated him to have it all. Was it possible?

Would she want to stay in Norak with him? She had made it clear before that she would return after they found that elusive door for the Soulstar.

The whirlwind of emotions kept him up rather than let him sleep peacefully. As he placed down the glass of water, a glint reflected from the window in the kitchen. A split second later, a ball of fire broke through the glass, landing in the kitchen. He doused it with water, but the curtains had caught fire. He pulled out the All-Extinguisher as two more fire bombs flew in.

Warcat growled and burst through the broken window, chasing after the suspect who had vandalized their home.

Teegan rushed out of the bedroom, covered in a robe. "What's going on?"

"Kill the fire with this." He handed her the All-Extinguisher while he grabbed a blaster from the cabinet, rushed out the back door, and shot at one figure running away. Warcat went after the other.

Kazstrom returned to the kitchen, and Teegan fled to him. "Are you okay?"

"I'm fine," he said. "Can you pack some clothes? We'll stay at El Lara's until the damages are repaired. I'll get someone here to work on it tomorrow."

While Teegan packed, Kazstrom surveyed the area. She'd extinguished the flames, but his floor, walls, couches, and curtains were damaged.

Curses flew out of him like a solar storm. Malastrom! Damn it all to void! Who in the black void did this?

When Warcat dragged the bodies back to the yard, Kazstrom went to check. These were three-eyed beings who lived in Norak. They belonged to a rebel group that didn't like government policies, yet they often relied on the government for their essential needs. They'd never been caught or accused of this type of crime before. He couldn't remember the last time he had any interaction with them.

He took images for his own record before notifying the Crime Division to retrieve the dead bodies. Fury rose in him as he vowed to pay the rebel group a visit tomorrow. Who had hired them to kill him?

THIRTY-ONE

Teegan

IN EL LARA'S YARD, Kazstrom showed Teegan how to whip out the smoke bombs he'd gotten from Plantiss. They looked like rocks, about the same size as the plastic balls she'd used before. She held one between her index and middle finger and pitched it out. The bombs smashed into the ground and exploded into a balloon of smoke.

"Just keep practicing. You'll get used to its weight," he said. "I need to follow up on what happened last night."

She traced a finger on the cosmic code on the side of his face. "Let me come with you."

"No, stay and practice." He kissed her.

Though she wanted to join him, she needed to practice as much as she could. The past few days had shown an increase in threats.

"I need you trained so we can battle." He leaned into her ear and whispered. "In bed."

Intrigued, she angled her head. "You're a very proactive student."

"Does that mean you have another 'reward' planned for me?" Friskiness laced his words.

She pursed her lips. "No. You need to focus on your tasks. Don't let me get in the way."

The playful gleam in his eyes changed like she had struck a sensitive chord. He considered her a moment. What was he thinking?

He rubbed his forehead. "We'll stay here until the damages are repaired in the house."

What was on his mind that he wasn't ready to talk about? Perhaps he didn't want to worry her. He did have a lot to work on. He had to investigate the damage on the Aurora Matrix, find out who had kidnapped her and stolen the moonstone, who had hired the Ensaab Rebels to come to his house, and now, who had destroyed his home with firebombs.

She was sure he had more on his mind that wasn't revealed to her. A part of her ached at that thought. She wanted him to share anything and everything with her. She wanted him to trust her.

Trust was a simple word that could transform a relationship. She had experienced that firsthand when abandoned trust had ruined her relationship with Josh. Kazstrom meant more to her. Could trust be the key that kept them together forever?

Forever. Where did that word, that thought, come from?

Nothing lasted forever, and because she knew that, she ignored the idea. She compiled a mental list of Kazstrom's responsibilities, and it gave her a headache, so she could imagine the stress he was under.

She understood stress well. Stress was her middle name when she was on Earth. She rose to her tiptoes, cupped his face in her hands, and gave him a gentle kiss. "Come back soon."

Teegan spent the next hour pitching smoke bombs. Plantiss stopped by to show her a few tricks. She wouldn't have thought the lean and lanky plant-being could toss out a smoke bomb with precision. "Can you teach me? I'll be happy if I get this bomb to land in half that distance."

"You're doing a splendid job." He twirled the bombs between his twig-like fingers. "Keep the vision of where you want it to go in your mind. Then with your mind, speak to your arms, muscles, hands, and fingers. All will connect."

Teegan wasn't sure what he meant. She studied how he positioned his posture, arms, and hands. That intense focus in his eyes was the most powerful.

She copied his steps, and when she threw out the bomb, it landed half his distance. She jumped with glee. "Yes, yes, yes! I did it."

"Keep practicing." He chuckled and returned to his work in the greenhouse.

Teegan sensed a peaceful energy around her. It surprised her that she was becoming more sensitive to things. Maybe that explained why she had picked up on Kazstrom's mood change.

"Kazstrom never said anything about you being a warrior." El Lara plucked some fruits from a nearby tree and dropped them into her basket. The star at her forehead brightened, casting a soft glow over her face.

"I'm not. I just learned how to punch and kick a droid and whip out some smoke bombs," Teegan replied with a half laugh. "My usual skills are monitoring and directing a bunch of second graders. I teach the basics of language, math, science, and social studies. I'm no warrior. I'm no fighter."

"A teacher wields exceptional power. Without the basic skills, a warrior can't function. And if he can't function, he can't win a battle." El Lara rearranged the pink grass stems in her basket. "A warrior isn't just a fighter with a weapon, but someone who truly believes in her mission. In her decision. In her purpose. You have courage that deserves my utmost respect."

Teegan didn't know how to respond as she watched El Lara fill up a bowl with cherry-looking fruits. In her palm, they glowed like little suns.

"We'll help you remember the fighter in you." El Lara gestured to the bowl. "Are you ready to try out some fire-cherries?"

Teegan beamed. "I've been waiting to get my hands on them."

"Hold these." El Lara offered.

Teegan hesitated from the flaming glow. "Will they burn my skin?"

"No, they won't." El Lara dropped a few into Teegan's palm.

Teegan bounced them in her palm. Their warmth sizzled against her skin, but not uncomfortably.

"Swiftness and good aim are key points to remember. They'll distract your enemy just enough for you to escape." El Lara tapped her temple. "Winning a battle isn't always about strength. In times of urgency, if you can get away, get away." She whipped the fire-cherry toward an open field. It exploded, blooming up an immense cloud of smoke that was three times larger than the other smoke bombs. "Try it."

Teegan stared at the fire-cherries that weren't that much bigger than the cherries on Earth. "Do you eat these?"

"No, we don't."

Teegan aimed for the pebbled area about thirty-feet away and pitched the fire-cherry forward. It landed on her target and exploded in a balloon of smoke.

Beaming, she said, "It's getting easier."

"See? The fighter in you is just remembering." El Lara

smiled. "Do you like being a teacher? Is that your dream occupation?"

Teegan twirled a fire-cherry between her fingers. "I love teaching, but I don't know if I'll be back in time to resume my job. I've always loved guiding children. I think kids need to feel safe to grow and learn." She missed these simple conversations with her friends. "I also love working at the bookstore. I'd be happy if I could do both: teach and own a bookstore." To affirm her dream out loud was so empowering, why she hadn't shared it before?

"That's a wonderful dream. As you can see from my library, I also love books. Perhaps we can collaborate in the future."

"I'd like that a lot."

El Lara left the bowl of fire-cherries on the table. "If you need more, feel free to pluck them from the tree. I need to get back to work."

"Thank you." Teegan continued her practice as she visualized her dream.

THIRTY-TWO

Kazstrom

KAZSTROM TOOK Warcat to the investigation. Arriving at the area where the three-eyed rebel group lived, Kazstrom got off his jaguar bike and surveyed the square-shaped homes made of rusty metal. A few large tents were scattered here and there. A garden bloomed on the side of one yard.

Kazstrom understood and respected individual views. He couldn't make someone believe in a cause, just as no one could make him do what he didn't believe in. Despite that, he didn't allow for different viewpoints as an excuse for creating calamity or violence on anyone.

Most of the three-eyed beings didn't create that much trouble. They just needed food and shelter, which Norak provided. The thing was, some individuals needed more assistance and didn't know where to get them. His government needed improvement. He could go on and on, but at the moment, his mind was on who was behind last night's attack.

Kazstrom was striding toward a home when a brown

humanoid with three-eyes, a large mouth, and a round belly emerged with a blaster.

Two more with narrow heads came and stood beside the brown humanoid. "Are you lost, Captain?"

"No. I'm here for a very specific reason. Two of your members ruined my home last night with fire bombs." Kazstrom's voice was calm and controlled. "They died at the scene."

Those words had several families coming out of their homes to stare at him. Some of them were children, and he hated the fear on their faces.

"I know you don't want trouble," Kazstrom said. "Neither do I. But a crime was committed, and whoever hired them wanted to kill me. So you see, it is very important for me to find answers. I'll sort this out one way or another." He scanned the crowd. "Do any of you know what happened last night? Did anyone come by here asking questions?"

The crowd of rebels whispered amongst themselves. For a few minutes, no one said anything, then a voice boomed from a nearby tent. "Someone stopped by a few days ago."

An older being with one missing leg moved forward with a crutch. Kazstrom recognized him from several solar cycles ago, when he had stolen food at a market for his children. Kazstrom had let him go and guided him to some food shelters. At that time, he had two legs.

"Who?" Kazstrom asked.

"Two Ensaab Rebels came and threatened our children." The male with the missing leg gestured to four young star-beings playing in the corner. "They said they would provide us food for one full solar cycle if we do one job for them. If we refused, they'd take our children and sell them."

"We had to protect the kids," a female being spoke in a soft tone, her hands trembling. "We had no choice."

"They didn't even follow through with the food." The three-eyed brown humanoid tucked his blaster back onto the belt below his belly. "If you want to punish anyone, take me. Leave them alone."

Kazstrom understood their situation. "The individuals who committed the crime are dead. There's no need to punish anyone here, unless you're hiding something from me."

"The two Ensaabs had a streak of orange in their hair." The disabled male squished his bushy eyebrows together. "They came with a cloaked being, but he didn't speak. He wore a silver mask and stood in the back, watching the Ensaabs making demands."

Another cloaked being? The pieces connected in his mind. Kazstrom glanced around, looking for any cameras in the area. "Do you have any videos or images of the visit?"

He shook his head. "We can't afford any cameras or droids. But I remember the cloaked person having uneven shoulders. I notice these things because of my own flaws." He gestured to his missing leg. "Maybe he has an injury somewhere."

Rage steeled Kazstrom's jaw and straightened his spine as he let out a loud curse.

What the hell was Bannon doing with Ensaab Rebels? Did Bannon want Kazstrom dead so he could easily attain the promotion? Was it that important to him? Though Kazstrom desired the promotion, he'd earn it with sweat, skill, and honor.

It was time Kazstrom dealt with Bannon.

THIRTY-THREE

Kazstrom

RAGE BOILED inside Kazstrom as he tried to figure out the best approach to deal with Bannon. He wanted to believe that the attack on him was a simple result of the competition for the General position. But the more he thought about it, the muddier the picture became.

Moraku was his superior, and although Kazstrom wasn't as close to him as he was to Atreyu, Kazstrom respected him for his skills. But Moraku's negligence regarding Bannon had Kazstrom pondering if Moraku was involved.

Did Moraku owe Bannon's family a debt? Why would Moraku let an inferior warrior—if one could even call Bannon that—influence his decisions? Had they always been a pair like this? Kazstrom couldn't remember. He'd never noticed until recently. Was Moraku being blackmailed?

Perhaps Kazstrom had let his guard down and became too trusting of those around him. It was time he stepped back and looked at everything carefully.

Kazstrom couldn't find a solution to his problems and decided a good sweat in the gym would release some tension. Also, he needed to train. He needed to increase his strength for when he pounded his fist into Bannon's face. This time, he would annihilate Bannon's shoulders and hands. The hands that had touched Teegan. The ones that had kidnapped her and left her in the field.

Thoughts about Teegan brought a smile to his face. He was in love with her. He had tried to avoid the topic, but the more he ignored it, the more it wanted his attention. So now, it was a blazing sun taking over his mind. This truth scared him more than any battle. With battles, he knew what to do, what steps to take. With love, it was an unknown galaxy. He had no clue.

All he knew was that he needed to keep her safe. Other than that, he wasn't sure. Did she feel the same way about him? Should he tell her? Would that frighten her? Moreover, she had to return to Earth. She had a life there. She didn't sign up for anything extra on Norak.

She had wanted an adventure and nothing more.

The last thing Kazstrom wanted was to give her anxiety. Just like him, she didn't need any more complications. She wanted an adventure, and he'd give it to her. He'd make her time here on Norak worthwhile. But anything more than that, he'd really have to think about it.

For now, he'd focus on Bannon and Moraku, finding Atreyu's killer, and helping Teegan search for the ambiguous door. That was more than enough for his overwhelmed mind.

THIRTY-FOUR

Teegan

ON EL LARA'S floating island, Teegan practiced with more fire-cherries. In the backyard, away from the Star Lagoon, she created clouds of smoke that made the area look like a storm of fog had arrived.

Her body, legs, arms, and hands were adjusting well to all the whipping of the fire-cherries. Her muscles remembered what they had to do, so she didn't have to think much.

Kazstrom had alerted El Lara that his home wasn't ready to return to yet. The Priestess didn't hesitate and offered her guest cabin again.

The flapping of wings signified Mimic's arrival at the front of the cabin, probably dropping off Kazstrom. When he entered the backyard, she whipped a fire-cherry at him. He avoided it with precision.

"I see you've improved." He smiled, but there was something different about his expression. She couldn't put her finger on it.

Teegan came up to him and placed a hand on his cheek. "How was your day? You look exhausted."

He wrapped his arms around her. "It's been a long day. I discovered some news."

They went inside the cabin, where he gave her details about the cloaked individual.

"Bannon?" Teegan turned and faced Kazstrom at the surprise. "He's part of your legion, isn't he? You guys are like part of the same team. Why does he want the Soulstar?"

"We'll find out." Kazstrom sat down on the couch. "But we have to tread carefully. I think it's more complicated than what we're seeing. I don't want to miss any crucial elements inadvertently."

"The next time I see him, this is going into his face." Teegan held up a fist. "Then I'm going to shove a basket of fire-cherries into his mouth!"

"I'll hold him down for you," Kazstrom said. "I think he's also responsible for damaging the Aurora Matrix. Warcat picked up the scent of Ensaab Rebels and another masked one. That could be Bannon. What I can't figure out is how he disguised his energy. He doesn't have that power. Maybe he's working with someone else. Or maybe he's been playing with dark energies."

Teegan sunk back into the couch while her mind sorted out the information. "Do you think Moraku knows about Bannon? Maybe he's in on it too. Does he have the power to disguise his energy?"

Delight glimmered in Kazstrom's eyes. "Aren't you the clever one? You know, I have a weakness for clever females." He gave her a soft kiss. "I can't seem to resist you."

"Why would you want to?"

Kazstrom gave her one long kiss. He got up from the couch

and went to pour two cups of water. When she came to the counter, he offered one to her and gulped his down.

He looked at her. "You're the only female who could make me want so much that it makes my corra hurt."

Teegan placed her hand on his heart and repeated his words. "Nona faiya, nona lux. Coma faiya, coma vita. No faith, no light. With faith, all life."

Joy and pride sparked in his eyes. "You remember..."

"Of course, I do. When you first said those words in Elseon, they stayed with me. I believe my ability to understand Norakian is for that sacred mantra: to know your light."

As he stared at her, the cosmic codes on his neck glowed, confirming her recital meant a lot to him.

"You once said, 'I've never given up on what matters to me.' I don't know what you're going through right now or what you're thinking. And I won't pressure you into telling me. When you're ready, I'm here to listen. In the meantime, I hope that you won't give up on me. On us. Because I won't give up on you."

Kaz pulled her in for a long embrace, as if what she said was exactly what he needed to hear. "No wonder the Soulstar chose you."

I choose you. Teegan wanted to say, but she wasn't sure if he was ready to receive it. Today, she had thought about her situation, what she wanted in the long term. When she first agreed to go on this mission, she saw an opportunity for an out-of-this-world expedition. But as time went on, she found herself attached to this place, attached to this magnificent blue being. He was a perfect day at the beach, a timeless book, a prince from fairytales.

She was in love with him.

This passion ran so deep that when she acknowledged it, it sang like a song throughout her body. The relationships she'd had prior to Kazstrom paled in comparison. Those failures led her to him, led her to where she was meant to be. If there was a moment in life where she knew the answer without a doubt, this was it.

Could she leave her old life behind and start anew here? She could, but would he want her to? Did he love her? Or was she just another female that was his adventure for the time being? She was afraid to find out.

Right now, they had more important things to deal with than personal relationships. When everything was resolved, Teegan would demand answers from him. If he didn't want her, she'd ask El Lara for a job so she could stay in Norak, where she would take her time convincing Kazstrom no one loved him more than her.

If previous relationships had taught her anything, it was the fact that males often miss the obvious even when it dangled in front of their faces. Teegan had patience.

Because Kazstrom had endured a long day and needed to check on the Aurora Matrix the next day, Teegan suggested he go to bed early. He didn't need to keep her company. She wanted time to connect to the Soulstar. Something about being in Elseon with its peaceful atmosphere made her yearn for the moonstone. She sensed the stone wanting to connect.

Outside on the purple grass, Teegan sat and breathed. The Star Lagoon glowed like a moon on the ground, illuminating everything with its softness.

Teegan closed her eyes. "Where are you, Soulstar?"

The quiet hum of the wind combined with cricket melodies eased her into a meditative state.

"I'm here with you," the Soulstar replied.

The moonstone's powerful essence pulled at her. "What do you need me to do? Where is the door you need me to find?"

"Your intuition will guide you." The Soulstar's voice resonated clearly.

She opened her eyes, and streams of golden stardust floated around her. "Are you safe? Where are you?"

"Yes, I am. I'm where I'm meant to be."

An image of a dark hole swirled like a hurricane in front of her. Darkness chilled her bones. Her body shuddered, trying to fight off a dark energy that wanted to suck the life out of her.

Gathering courage, Teegan inhaled a breath and stared at the dark swirl.

"Take me there. That's where I'm needed. That's where *you're* needed." The Soulstar's energy faded, and the connection did too.

When the dark swirl disappeared, Teegan released a loud breath as her heart thumped with excitement. The Soulstar just showed her what the door—or rather, the portal—looked like.

THIRTY-FIVE

Kazstrom

KAZSTROM LEFT for the Aurora Matrix before Teegan woke. He didn't want to disturb her sleep, and he needed time to think. When she had recited the Norakian oath back to him, his corra collapsed in total surrender. She brought him to his knees. She could destroy him without intention. And that was more powerful than any warrior, any weapon.

Though he possessed strength and fortitude, he relinquished them all for her.

His allegiance had always been to Norak and its citizens. But recent days had shown him another facet of allegiance. Where did his loyalty, his faithfulness lie? What was he most devoted to?

What would give him the true meaning of life?

Who would he die for? What would he give up his life for?

He had many things to think about as he walked the length of the Aurora Matrix with Warcat. Kazstrom wandered to the damaged area, but didn't jump down to the disturbed ground.

From where he stood, he sensed it was healing slowly. The density of dark energy had lessened a good percentage.

"It feels better, but darkness still lurks," Warcat growled.

"I agree. Something's still not right, though." Kazstrom glanced at the small two-headed bug-droid he'd let loose. Perhaps the droid would capture something important. "Maybe the Aurora needs more time to adjust and recalibrate."

"I figured you'd be here."

Kazstrom whirled toward Bannon. "You saved me time by bringing yourself to me." He willed himself from destroying Bannon on the spot.

Tension stretched across Bannon's face as the light from the bridge gleamed on his bald head. He wore a black armor with plates tipped in metallic blue. "We have to talk."

That piqued Kazstrom's interest. "Do we have something to talk about? Where's your cloak?"

A sly smile formed on Bannon's lips. "You've always been a talented investigator."

Because Kazstrom understood Bannon, he knew the selfish asshole wouldn't want a discussion unless it benefited him. Bannon would do anything to save his ass.

"I should kill you right now for what you did to Teegan. Where's the Soulstar?"

"I only wanted the Soulstar." Bannon took two steps back when Warcat bared his fangs. "If she had given it to me in the conference room, I wouldn't have gone after her. I need that moonstone."

"It's not yours to have. What I don't understand is why you hired the Ensaab Rebels to come searching for it after you already had it. Then you hired Norakian citizens to torch my place? Give me a reason why I shouldn't rip off your limbs right now."

"The Soulstar doesn't belong to a human. It belongs to

Farra, our moon." Bannon threw out his hands in frustration. "It belongs to star-beings from the Alarus galaxy, not the Milky Way. Also, the one she had was a fake!"

"Impossible." Kazstrom paused in shock. How could that be? He saw with his own eyes how Teegan had connected with the stone, how it had glowed and pulsed.

"The one she wore in the conference room was real. The one she wore at the Shopping Plaza was a replica. I took it apart and tested the properties." Bannon gritted his teeth. "It's made from minerals that aren't from Farra."

Kazstrom's mind spun with theories. He knew Teegan had no idea someone had switched her moonstone; she had been trying to connect to it. Who had switched it? And why? When did this happen?

"That's why I hired the Ensaab Rebels to kill that homeless male and infect him with the parasites," Bannon said. "I needed to get you away from her so I could search for the real Soulstar."

Kazstrom had speculated that. He could say many things to Bannon, but they would only anger him. Kazstrom needed straightforward answers. "I don't know what to tell you. Someone probably took it from us without us knowing. We've been trying to locate it."

Bannon paced back and forth, cursing. "Moraku. He must have taken it first."

"You've been collaborating with Moraku? Why does he want it?"

Bannon let out a roaring laugh. "Moraku owes me a big favor. He said I could be General. He promised me the position. You had no chance."

Kazstrom's suspicion had been right all along. "So you and Moraku concocted an untrue story about the Soulstar healing my wounds. You sent me off to search for the unsearchable. But somehow, fate led me to the real thing."

"I wanted the poison to damage you for the competition. You'd be too weak. You wouldn't have time to train."

"I didn't realize you were that afraid of me."

"I'm not," Bannon retorted. "It was Moraku who suggested those details."

"You got played." Kazstrom enjoyed Bannon's frustration. "You didn't answer my question. Why does Moraku want the Soulstar?"

Bannon's face twitched with anger. "To absorb its energy. To be the most powerful being within the Cosmos. To destroy the Galactic Coalition of Truth." He flicked a desperate look at Kazstrom. "He wants to create his own version."

The truth of those words punched Kazstrom in the gut. Kazstrom didn't know Moraku had these dark ambitions. Was Kazstrom blind all these solar cycles? How did he not see any of this in Moraku? Were there others like him?

Kazstrom's mind swerved to the Soulstar. Was it possible for an individual to siphon the moonstone's energy?

Power elevated an individual to a place where he *believed* anything was possible. It gave him the stamp of approval, of recognition, of worthiness. Wasn't that the exact reason Kazstrom wanted the promotion? So that he could create his own version of punishment, of catching criminals, and of keeping the citizens safe? He was no different from Moraku.

The thought troubled Kazstrom, so he pushed it aside for now. "Why are you here looking for me?"

Bannon smirked. "Because I think if we work together, we can both destroy Moraku."

Kazstrom held back a laugh. "What makes you think I want to work with you?"

"Don't you want to be General?" Bannon's spine snapped straight. "We can both be Generals, working side by side. My family can give you all the universal credits you want."

Kazstrom let the insult slide off of him. He always knew Bannon wasn't the brightest individual, but he didn't understand the caliber of his stupidity until now. In a way, Kazstrom pitied him. Bannon was an opportunist who latched onto whoever could benefit him.

"You don't know me or what I believe in," Kazstrom said. "I'm Captain of the Norakian warriors. I take my responsibility with honor. I have an allegiance to Norak and its citizens." His voice rose like a wild torrent. "There's nothing you can say or do to make me believe otherwise."

Bannon threw up his hands in defiance. "You're just going to let Moraku do whatever he wants? He's been avoiding me, not letting me in on his plans. He's going to kill me." He pointed at Kazstrom. "He'll kill you and that lovely female of yours. Speaking of her, I would've spent more time getting to know every inch of her if those idiots hadn't interrupted me." He licked his lips. "Tell me, does she taste like the female star-beings on Norak?"

In half a second, Kazstrom's fist flew into Bannon's face, cracking his cheek. Another blow broke his nose.

Unprepared, Bannon fell to the ground, but he pushed himself up, cursing at Kazstrom. "Let's battle this out." With his hand, he wiped the blood dripping from his nose and mouth.

Kazstrom welcomed the opportunity to beat the shit out of him. "No weapons."

"No weapons," Bannon agreed.

With a fist, Bannon whirled at Kazstrom. Kazstrom clutched it, twisting it until bones cracked. "That's for torching my home."

For the next ten minutes, the two warriors clashed with their knees, legs, and whatever body parts weren't already damaged. Kazstrom got hit in the jaw, but that was nothing compared to the injuries he inflicted on Bannon.

Bannon sprawled on the Aurora Matrix, gasping for air. Getting his second wind, he jumped up, grabbed his blaster, and shot at Kazstrom. Warcat leaped and latched onto his arm. Bannon wailed from the Warcat's fangs penetrating his flesh.

Kazstrom held up his hand to Warcat, preventing him from devouring Bannon. "Give me a reason why I should save your ass? Give me a reason I should stop Warcat from tearing you apart." He snarled. "You can't even keep your word in a small fight, and you want to be General? You're a pathetic piece of shit."

Warcat sunk his fangs in deeper, cracking bones. Bannon screamed in pain and glared at Kazstrom. "If you kill me, you'll never find out who killed Atreyu." A bloody smile bloomed on his face.

Kazstrom gripped Bannon's armor, pulling him upright. "Who killed him? Tell me, or I swear I will skin you alive."

Bannon didn't have the brains or the ability to kill Atreyu.

Bannon opened his mouth to say something, but Warcat growled and pushed Kazstrom aside, just in time to avoid a blaster. Bannon's face wasn't so lucky. It exploded with flesh flying everywhere.

Kazstrom dropped below the Aurora Matrix, concealing himself from more blasts. Warcat joined him. He couldn't tell what direction the blasts came from. He listened to the sounds until they stopped.

When silence came, he waited a minute longer before returning to the Aurora Matrix. He found Bannon's body destroyed by the blasters. The bloody mess was the by-product of someone who had heard the conversation and wanted his identity hidden. He had murdered Bannon to ensure that Atreyu's killer would not be found.

Too late. Kazstrom already knew who it was.

His mind spun as he considered the best approach, the best

move to continue playing this deadly game. Too much was at stake for him at the moment. Kazstrom needed to keep Teegan safe while he dealt with his mentor's killer. He needed proof. His words would mean nothing in front of the Elders and the Officials. After all, Moraku was a respected warrior and politician. Kazstrom had to move with caution.

Not only had Moraku eliminated a thorn in his side, he'd also turned Kazstrom into a suspect in Bannon's death. There was no one else on the bridge except Kazstrom, Bannon, and Warcat. Malastrom!

Well played, he thought.

In all his years of battle, Kazstrom had learned a few strategies when dealing with his enemies. One of his tactics was feigning weakness or ignorance to create overconfidence in the enemy. Kazstrom would pretend he was cornered, had nowhere to go, and had no proof. This would give him time to gather information to support his theory.

THIRTY-SIX

Kazstrom

KAZSTROM RETURNED to his office inside the Norakian Palace, contacted Magnetti and Aleeya, and told them what just happened with Bannon. "The Crime Division is cleaning up the bloody mess right now."

"You look distressed," Aleeya said.

He should have deactivated the video mode and left on audio, but he wanted to see their faces. They were his legion, a reminder of what was true.

"You're going to need to give a report of what happened," Magnetti said. "His uncle is Elder Kai. He won't let this go easily."

"I know. I've got it covered." Kazstrom looked over at Warcat who sat by the window, waiting for the spy to return. "He's going to think I killed Bannon. Everybody knows we hate each other. They know we're competing for the same title."

"I can't believe Moraku set you up." Aleeya crossed her arm.

"To think we considered him our mentor. He was our superior. What else did he screw us with?"

"He's probably the reason the Aurora Matrix is damaged. I didn't get a chance to ask Bannon about that." Kazstrom pulled up the files regarding Atreyu's death. "Thanks for the research on Atreyu. I'm looking at it now. Please inform the others and ask them to be careful. I'll keep you posted."

"Are you going to be okay until next week?" Magnetti asked. "I won't be able to return to Norak for a few days. I've got a few issues to resolve near Falera."

"Me too," Aleeya added.

"Don't worry about me. I can always recruit the soldiers. I've got it covered." Kazstrom didn't want to add an extra burden to anyone.

For the next hour, Kazstrom reviewed the files on Atreyu's death. The doctor stated he died of a natural corra attack. Kazstrom read the reports over and over again, but didn't see anything abnormal pop out at him. Next, he reviewed the information provided by Atreyu's family members.

Atreyu had made several trips to the Aurora Matrix in the months prior to his death. He had gone with Moraku to investigate. Kazstrom sat back in his chair and considered the information. Moraku had mentioned nothing about this to him or any member of the Norakian warriors. What were they investigating on the bridge? Did Atreyu discover the initial energy damage?

Kazstrom dug further. Atreyu was always organized and kept a log sheet of where he went. Perhaps Moraku didn't know this. Kazstrom did because his mentor had taught him organization was key to winning battles, to living life. He said you needed to see where everything was to know where to go, where to step, and so on.

Atreyu's wife had provided a copy of his log. Sure enough,

Atreyu and Moraku had made three visits to the Aurora Matrix. In his notes, Atreyu said he noticed the energy to the bridge was off in a small section. When he went to review with Moraku, it had disappeared. But then he went back another time by himself, and saw that it was still there. He didn't know why it wasn't visible when he and Moraku had made the visit.

According to the notes, Atreyu and Moraku had traveled on a mission somewhere near the Ensaab border. Perhaps it was to investigate the bridge? It was just a one-day trip, but when he returned, he felt ill the next day.

Kazstrom flipped through more files. What he read was circumstantial information. Could any of this truly tie Moraku to Atreyu's death? As Kazstrom looked back at the coroner's death file, he noticed in the details that there was residue of an Ensaab parasite in his corra. The coroner had left the information with a question mark.

Kazstrom contacted the coroner's office and discovered that they had looked further into Atreyu's body, and that there was an Ensaab worm in Atreyu's corra. It had been there a while. The coroner gave Kazstrom an estimated timeline of when the parasite could have infected Atreyu. If the timeframe was correct, it coincided with Atreyu's visit to Ensaab with Moraku.

Kazstrom scrubbed a hand down his face. How long had Moraku been planning this? Bannon mentioned that Moraku wanted to demolish the GCOT. But so many enemies wanted that. Had Moraku been this way all along? He had deceived everyone around him.

Warcat made a noise when the bug-droid flew in the window. It landed on Kazstrom's desk. He retrieved a drive from the two-headed bug and inserted it in his computer. Kazstrom scanned the videos and images. Relief settled in him when he saw his battle with Bannon play out, and how he was killed. This was evidence Kazstrom needed to support his innocence.

Perhaps this evidence could also show that Moraku was involved. Kazstrom contemplated how he could use it, and formed a plan. The element of surprise had always worked well in battles; it was time to apply that now.

THIRTY-SEVEN

Kazstrom

THOUGH HE DIDN'T HAVE time to waste, Kazstrom took two hours to sort out his thoughts coherently. He needed to form a clear picture in his head before he confronted his enemy. Moraku was not Bannon. He was more cunning, therefore, more dangerous.

When Kazstrom had a solid storyline, he went to search for Moraku. He found Moraku in his office, sitting at his desk. Though the door was open, Kazstrom rapped a knuckle against the door, catching Moraku's attention.

Moraku smiled, rose, and waved him in. "What brings you here, Kaz?"

Kazstrom tried to read his energy, but he didn't pick up any negative vibrations. Moraku could have concealed it. His civility was normal. The way he conducted himself had always been proper. Polished. Perfect. Perhaps it was that untainted facade that had fooled everyone.

How could General Moraku create such an atrocious

crime? Bannon must have framed him. Kazstrom could already hear that from the Officials.

"I have something to discuss with you." Kazstrom sat down in the chair across from Moraku and looked him in the eyes. "Did you hear about Bannon?"

With his red hair swept back into a tail, Moraku intertwined his fingers, sighing. "I did. He didn't listen to me. He came to me earlier today, asking me to give him the promotion. I didn't agree with him. I told him that would be wrong, and there's an honor to dueling a fair match to win that title."

"So when you denied him, he got angry and came for me?" Kazstrom asked, studying the General's eyes. Moraku revealed nothing except genuine sorrow. Either Moraku was an outstanding actor, or Kazstrom had underestimated Bannon. Could Bannon have misled him about the entire situation? Kazstrom let that theory marinate in the corner of his mind.

"I'm sorry he came after you," Moraku said. "If I had known, I would have stopped him. He still had potential if given the direction and guidance."

"Like how you directed and guided me to search for the Soulstar?"

Moraku's eyebrows pinched together. "What are you hinting at?"

"You told me the Soulstar was the only solution to healing my poisonous wound. But in reality, El Lara could've easily healed me. Why? Why did you send me off?"

"Your wound was horrendous. I assumed the moonstone was the only option."

"That's not what Bannon said."

"What did he say?" The corner of Moraku's lips twitched. "From my experience, everything that comes out of his mouth is full of shit."

"Then why did you keep shit around? He said the two of you were partners."

Moraku leaned back in his chair. "I respect Elder Kai, and I thought I could help him train his nephew. I was wrong." He met Kazstrom's gaze. "I know you and Bannon disliked each other. I'll perform a thorough investigation so the Elders and the Officials will know you didn't kill Bannon on purpose. I don't want to lose you as Captain of the Norakian warriors."

Those were crafty words that could gain Moraku support if someone were to eavesdrop.

"I didn't kill him." Kazstrom didn't plan on sharing the video he had.

"I believe you," he said with sincerity.

For a second, Kazstrom speculated if the situation involved a third individual. His mind turned and tangled, bringing him back to this moment.

"I looked into General Atreyu's death." Kazstrom pulled out some copies of the coroner's files from his vambrace. That information was public, so Moraku could have seen it already. But Moraku didn't know about Atreyu's organized log. "It appears that you and General Atreyu discovered something was wrong with the Aurora Matrix before I had any knowledge of it. Why didn't you share this information?"

A slight movement of his jaw was all Kazstrom needed to confirm that the data unsettled him, made him uncomfortable enough that his perfect facade cracked a little.

"I wanted to be sure it was real first," Moraku said. "And when I went to see it with him, there was nothing wrong with it."

Atreyu did mention the damage had disappeared when he reviewed it with Moraku.

Moraku pursed his lips. "Look, I know this is a sensitive time for you. Everyone will ask questions about Bannon's death.

They'll want a report from you and your version of what happened. I've seen you grow into a fine warrior, and you'd make a remarkable General. I'll put in a kind word for you to ensure you can still compete." He rose from his chair and glanced at his vambrace. "I've got to attend a meeting with the Elders and the Officials."

Kazstrom got up from the chair. "Thank you for your time. I guess I just needed someone to talk to. Bannon said a lot of things that got me thinking."

Moraku walked around his desk and placed a hand on Kazstrom's shoulder. "Talking nonsense was one of his actual skills. Go home and get some rest. The Elders and others will want to hear from you soon."

"They have to believe that I didn't kill Bannon."

"You know how these things are. They'll want proof. They'll want to hear from witnesses. Do you have any?" The slippery question slid out of Moraku's mouth like a venomous snake that thought he had just won the battle.

Kazstrom offered an answer full of defeat. "Warcat was the only one with me. They won't believe him."

Moraku pressed his lips together. "You've done plenty for Norak. I'm sure they'll take that into consideration."

"One can only hope," Kazstrom said. "They're strict with horrific crimes. Your title and position mean nothing for something like this. If Atreyu was here, he could help them see the truth."

"I can do that for you. Like I said, I'll remind them of all your accomplishments."

"Thank you." Kazstrom headed toward the door, but stopped and turned around. "One more thing. I noticed the coroner's report stated that General Atreyu had Ensaab parasitic traces in his blood. How was that possible? I don't understand it. Do you know if he ever visited Ensaab?"

"You're thinking too much, Kaz." Moraku straightened a fortisium plate on his uniform. "Go home and rest. And no, I don't recall him mentioning anything about going over to that region. Why would he? We didn't have any issues or business to discuss with them. Perhaps the coroner's report is inaccurate. Those things happen."

"You're right. It's time I stop thinking, time to stop this nonsense."

Kazstrom left Moraku's office and returned to his. He dropped down to his chair and took several deep breaths to calm the anger he had contained.

Moraku was crafty with his words and demeanor. It would take more than Kazstrom's video to make a solid case. Moraku could have used this opportunity to redeem himself. But instead, he gave Kazstrom everything he needed to implicate and apprehend Moraku.

Kazstrom took a few minutes to gather himself before he interrupted the meeting with the Elders.

THIRTY-EIGHT

Teegan

THE ENERGY of the Soulstar swirled around Teegan as she sat in the backyard of the guest cabin. The potency brushed her face, shoulders, back, arms, and hands.

"Where are you?" Teegan asked. "Are you safe?"

"Yes, I am," the Soulstar replied. "Kazstrom needs you."

Teegan sucked in a breath as her chest constricted. "What happened? Where is he?"

The Soulstar gave her Kazstrom's location, but didn't mention why. Then her energy vanished as if she had come to deliver that one message.

Teegan called for Mimic, who arrived right away. "Can you please take me to the Norakian Palace?"

Mimic didn't question and lowered her body for Teegan to hop on. She hesitated a moment, remembering the first time she had sat on the purple parrot. Being up so high in the sky and unprotected had overwhelmed her. At least with a spaceship, she was inside something and felt safe.

Sitting on a bird—exposed to unforeseen danger—was different. Not to mention it had been uncomfortable. But she thought of Kazstrom and his need for assistance. She scrambled for courage and got on. She gripped the side handles on the saddle and faced forward, contemplating what was happening to Kazstrom.

Teegan held her breath as Mimic took off. The strong wind whipped her hair across her face. The gusts howled in her ears and rattled her nerves. Teegan's spine stiffened as her hands clenched around the handles until her knuckles turned white. Her legs tightened around Mimic's body.

The bird swiveled its head. "You can relax. You won't fall unless you jump off, and even if you did, I'd catch you."

Mimic's acknowledgment relieved Teegan. Releasing a slow breath, Teegan regulated her breathwork. She inhaled and exhaled at a pace that kept her mind on the breath and away from the fear of falling. All those yoga practices came in handy.

She loosened her grip on the handles and relaxed her legs. "Sorry, it's going to take me a while to get used to this. I've never ridden a bird before."

"There's a first for everything. You'll be seeing and doing a lot of unfamiliar things here."

"You're right about that. For instance, I'm talking to a bird right now. It's amazing and strange all at once." Teegan brushed the feathers. "But I wouldn't change it for anything."

The powerful wind subsided, and Mimic slowed her flight, allowing Teegan to see the city before her. Nerves tangled in her stomach as the Norakian Palace came into view. At the moment, she didn't sense that Kazstrom was in danger, but something was about to happen.

She looked up at the sky, glanced toward the two suns, and imagined the three moons. "Please keep him safe."

THIRTY-NINE

Kazstrom

KAZSTROM STRODE into the conference room where Moraku, several Elders, El Lara, the Masters, and the Ambassadors were gathered. This meeting didn't involve anyone below the General position.

"I'm sorry for interrupting your meeting." Kazstrom looked at everyone and placed a fist to his chest.

Moraku rose from his seat. "What's this about, Kazstrom? I thought you went home to rest." He glanced around the table. "Like I said, he's tired and sensitive to what occurred today with Bannon."

"I am tired, but I'm more determined to resolve some important issues. I'm here because of you." Kazstrom walked to the front of the room where a large virtual screen displayed a map of Norak, its buildings, and landscapes.

"Me?" Innocence coated Moraku's words. "I have no idea what you're referring to. We have important things to discuss in this meeting. We don't have time for your nonurgent topics. Come back when we're done."

"This is of extreme urgency. What I have to share with you has to do with two murders. One is Bannon's; the other is Atreyu's."

"How dare you disrupt this meeting for crazy accusations?" Moraku looked over to the Elders. "He's mentally unstable."

"I didn't accuse anyone." Kazstrom held up a finger. "Not yet, anyway."

"Do you have the reports from Bannon's death?" Moraku's voice surged with frustration as the polished facade crumbled.

"I have something that can prove I didn't kill Bannon. It has great audio."

Noises erupted in the room. El Lara met Kazstrom's eyes, warning him to be extra careful as she glanced at Moraku and the Elders.

Elder Kai, Bannon's uncle, got up from his chair. His white hair hung in a braid that came past his shoulders. Like Bannon, he had orange, scaly skin. Rows of cosmic codes covered his neck, but none on his face. He wore a white cloak with an energy belt circling his waist.

With his hands behind his back, Elder Kai walked around the long conference table to stand fifteen feet away from Kazstrom. "I'd like to hear what our Captain has to show us." He turned toward Moraku. "Before Kazstrom showed up, you told us he came to you and appeared unsettled. That you're worried he could be a threat to others. That we should evaluate his capacity to lead. This is me evaluating." He looked at Kazstrom. "Show me."

"He probably made up something," Moraku interjected.

"Let him entertain us." Elder Kai lifted a hand to silence Moraku. "It appears you're extremely bothered by Kazstrom. Why is that?" When Moraku didn't reply, he continued, "If anyone should be troubled, it should be me. Someone murdered my nephew. I have a lot of questions."

Kazstrom pulled up a blank screen from his vambrace, preparing to show the video. "To be clear, I did not kill Bannon. Yes, we had our differences, but those differences would never lead me to killing a member of Norak."

He met Moraku's glaring eyes, and the controlled pretense collapsed. In that moment, the two exchanged a silent understanding of the masquerade that had transpired inside Moraku's office. It was as though Kazstrom's hand was pulling off Moraku's mask, and there was nothing Moraku could do about it. A muscle in his cheek flexed, revealing the fury and hatred he had toward Kazstrom.

Kazstrom began his speech. "As most of you know, I was injured a while back. Moraku told me that my injuries were extreme and that I needed to find the Soulstar to live. That the Soulstar would remove the poison inside me. He led me to believe I had no other choice. He was my superior, so I had no reason to question him. I had no reason to believe that my mentor would deceive me."

"I did no such thing!" Moraku spat and everyone examined the outburst. "You lie. Your injuries were dangerous. The moonstone could have saved you. That's the truth."

"The Soulstar is a rare stone. Yes, it could've saved me. But so could El Lara's healing abilities," Kazstrom said. "He led me to believe I had no choice but to chase after an elusive stone that took me to planet Earth, where I found it and brought it back here. When my injuries got worse, I asked El Lara for her opinion. Not only did she heal me in a day, she said the poison could have been easily remedied if I had treated it earlier. Now, I carry a long scar, a reminder of deception."

The Elders, Masters, and Ambassadors looked at Moraku.

"He's lying." Moraku jutted a finger toward Kazstrom.

"Can't you see it? He wants the promotion so bad that he's making things up. He killed Bannon."

El Lara rose from her seat. "I can verify that Kazstrom's injuries could have been treated easily if he had come to me sooner."

"Bannon and I battled, but I didn't kill him," Kazstrom said. "See for yourself."

"How?" Moraku asked with a clenched fist.

"Watch and you'll see. The audio is crystal clear." Kazstrom gestured to the screen. The look on Moraku's face changed when the video showed Bannon interrupting Kazstrom and Warcat on the Aurora Matrix.

Moraku walked closer toward the screen. "That's a fake video. Anyone could have composed it."

"Stop the video. I've seen enough." Elder Kai lifted a hand. "I don't need to see how his body was desecrated." He whirled, facing Moraku. "You're quick to make assumptions. Do you think we're blind or easily deceived? This video proves Kazstrom did not kill Bannon. Bannon's words show that the two of you were concocting many things."

Moraku scowled and moved away from the conference table. "Kazstrom created this video to vilify me."

"If I had made this video, then I would have added all the other facts to get this over with." Kazstrom looked Moraku in the eye, showing no fear. No respect. "For instance, you told Bannon to kidnap Teegan and steal the Soulstar. You sent the Ensaab Rebels to hire Norakian citizens to kill me and torch my house."

More noises erupted as Elder Kai whispered something into another Elder's ear.

"You're not worthy of being General," El Lara said to Moraku.

"You know nothing." Moraku slammed a hand on the table, rattling the mugs and tablets.

"There's one more thing I didn't get to yet." Kazstrom leaned into the table on the opposite side of where Moraku stood. "You killed General Atreyu."

This time, everyone in the room rose. Atreyu was loved and respected by so many.

"You conspired with an Ensaab Rebel and infected him with a parasite that took its time poisoning his corra. I found record of residue of an Ensaab worm in the report. Atreyu knew you were tampering with the Aurora Matrix, and you killed him."

"You have no proof." Moraku's words dripped with disdain. "Atreyu could've gotten infected when he went to Ensaab."

"How do you know? Did he have any reason to go there? Any business conference to attend? Can anyone prove that he went there?" Kazstrom looked Moraku square in the eye.

"I can," Moraku said. "We went to investigate to see if the Ensaabs tampered with the bridge."

"But you told me something different when I inquired about it in your office," Kazstrom said. "Or are you 'mentally unstable' now?"

"I don't know what you're talking about."

"Let me remind you." Smiling, Kazstrom pulled up another screen from his vambrace where he had uploaded the new video he had taken from inside Moraku's office.

Kazstrom understood that when he entered enemy territory, he had to be prepared. He strategically placed his two-headed bug-droid on his uniform where it was hidden from view. Kazstrom replayed the part where Moraku denied knowing anything about General Atreyu's visit to Ensaab.

Kazstrom showed everyone Atreyu's organized log. "He

went with you to Ensaab. He treated you like a brother. Why did you kill him?"

Moraku's face strained with animosity. "He was no brother of mine." He glared at everyone, probably blaming them for his situation. "The power of the Aurora Matrix is divine. We could use this power and rule all of Alarus. We'd be the most powerful galaxy within the Cosmos. We can rule the GCOT."

Moraku took the bait as Kazstrom had hoped. Moraku had expected Kazstrom to go home and rest. He didn't expect Kazstrom to disrupt the meeting armed with this information.

Kazstrom didn't have enough proof regarding Atreyu's death to pin it on Moraku, so he wanted to corner the evil bastard. The truth was, the coroner couldn't conclude it was the parasite that truly killed Atreyu.

Though Kazstrom knew it was, he couldn't prove it. But Moraku proved it for him with his words.

Moraku let out a laugh that didn't belong to him. "I did what I had to do." His face darkened and his eyes hollowed. "This is what genuine power looks like." In a flash, he wrapped an arm around El Lara's neck and held a knife to her throat. "Anyone gets close to me, she'll die. That's a promise."

"You won't get away." Kazstrom's mind raced for a way to save El Lara.

"If I die, she'll come with me." Moraku pressed the knife closer. "You should thank me for proving that the energy of the Aurora Matrix could empower anything it touches. We could use the energy to bargain with other regions, planets, galaxies." He kicked a chair away. "But you're all stuck to the old ways that no longer serve Norak."

Elder Kai shot out a light beam at Moraku's feet, making him jump. Elder Kai was probably afraid to use more force, fearing Moraku's knife could slip toward El Lara's neck.

"The next blast from you will have my knife into her throat." Moraku moved toward the door.

Kazstrom met El Lara's eyes. An inner light gleamed in them, revealing no fear. One corner of her lips curved. Her pet snake, Sizzler, peeked out from her sleeve. It slithered up her arm and bit Moraku's hand. He flinched and dropped the knife. Blasts of power came at him from several directions. Moraku got hit, but he escaped the room.

Kazstrom chased after Moraku as he ran toward his office. Kazstrom kicked the door open, rushed in, and saw Moraku disappear into a portal that opened on his wall.

Kazstrom raced to the wall, but the portal had closed. He ran a hand all around the wall. He had a feeling the portal wasn't a physical door that could be opened with a key or a hidden latch, but he searched anyway. Heat warmed his hand where the portal had been.

Then a theory popped into his head. Could the elusive door Teegan was searching for the Soulstar be a portal like the one Moraku just escaped through? It was something to consider.

Kazstrom returned to the conference room and notified everyone that Moraku had escaped. They sent a team of soldiers out looking for him. Kazstrom also notified his brothers and sisters of what had transpired.

"Are you okay?" Kazstrom asked El Lara.

"I'm fine." El Lara tucked Sizzler back into her wide sleeve. "Moraku seeps with dark energy. He's been concealing it for a while. I also sensed the energy of the Aurora Matrix in him. He's been siphoning it into himself. The crystal grid I created won't be able to stop it."

"Why not?" Kazstrom asked.

"There's too much dark energy in him. It's like your wound —if we'd caught it earlier, we could've stopped it. But this has been going on for several solar cycles. He's been hiding it well.

THE ALIEN'S ALLEGIANCE   221

He now has a strong connection to the bridge. It's very hard to detach it. My crystal grid is too weak to cut off the siphoning. But I have a plan."

At that moment, Elder Kai emerged. "Thank you, Kazstrom, for what you did today. The truth is hard to accept. But it's the only thing that keeps us on our path. I'm sorry for what Bannon did to you and Teegan. My family apologizes to you and to all of Norak." He placed a fist to his corra and tapped two times.

"There's no need for any apologies. None of this is your fault." Kazstrom returned the warrior gesture.

"I'm his uncle. I feel responsible. I know you have a lot to do, so I won't keep you from your responsibility. The Elders and I have important things to discuss." He turned to El Lara. "Will you join us? We'll need your opinion."

"Absolutely," El Lara said and turned to Kazstrom. "We'll resume our plan soon."

On his way back to his office, a cry reached his ears. Kazstrom whirled as Teegan ran toward him, with Warcat by her side. He had left Warcat in the lower level in case Moraku ran in that direction.

His corra thudded at the sight of her. Today had taught him that nothing was more important to him than her. He was exhausted, but seeing Teegan brought on a new energy that he needed in order to survive the next few hours.

Her body barreled into him, and he welcomed her.

FORTY

Teegan

TEEGAN SLAMMED INTO HIS BODY, wrapping her arms around him. For a minute she inhaled his scent. Then she veered back, staring at him.

"Is something wrong? Why are you here?" Kazstrom searched her face and body.

"I'm fine. Are you?" She examined him just the way he studied her. She twirled him around and she didn't see any physical injuries. "You scared me."

He placed his hands on her shoulders and smiled. "I didn't realize I was that scary."

"That's not what I meant," she said. "I came because I connected with the Soulstar. She told me you'd be in danger. Well, I assumed, from her comment."

Kazstrom led her back to his office. "Have a seat and tell me everything. Do you need water?"

Teegan sat down on the chair while Kazstrom went to pour her some water. "I spent most of the day connecting to the Soulstar. On and off. The Soulstar said she was in a safe place. That she's where she's meant to be. She talks in riddles, so I'm learning how to decipher her. I don't think Bannon stole her."

"Bannon is dead."

Her mouth dropped. "What? How?"

Teegan's heart raced as she listened to Kazstrom. "The Soulstar was right. No wonder the nerves in my stomach were erratic. You were in danger. What else happened?"

As Kazstrom described what had occurred in the conference room, a fluid image appeared before her. It was a translucent figure.

She jumped up from the chair. "Do you see that?" She pointed to the figure.

Kazstrom glanced in the direction she pointed. "No, what is it?"

The figure became more solid, holding a bright ball in his hand. "Moraku!"

Moraku whipped out an energy and Teegan leapt in front of Kazstrom, blocking the blast with her body. Kazstrom caught her, and she looked at him. Fear, concern, and desperation overwhelmed on his face, confirming that he loved her. She saw it written in the fear in his eyes.

"Teegan!" Kazstrom scooped her up and brought her somewhere.

Her vision blurred. She tried to look at him once more because she feared it could be the last time, but her eyelids weighed like rocks.

She shifted for a glimpse of him. Pain spiked as something cracked in her body. The agony overwhelmed her, and she began to shudder.

"Stay with me." Kazstrom's words sounded far away. "I love you, Teegan."

She opened her mouth to reply, but pain constricted her

chest and throat. She couldn't breathe.

Her heart stopped.

And darkness dragged her down.

FORTY-ONE

Kazstrom

WHILE MOST OF Norak searched for Moraku, Kazstrom monitored Teegan as she lay in bed at El Lara's. Teegan had several broken ribs. When she blocked Moraku's blast, Kazstrom thought he had lost her. That power could have killed any warrior. But she was alive, even though her corra was weak.

As long as it kept beating, there was hope for her recovery.

Kazstrom held her hand. "Come back to me." He envisioned the two suns and the three moons and prayed for an opportunity to tell her what he felt. "We have important things to discuss. I have more adventures to show you. Places to take you... things to say to you."

His chest ached from replaying the scene repeatedly. He couldn't imagine life without her. It was all his fault. He had placed her in danger. If he hadn't been so adamant about being General, he wouldn't have brought her to Norak, hoping to use the Soulstar. At that time, he wasn't in love, and his priorities were different.

But now, his entire world was lying in front of him. She was his priority. Kazstrom only wanted Teegan to wake up and regain her strength.

Fury crawled back in him when he replayed what had happened. Kazstrom got up from the chair and paced the room. How had she been able to see Moraku's figure before he did? When Kazstrom finally saw him, it was too late. He had underestimated Moraku's abilities.

Soldiers were out searching for Moraku. They sent images of him to every citizen. The Officials even sent his image and info to nearby regions. The GCOT were also notified of the event, but they normally preferred that the regions resolve their own conflicts.

Kazstrom stared out the window. Where could Moraku be? Rage roiled in him as he envisioned a thousand ways of torturing Moraku.

El Lara placed a hand on Kazstrom's back, getting his attention. "She's going to be all right. She'll wake up when her body is ready. The broken ribs need time to heal."

"What about her corra? Is it strengthening? Can you tell?" Kazstrom asked, looking over at the monitor.

"It's quite a miracle, I'd say. Her corra is recovering slowly. That's what matters."

The news removed a heavy burden from him.

"I have something to tell you." Guilt spread across El Lara's face.

"What is it?"

"First, I want to say that what I did, I did to protect the Soulstar. It asked me to." El Lara dug into the pocket of her dress and pulled out the Soulstar pendant, hanging from a different chain. She dropped it into his palm.

A storm of betrayal, disappointment, and anger whirled around him. He tensed from the cauldron of emotions. But as the Soulstar pulsed in his hand, he remembered Teegan's words: *she's where she's meant to be.*

"When Teegan gave it to me to review, I made a replica of the moonstone. I could connect to it. It told me to keep it with me in Elseon. That more was at stake." El Lara glanced out the window, where birds flew into the roots of the floating island. "I don't know if it would've changed things if I had left it on her. I'm sorry for not telling you or Teegan."

Kazstrom understood more than he thought. Sometimes he did things that he believed in and didn't have an explanation for it. He just knew that it was the right thing. The more he analyzed the situation, the more he agreed that the Priestess had done what was right.

"Apology accepted. I know you did what the moonstone asked you to do. You saved the Soulstar from getting into the wrong hands. If it had been on Teegan at the Shopping Plaza, Bannon would've gotten it and given it to Moraku. Where would we be now? Moraku wouldn't be the fugitive we're after. He'd be the one after us."

Kazstrom didn't even try to imagine the consequences of that dire scenario.

"The Soulstar knew it was in danger and asked you to keep it safe." Kazstrom caressed the stone. "This moonstone is sacred to our Farra. So I'm not angry at you."

Kazstrom placed the necklace over Teegan's head, positioning the Soulstar close to her corra. "Teegan said she connected with the stone while she was here in Elseon. It told her I was in danger."

El Lara nodded. "They have a sacred connection. Her mission is to finish what she didn't get to do in a previous lifetime."

"You think so?"

"I know it." El Lara gave him a warm look. "The Soulstar

confirmed it to me. Life is mysterious and interesting. The star-beings we encounter, the other life-forms we meet, the places we attend, the purpose we have, they're all connected to us at some point in time. It's one huge energetic grid that's interlaced with the past, present, future." From her hands, a sparkling grid emerged and floated in front of him. Its pattern shifted as energy moved like waves. "We're all connected on an energetic level. There's a certain beauty to it. Another chance to heal, love, and make things right."

El Lara's words soothed him. With a wave of her hand, the grid disappeared.

"My desire to become General blinded me. Before today, I would have given anything to get that position, that title. I thought I needed that power to do more. I thought that power could replace the pain I had experienced as a child."

"Your parents' death wasn't your fault, Kaz. You were a child. You couldn't have done anything."

"I know that. But that experience left this imprint in me. Fear, helplessness, abandonment, loss, grief—so many dark emotions that I don't want to ever feel again. I thought that if I had more power, I could mold the system. Change the way we catch criminals or deal with them."

"You still can." El Lara lifted an eyebrow like he grew a third eye. "You have that power now."

"I know, but I didn't see or understand that until now. I thought the promotion allowed me to make more rules and regulations." He let out a laugh. "I make those now."

"Being General has its advantages and disadvantages. You're forced to attend meetings after meetings. Sometimes they're productive, sometimes they're not. The politics can drive you crazy." El Lara dug her hands into her pockets. "For what it's worth, you're a fantastic leader. You'd make an admirable General. The best one yet."

Kazstrom squeezed her shoulders. "Your support means more to me than you know. But at this rate, I don't think I'll be competing anymore. Furthermore, who will I duel with? My superior is a criminal on the run. My opponent is dead."

"Then that position should be yours automatically."

"I don't want it like that."

"Your stubbornness hasn't changed one bit." El Lara smiled. "Your integrity is why you deserve it. At least in my eyes. Your allegiance to Norak is unbreakable. It's an honor to serve Norak with you."

Kazstrom paused a moment. He'd never heard El Lara speak this way to anyone before. The pride in her voice was like the pride from a mother. He pulled her in for a hug. "Thank you for all that you've done for me. I appreciate you more than you know."

"I know your appreciation, Kaz." With that, she turned and headed out the door. "I have another conference with the Elders in a few minutes. You should try to get some rest."

Kazstrom continued staring out the window where the peaceful scenery helped him think.

Warcat's tail curled around his hand. "How are you?"

"Okay, and you?"

Warcat snarled. "I'll be great if you promise me I get to have a piece of Moraku."

Kazstrom chuckled. "You can have whatever is left of him after I have my revenge."

"He deceived us all," Warcat growled.

Deception was a cruel weapon that cut deep, especially when it was used by someone close to you. But in war, deception was a key component to victory. If you could make your enemy believe you were weak, then you had an upper hand. The thing was, Kazstrom and Moraku had been on the same side. The sting of that betrayal taught him a lesson.

If he hadn't been focused on his training for the competition, would he have seen the lies and betrayal from Bannon and Moraku? Probably.

Moraku's outburst in the conference room flashed across his vision. Moraku went from being someone Kazstrom recognized to a monster in seconds. It wasn't just his facial features that astounded Kazstrom; it was the revelation of true character. Greed and power had transformed him into someone unrecognizable.

"I compared myself to Moraku, you know. I had thought I didn't differ from him. He had a strong desire for something," Kazstrom said. "He believed in it, and he went after it with all his might. In doing so, he disregarded the effect it had on others. His desire consumed him. I hate myself for seeing me in him."

Warcat made a disapproving noise. "You're not like him at all. Yes, you go all-in when you believe in something, but you have regard for people. You have a conscience. And you have limits to what you would do."

Kazstrom rubbed the top of Warcat's head. "I see that clearly now. It would have been easy for me to follow Moraku's footsteps. But I had a wonderful home at the Cosmic Corra, exceptional mentors like Atreyu, and good friends like you. People who cared for me reeled me in." He let out a sigh, releasing all the negative thoughts. "And that saved me. I'm not like Moraku or Bannon. The only thing I have similar to them was the mental drive. My reason was different."

Warcat nuzzled his face into Kazstrom's leg. "It's a good thing we found each other back then."

Smiling, Kazstrom remembered finding an injured jaguar while he was hunting with the Cosmic Corra group. He had brought Warcat back, and the teachers helped him repair his pet by adding metal parts that made him whole. "You were the best gift for any child."

FORTY-TWO

Teegan

TEEGAN'S BODY ached like she'd fallen off a cliff. Faint noises sounded, like someone talking, but the sounds appeared far away. Opening her eyes, her vision blurred, making out abstract shapes. She blinked, and the vision cleared to gray images. She was wearing the Soulstar necklace, which wasn't gray. It pulsed in her hand. Energy swirled around her body, her heart. She glanced at the glow from her chest. It reflected the color of the Soulstar. Energies exchanged between her and the moonstone.

In seconds, she was no longer in pain. She pushed away the cover and stood up beside the bed. Then the bed vanished. She recognized the room. But all her images were in gray tones except the radiance from the Soulstar and her heart. Turning toward the faint noises, she looked to the other side of the room and saw Kazstrom and Warcat beside her bed. She was sleeping and making strange noises.

"It's time to go," the Soulstar said. A portal the size of a door opened right beside her. Rainbow lights burst from it, welcoming her.

Concerns floated in her mind. Was she dying? Was this the light at the end of the tunnel? She wasn't ready to go anywhere. She stepped toward Kazstrom, but she couldn't move. She needed to touch him. Was he hurt during the attack? She couldn't remember much.

"It's not time yet." The Soulstar warmed her skin. "He will be fine. Come with me."

"Where are we going?" Teegan asked, even though her body was moving toward the bright portal of soft colors. As she neared it, the energy lured her in. The feeling wasn't uncomfortable; it was familiar in some strange way.

"You will understand when you see it." The Soulstar's voice vibrated inside the portal.

Teegan looked back at Kazstrom and Warcat once more. Kazstrom adjusted the blanket over her unconscious body, and Warcat placed a paw beside her leg. Satisfied that they were safe, she entered the portal.

She walked through a tunnel full of colors and images of herself and Kazstrom in various physical forms. She saw the familiar eyes on the different people and star-beings. She recognized the version of herself from that dream she had with him. Were these snapshots of her previous lives? Each of them had Kazstrom in them. Her heart thudded seeing these images.

She was walking through a memory book.

In a second, Teegan stood on the Aurora Matrix. Its energy circled around her. Before she knew it, the energy cloaked her like a dress. It surged through her, remaking and restoring her. She knew she was in between dream state and reality, so perhaps the disappearance of the pain was only temporary. It didn't matter; she'd take it.

The Soulstar nudged her forward until they came to a

section with trees. She jumped down and was shocked that she landed gracefully.

She glanced back up at the bridge and pondered why she didn't even flinch or hesitate at the high drop. It wasn't a short distance from the top of the bridge to the ground.

Teegan didn't have time to contemplate further when dark energy yanked at her. She walked toward some shrubberies. With her hand, she waved them off. Immediately, the shrubberies flew away at her command. Teegan glanced at her palm. Had she really done that?

"Yes, you did that," the Soulstar answered her thought. "You're picking up attributes from previous lifetimes. These are talents and skills hidden within your DNA. You're just remembering."

Part of Teegan didn't understand what she was referring to, but another deep part of her understood it like a dormant remembrance waking up. Just like how her body knew what to do while her mind took the time to analyze and catch up.

A large black hole appeared in the ground where the shrubberies had been. The force of the spinning energy almost pulled her into it. The dark portal gave her chills. It felt like a combination of greed, hatred, violence, blood, temptation—all the sinful things of evil.

As she stared at the dark whirlpool that could swallow her with its size, an epiphany occurred to her. She recognized the black hole from one image that had flashed across her mind. But it was the absolute inner knowing that told her this dark portal was the elusive door.

Darkness enticed and seduced her. She understood its energy as though she understood a foreign language. It wanted her to kill for it. It wanted her to kill Kazstrom and El Lara.

Remove these obstructions. If you don't comply, I will kill them. And I will kill you.

She shivered at the cold threat that came from the depths of hell. Her trembling body confirmed that the darkness would carry out the threat.

Out of nowhere, a voice said, "When you choose to become fearless, you choose to replace 'fear' with 'limit.' That's how you become limitless." Though she didn't recognize the voice, she resonated with the familiar energy like a recollection from a long time ago.

Teegan whirled to see who it was. But there was no one around. "Who's there?"

"It's just us," the Soulstar said. "Those were *your* words from another time, in another place. They're reminding you of what you need to remember now. Do not let fear stop you from doing what you need to do."

The black portal grew larger and larger, forcing her to step back.

Then Teegan understood. This black portal wasn't the elusive door she needed to open. It was the one she had to close. She had to stop the influx of darkness flowing into Norak.

The Soulstar sighed with joy at Teegan's realization.

Teegan clutched her moonstone as black snakes with three eyes poured out of the opening, slithering toward her. She didn't flinch. She didn't surrender to fear. She stood her ground and faced the darkness.

FORTY-THREE

Kazstrom

KAZSTROM WIPED the sweat from Teegan's forehead as distress tensed on her face. What was she dreaming about? He wished he was in there with her so he could help her.

He walked to the window and looked out at the three moons that adorned the evening sky. He prayed to Farra, Yarra, and Jarra. Teegan didn't deserve this. She had come to Norak to help him and his home. "Please heal her."

Teegan shuffled and he rushed over as she opened her eyes and turned to him.

Concern flooded him when she sat up without regard to her injuries. "Are you in pain?"

"Just a slight discomfort." Her face had more color, and her eyes were vibrant.

"But you broke some ribs. You should be in pain." Kazstrom searched her face while he pressed something on his vambrace.

El Lara arrived and checked on Teegan. She used a portable

bone scanner that gave her an instant reading. "That's incredible. Your ribs are ninety-five-percent healed."

"How's that possible?" Kazstrom grabbed the device to review it himself.

Teegan rearranged the pillow behind her. "I think my spirit went somewhere while I was in and out of consciousness. I entered a portal."

"Were you in pain when you went in?" El Lara asked.

"Nothing horrible." Teegan clutched the Soulstar. "How did the moonstone get back to me? Did you find it, Kazstrom?"

He sat down beside her. "No, El Lara returned it."

El Lara pulled up a chair and told Teegan the story.

Teegan reached for the Priestess's hand and held it tight. "I'm not angry or disappointed. The Soulstar knew what had to be done, and it asked you to do it. We're all serving it in different ways. You did what was needed. You saved it from Bannon, from Moraku. Therefore, you saved us all."

"I shouldn't have kept the truth from you," El Lara said.

Teegan stared at their clutched hands. "You were trying to tell me that in the garden the other day, weren't you? About some things aren't what they appear. And that I should trust the process."

Smiling, El Lara replied, "You connect the dots very well."

"I learn from the best." Teegan looked at Kazstrom. There was so much in her eyes. He could tell she had things to share.

He had things to confess too.

El Lara got the message and got up from the chair. "It appears you're healing extremely well. There's nothing to worry about. Take it easy today. I'll be back to check on you."

"Thank you for all that you've done for me."

"No, *thank you* for what you gave back to Norak." El Lara placed a hand on Kazstrom's shoulders. "We would have lost a wonderful warrior if you hadn't been there."

When El Lara left, Kazstrom brushed a hand over Teegan's cheek. "You scared a hundred solar cycles from me. I thought I'd lost you." His hand trembled when he could no longer hold back his emotions.

Teegan tightened the grip. "I couldn't lose you. So I did what someone in love would do."

Kazstrom inhaled a breath to calm his erratic corra. "What... What did you say?"

Teegan smirked. "I love you. I fell in love with you the moment you stepped into the bookstore. But I didn't want to admit it. I was scared to admit it. You were a star-being from another planet. I thought my attraction to you was just on a physical level."

Intrigued spiked in him. "Oh yeah? Like what parts?"

She waved his tease away. "I thought my brief trip to another planet would be a fun adventure with a beautiful blue man. But as I spent more time with you, I fell for your heart and your dedication," she said. "I didn't know if I could love again after my failed engagement. But you opened me to possibilities I once thought were impossible. You helped me remember who I am." Tears rolled down her cheeks, and he brushed them away.

Kazstrom placed her hand to his corra. "Can you feel that?"

She nodded.

"It beats for you, and you only," Kazstrom said. "I love you as well."

She fell into his embrace. "I know. I've never been so happy." Then she veered back. "What has been bothering you lately? I've been meaning to ask you, but I didn't want to add more stress if you weren't ready to tell me."

"I've been struggling to find the best solution for us. This was before I knew you loved me. I knew your stay in Norak was temporary. The thought of you leaving tore me up inside. I didn't know how to ask you to stay."

"I'm staying no matter what." She pulled him down for a kiss. "When I was unsure about us, I thought about asking El Lara to hire me so I could work and continue living here while I convinced you that no one else loves you more than me."

Charmed, he stared at this precious female who continued to surprise him. "Is that so?"

"Yep. I had to make sure you can't escape me."

The idea of being stuck with her forever elated him. "I never expected love to find me. I was focused on my career and my promotion," he said. "But then you entered my life and turned it inside out, in a good way." He smiled and looked into her eyes. "I found something priceless. Something that made me whole again. I no longer want or need a title or a position to make me feel worthy or powerful anymore." He rubbed her cheek with his thumb. "You strengthen me more than any weapon, any title. You make me happy. I found the true meaning of allegiance through you. You have my love, loyalty, and dedication in this lifetime and all the lifetimes to come."

"You sure know how to break down barriers and make a woman vulnerable." She stared at him. "I found myself because of you. I've learned to trust myself again. Before you, I didn't think it was possible."

Kazstrom closed his eyes to acknowledge the joy stirring within him.

Opening his eyes, he said, "I believe the moonstone exists because it's showing me that *you* are my Soulstar. With you, I'm better in every way. Without you, my soul doesn't exist. The Soulstar connected us. It led me to Earth. To you."

Teegan wrapped her arms around him. "I love you so much."

"Same here. But if you don't stop squeezing me, I'll suffocate." Kazstrom chuckled. It was time he ended the darkness so she could be safe. "What were you dreaming about earlier? You kept fidgeting."

She straightened her back. "I saw you and Warcat watching over me, but the Soulstar wanted me to go somewhere important. I went into a portal and arrived at the Aurora Matrix."

As she continued to share her story, Kazstrom realized what she was experiencing. "You bilocated. You were in two places at once. Your etheric body astral traveled, while your physical body stayed in the bed."

Teegan's eyes widened. "Is that something all star-beings do?"

"No, only very special beings," he said. He'd never done it before. "Perhaps that was how you could see Moraku's figure before I did."

Nodding, she muttered. "I wondered about that too. I know what the Soulstar wants me to do. I know where the door is, Kaz." She gripped his hand, and her eyes brightened with hope. "The Soulstar doesn't want us to open the door; it needs us to *close* the door."

"Close what door?"

"There's a dark portal at the Aurora Matrix. It's sucking the bridge's energy." She shivered, and he wrapped his arms around her. "I felt its energy as I stood near it. It wanted to pull me in."

An image of the portal that he and El Lara had been trying to destroy popped into his head. "I know exactly what you're referring to." He rose when her stomach growled. "I'm going to get you something to eat. Then we can continue planning. We'll need an error-proof strategy if we want to stop Moraku."

Kazstrom had to protect what was his at all costs. To do so, he'd request the assistance from his legion.

FORTY-FOUR

Teegan

TEEGAN, Kazstrom, and El Lara sat at a round table in her office. From the window, Warcat chased Nari outside in the yard.

"In two days, Farra is full. The full moon's energy will make the Soulstar more effective. We can use this opportunity to maximize its powers and destroy Moraku's portal."

"And obliterate him," Teegan said, taking a sip of a green healing liquid El Lara had made for her. Interest bloomed regarding the other moons' orbits. "If Farra is full, what about her moon friends? Do they have similar phases?"

Kazstrom smiled at her desire to learn, but he let El Lara speak.

"Each moon has different energies, orbits, angles, and locations. Some move faster than others. But like anything, they're made of energy," El Lara said. "They have a divine consciousness within them, so sometimes they can slow or quicken their phases to create this cosmic dance with their peers." She shrugged. "I don't analyze it too much. It's just something that happens. We accept it and trust that the Cosmos has our back. Does that make sense?"

Teegan thought about it for a moment. Ever since she came to Norak, she had witnessed countless magical things that were unbelievable. Right now, she was sitting and talking to star-beings who—a few weeks ago—did not exist in her life. The possibility of their existence hadn't even occurred to her. So yes, she was open to the inexplicable phenomena, even if she couldn't fully grasp their meanings.

She felt the truth.

"Yes, it does. Sometimes, the truth speaks in here." Teegan placed a hand on her heart.

"If we wait two days to close that portal, I fear Moraku will have used that time to expand the darkness. Or increase his powers." Kazstrom pulled out a virtual screen, showing the Aurora Matrix.

"That's a possibility," El Lara said. "If we go now, the Soul-star *might* close the portal. But what if the closure isn't permanent? What if the closure is just another bandage? We have to remember: Moraku has been siphoning energy for a while now. His portal is powerful. But if we wait to ensure the Soulstar is at its peak potency, we have a better chance to obliterate that opening once and for all. When the moon is full, the Soulstar is full."

"Why don't we ask her," Teegan suggested, pulling out the necklace from under her shirt. She held the moonstone in her hands, took several deep breaths, and focused on it. "Soulstar, should we wait for the full moon to close the portal?"

A lovely melody hummed around the room. "It's time for me to go home."

Kazstrom displayed a slow, disbelieving shake of his head at what he'd just heard from the Soulstar. "What does that mean?"

The moonstone repeated, "It's time for me to go home. The Soulstars have found each other."

The message sank into Teegan as she exchanged a glance with Kazstrom.

She understood the moonstone. "The Full Moon is the reflection of the Soulstar, the entire entity of her. That is her home." She met Kazstrom's eyes. "We wait for the full moon."

El Lara said, "The Soulstar is correct. You both found each other. You came together to help Norak, help her. Her mission is complete."

It was now Teegan's turn to complete hers.

Kazstrom showed them how they should approach the portal. "Magnetti and Aleeya will stay close to the portal and ensure your safety." He glanced at Teegan. "I'll deal with Moraku."

"I'll create a crystal grid to empower all of you. You'll need the recharge."

"How can we be sure Moraku will be there?" Teegan asked.

"He'll be there," Kazstrom said. "As soon as we blast his portal, he'll come. He has nowhere else to go, and he wants to kill me. He missed once, and, knowing him, he'll try again."

While Kazstrom alerted Magnetti, Aleeya, and soldiers she didn't recognize on the screen, Teegan followed El Lara to a cabinet. El Lara opened it, pulled out a box, and offered it to Teegan. "For you. You'll need it for Moraku."

Not knowing what the Priestess meant, Teegan furrowed her eyebrows. She opened the box and glanced at the beautiful jewelry. Now, she knew what El Lara meant and smiled. "Thank you. This will be useful."

"Sometimes, you just have to give the enemy what he wants." El Lara smiled

"Or what he deserves." Kazstrom stood beside her. "Magnetti and Aleeya will gather some of their soldiers to assist. I'll have a dozen soldiers from my end. I don't want to pull them all from their duties. Moraku would love knowing that all of Norak has stopped functioning because of him. That's not going to happen."

Teegan couldn't stop worrying about Kazstrom's safety. He was her warrior, her everything. She'd do anything to keep him safe. She tucked the jewelry into her pocket and returned to finalize Moraku's death plan.

FORTY-FIVE

Kazstrom

TWO DAYS LATER, Kazstrom gave Teegan a smart-tech undershirt and a high-performance jacket to protect her. He didn't want her near any danger. If he could, he'd tuck her in a safe place until everything was dealt with.

But he knew she wouldn't settle for that. His female warrior wanted to fight beside him. She wanted to help Norak and fulfill her promise. He respected that.

She stuffed her jacket with fire-cherries. "I can't wait to use these." She gave him a once over. Their eyes met, and they both acknowledged the danger that lay ahead.

"Be quick, and do what you need to do. Once it's done, I need you to find a safe place and stay out of sight." He stepped closer and tipped up her chin. "You're my strength, but you're also my weakness. Moraku knows this."

Teegan nodded. "I won't give him an opportunity to use me against you."

They shared a kiss that promised a lifetime of happiness and prayed for their safety.

Fully dressed in his armor, Kazstrom secured his sword on his back along with the blasters on his belt and went to review the plan's details once more with his soldiers.

When they were ready, they left in separate groups. Kazstrom had alerted the Elders, Masters, and Ambassadors of his strategy. The citizens who lived near the bridge were temporarily evacuated to avoid casualties.

El Lara would meet them at the bridge along with Magnetti and Aleeya.

Kazstrom and Teegan took his spaceship to the Aurora Matrix and landed on it. Clouds loomed over the area, foreshadowing the doom that was about to occur.

Warcat raced up and down the bridge, sniffing out danger, and growled. "You need to see this."

Kazstrom and Teegan rushed over to find large sections of the bridge had turned black. Unlike before, where the damaged area possessed dull colors, the dullness was now ebony. The darkness ate the bridge in sections. El Lara was right; her crystal grid couldn't stop the funneling of energy.

"Let me close it now." Teegan clutched the moonstone from her necklace.

"Close what?" An Ensaab Rebel with one eye grinned, revealing sharp fangs.

About fifty more Ensaab Rebels appeared on the bridge, surrounding them. One rebel tried to grab Warcat and lost a hand. The rebel screamed as blood sprayed everywhere. Warcat chewed the hand and spat it out with disgust. He growled at anyone else who came near him.

Kazstrom glanced at the blood desecrating the Aurora Matrix. He wanted to kill them all. He didn't want their filth on the sacred bridge. Rage spiked in him as the bridge's energy flowed out of balance.

A second later, the Ensaabs parted, creating a clear path for the monster that came forward.

Moraku strode forward in a new armor of gunmetal from top to bottom. His body had grown in size from a few days ago. Muscles made his shoulders, arms, and legs appear twice as big. Scars etched his face like lava had singed his skin. His electric eyes warned Kazstrom that this monster was a lethal version of Moraku.

"It's good to see you one last time, Kazstrom." Moraku grinned, and the rebels laughed. "Anything you'd like to know before I destroy you?"

"There's not much to say to a traitor. I don't believe words from a traitor," Kazstrom replied. "But you can prove me wrong. How did Bannon get involved with you? We both know he's not the smartest individual."

Moraku waved a dismissive hand. "He was useless. He got lucky. He spied on my conversations with my Ensaab friends. He threatened to reveal everything if I didn't make him General. He wanted that position as much as you did. I thought of killing him to remove all threats, but then I realized I could use him as a distraction. He was very good at that." The electric blue eyes flickered with hostility. "He would have made the perfect General."

"One you could control," Kazstrom said, seeing through the truth.

Moraku laughed. "You were always the quick one—one I could not control. Atreyu loved you like a son. Did you know that? He saw great things for you. He even mentioned that to the Elders. He wanted them to create a new position tailored to you. He thought that you were better than him and me put together." A thousand curses erupted from Moraku. "How dare he compare me to you?" His bony finger jutted at Kazstrom like an arrow. "You're nothing. You're just a Captain of the Norakian warriors. You're just an orphan who got saved."

At one point in time, those words would have bothered Kazstrom. But over time, his skin had thickened and grown impervious to those insults. Kazstrom imagined what Atreyu did for him, and emotions filled his corra with love and gratitude. He didn't know Atreyu had gone to the Elders for him, but that didn't give Moraku the right to kill him.

"So you killed him because he favored me? Sounds like jealousy. Seems to me you have childish tendencies." Smiling, Kazstrom delivered a powerful blow. "Seems to me you're just like Bannon."

Moraku flared his nostrils and whipped out a blue streak of power from his hand that landed a centimeter from Kazstrom's boots.

Kazstrom didn't flinch. Instead, he studied how Moraku's desire for power had morphed him into a distorted beast. If he hadn't wandered off his path, he would've made a decent warrior.

Moraku's eyes wandered over to Teegan and the Soulstar dangling from her neck. "Thank you for bringing that to me. Get her." He ordered the Ensaabs.

Three rebels reached for her, but she whipped out several fire-cherries that startled them. The smoke allowed her to run toward the portal's location. Kazstrom rushed after her, but Moraku stopped him with his electric blasts. Kazstrom drew his sword, deflecting the blasts.

After killing two rebels, Kazstrom and Moraku considered each other. Behind Moraku, Magnetti arrived with his soldiers and battled the rebels. Aleeya's spaceship hovered in the distance as she jumped down with her soldiers to assist

Magnetti. She shot out her golden arrow, which multiplied, sending a shower of death into the rebels.

El Lara was somewhere around the area, creating a crystal grid that kept the violence contained within the perimeter.

Moraku leaped and charged at Kazstrom. Kazstrom jumped out of the way, swinging his sword, which sent a powerful force into Moraku. The force pushed him back ten feet. Frustration flared as Moraku shoved out two powerful beams of blue light that cracked the bridge.

The bridge's energy swerved and dipped, making it difficult for everyone to stand. The ground below the bridge shook like an earthquake. Then more Ensaab Rebels arrived and attacked Kazstrom.

Moraku's attention went to Teegan as she neared the portal. He sent another blast toward her. It missed her and landed on the bridge. The motion tossed Teegan forward, and the Soulstar that was in her hand flew into the air.

Using his power, Moraku leaped to catch it with his hand. He let out a victorious laugh. Kazstrom plunged his sword into two rebels, sliced another, and blasted three more as he tried to make his way toward Teegan. Aleeya destroyed several rebels and rushed over to Teegan, who was having a hard time stabilizing herself on the shaky bridge.

Kazstrom got a glimpse of Teegan rolling off the bridge as it tilted at an angle that was too difficult for her to hold on. Aleeya tried to catch her, but failed.

"Teegan!" Kazstrom shouted as fear and fury slammed into him.

FORTY-SIX

Teegan

THE INSTABILITY of the Aurora Matrix illustrated the danger everyone was in. It meant the dark portal was growing stronger. Teegan had to get to the portal, but she didn't know if she could jump that far down without killing herself. What she did when she experienced bilocation happened in a dreamy state. This was reality.

What was the point of her jumping and then dying before she could complete her mission?

So many people were depending on her. Kazstrom needed her. She had to find a way to get down to the ground safely.

But as the Aurora twisted and quaked, Teegan had to decide. The trees around the dark portal fell on top of each other. This gave Teegan an idea. When the next ripple of energy from the bridge pushed at her body, she rolled with the motion and fell over the bridge.

Her body landed on a tree branch, and the pain was surprisingly tolerable. She muttered a gratitude to the Soulstar, believing it had cushioned her fall. She jumped to another tree branch until it was safe for her to leap to the ground. She glanced back up, but it was hard to see from all the fallen trees.

The dark power pulled at her before she saw it. An icy chill ran down her spine as she neared the spinning whirlpool. The portal was the size of her house on Earth. Just as she had seen in her vision, black snakes with three eyes spiraled from the portal, glaring at her. Their red eyes gleamed, and their fangs glinted as they slithered toward her. She dug into the inside pocket of her jacket, where she kept the real Soulstar hidden. The one that had escaped her hand was for Moraku.

El Lara, Kazstrom, and Teegan all knew he wouldn't be satisfied until he had the moonstone in his hands. She'd do anything to see his face when he realized it was a replica.

With two hands, Teegan held the moonstone in front of her. Her hands trembled as the Soulstar brightened. To her surprise, the moonstone grew in size as it pulsed, sending out an auric field around her. The pull from the portal weakened. The snakes hissed and retreated from the brightness. The howling wind that whipped the debris didn't affect her. Teegan moved forward, using two hands to hold the Soulstar like a torch that lit the way.

By the time she stood a foot from the portal, the moonstone had grown to the size of a large yoga ball, solid and heavy. Yet, somehow, she was still cradling it with ease in her arms. She knew her limits; her strength training had never been more than the five-pound dumbbells. This massive ball of radiance was nowhere near five pounds.

The stone became translucent, so she could see what was in front of her.

She knew there was a higher power with her at the moment. "This is it, isn't it?" she asked the Soulstar.

"Thank you for taking me home. Offer me into the portal and hide among the trees." The moonstone grew a few more inches in diameter as its luminescence intensified. Teegan's arms tightened around it like she was embracing a real moon.

Teegan didn't know why, but she glanced up at the sky, looking for the moon. Although it was daylight with intermittent clouds, she saw an image of the full moon. She stared at the energy of the Soulstar connecting to its source in the sky. She didn't know if anyone else could see it. But the power and brilliance of it forced Teegan to close her eyes.

Something lifted the Soulstar from her hands. When Teegan opened her eyes, she saw that it was her own arms that were pushing the Soulstar forward.

"Thank you." Those were the last words from the Soulstar as it dropped into the portal.

A moment of silence pulsed in the atmosphere, and everything froze, and the land held its breath for this incredible moment.

Teegan rushed over to the fallen trees and found a spot to watch the event unfold. A tubular tunnel of light from the sky anchored into the dark portal. Thunder roared like a tantrum as lightning flashed from the portal. A second later, a potent wave of light shot down from the sky and a large explosion burst from the whirlpool. With her hands covering her head, Teegan ducked behind a massive trunk.

When the debris stopped flying around, she snuck a peek and found the dark portal had sealed up. In its place was a sacred circle with cosmic codes that reminded her of the ones on Kazstrom's body. In the distance, Teegan saw El Lara on her parrot, Mimic. The Priestess waved her hand around, and various crystals formed an interesting pattern in the sky. Energies pulsed from the crystals.

"There you are!" Aleeya rushed over to Teegan and grabbed

her hand. "You did it! Let's get back up there so Kazstrom's not worried about you."

FORTY-SEVEN

Kazstrom

KAZSTROM'S CORRA dropped when he saw Teegan fall over the bridge. What had simmered, cranked to a full boil. With his sword, he vaulted out his wrath at Moraku. Moraku dodged out of the way.

Teegan didn't have the power or experience to land without breaking a bone or smashing her head against a rock. But when the air and the trembling ground paused and the energies on the bridge slowed, he knew something extraordinary had happened.

Though concern clawed at him, he knew Teegan wasn't dead. He just knew it. If something terrible had happened to her, he would have known it in his gut.

Kazstrom whipped out another energetic force from his sword. Moraku met it with two of his electric blasts. The explosion killed two rebels who stood nearby.

Moraku threw his head back, and a belly-shaking laughter exploded with delight, probably thinking Teegan had died. Thinking he had the real Soulstar in his grip.

Moraku shouted to his rebels. "The Soulstar is mine. Power is mine. You will all kneel before me." He lifted the Soulstar, and a burst of energy erupted from where his portal had been. The smile that had been on his face turned into a grimace. Moraku glanced at the Soulstar, studied it for a second, understood, and met Kazstrom's gaze with rage.

"Looks real, doesn't it?" Kazstrom offered the widest grin he could produce.

Moraku glowered as the veins on his face swelled like fat worms. "I'll break your bones and burn you alive."

Kazstrom pointed his sword. "Highly unlikely. Especially when I'll kill you first."

Moraku gathered his energy and was about to pitch out another blast at Kazstrom when a massive tunnel of light came down from the sky, connecting to the portal. Energies spiraled within the tunnel, creating high sonic frequencies. Although the tunnel spun with energy, it didn't create mayhem like a tornado or any wind storm. Everything was contained within that tube.

The battles stopped. Everyone stared at the unbelievable beam of light. There was no question this was the work of the Cosmos.

The cosmic codes on Kazstrom's body and face glowed from the energetic upgrade. This reception told him that the Soulstar was returned to its home. That the dark portal had closed, which meant Moraku was weakened.

Moraku shouted to the few rebels that were still alive to continue fighting. Magnetti and his soldiers took care of them quickly.

The remaining audience stood on Kazstrom's side. As he glanced around, a realization hit him. This battle with Moraku was symbolic of what should have occurred a week from now if he hadn't been a murderer and a traitor. Though Kazstrom couldn't fight him in the arena, he would defeat him here.

Kazstrom no longer had the desire for the advanced title. Moraku had shown him what corrupted power looked like and that had put a distaste in his mouth.

"We battle at last," Kazstrom said.

Moraku cursed and sent a bolt of lightning to Kazstrom. Kazstrom blocked with his sword and returned a force that slammed into Moraku's gut. Moraku raged forward, and Kazstrom jabbed his forearm into his opponent's chin and spun with a kick to the neck. Moraku flew to the ground.

Moraku pushed himself up from the fall. The scars on his face broke out, and blue secretion dripped down his face. He wiped it with his hand, glanced at it, and snarled. The muscles on his body diminished in size. His source of power weakened, leaving him vulnerable.

In warfare, when an enemy revealed his weakness, you had to strike. A warrior recognized his opportunity, and attacked before the enemy could recover his strength. Kazstrom understood this and lifted his sword. He swung a massive blow of energy into Moraku, slicing off a shoulder and arm. Blood seeped out of him and sizzled against the sacred energy of the bridge.

Then the cloud-mobile hovered onto the bridge, and Kazstrom saw Teegan's face. His world brightened. Her smile told him everything he needed to know. Joy and pride coursed through him.

She had succeeded.

With his shoulder and arm missing, Moraku gathered a blast with his other arm and whipped it at Teegan. Kazstrom sent another energetic blade right into Moraku's corra. Energy spider-webbed out from that center, cracking his body. He collapsed onto the bridge. With swiftness, Kazstrom's soldiers removed the dead body, not wanting to taint the Aurora Matrix that was recalibrating.

Teegan fled over to him, putting a hand on the opened wound on his stomach. "Are you all right?

"It's just a minor cut. Nothing El Lara can't fix." Kazstrom glanced up at the Priestess flying around with Mimic, empowering her crystal grids.

Energies formed sacred patterns that shifted into different shapes as they rectified and healed the Aurora Matrix. The surrounding area illuminated with soft, soothing colors. The birds chirped in celebration. The clouds turned into fluffy, cheerful shapes instead of the dull gloom from earlier. Everything appeared vibrant and full of life.

Kazstrom inhaled a deep breath, and the air smelled sweeter. He glanced around at the dead bodies of the Ensaab Rebels that were being gathered by the soldiers. He'd have to alert Brixx about what had occurred here today. Brixx could inform his Ensaab government and maintain a cordial relationship with Norak.

"Look!" Aleeya pulled up a virtual screen from her vambrace, showing the map of the Aurora Matrix. "It's extending beyond its normal location."

Kazstrom and Teegan walked closer to the screen to see that the bridge had created a full circle, looping back to its beginning. That image portrayed how the beginning met the ending, and how the two had created a new beginning.

Something settled quietly in him as he watched Teegan's eyes shimmer with happiness.

"The closure of one book allows for another to begin," Teegan said.

Kazstrom placed both hands on Teegan's shoulders and looked at his future. "It's time for us to write our own book."

FORTY-EIGHT

Kazstrom

A FEW DAYS LATER, when everyone had recovered from the aftermath of the battle on the Aurora Matrix, Kazstrom and Teegan attended a gathering at Elder Kai's courtyard. Kazstrom had never been to any of the Elders' homes inside the Norakian Palace.

Kazstrom wore a new armor of metallic navy and gold that had arrived yesterday. He had almost forgotten about the order, which had been placed almost three months ago.

"Norak has such interesting life-forms." Teegan touched the beautiful plants that draped from canopies. The flower buds produced music, creating a lovely ambiance. She wore a lilac dress with a leather belt that had an attached pouch for her fire-cherries.

"Well, you'll have all the time in the world to discover its magic now." Kazstrom plucked a pink rose from a floral bush and tucked it behind her ear. The petals swirled as it moved to the music of the area.

Teegan sucked in a breath and whispered. "This isn't your backyard. You need to respect people's property."

"Elder Kai won't mind," Kazstrom said. "Look, the bloom's already replaced. This is one of El Lara's new plant species." He pointed to a blue rose that had grown in place of the pink one he'd picked.

A robotic humanoid pushed a cart full of refreshments and delicacies and offered them some. Teegan took a Venusian fruit tart and a Neptunian coffee. "I can't resist this coffee."

Kazstrom opted for a Lion's Gate Roar cocktail.

"Kazstrom and Teegan, it's good to see you both. How are you?" Elder Kai wore his silver and gold armor, which differed from his normal white Elder cloak.

"We're fine, thank you." Kazstrom lifted his drink.

"Thank you for inviting us here," Teegan said.

"This small party wouldn't exist without you both." Elder Kai took Teegan's hand in his. "Teegan, on behalf of all of Norak, thank you for your selfless action that restored the Aurora Matrix. You have my respect and my gratitude. Norak is your home for as long as you want."

"You're welcome. It's everyone's responsibility to do what's right when the time calls for it." She tapped his wrinkled hand. "I've fallen in love with Norak, and I would love to call it my permanent home."

Elder Kai turned to Kazstrom and placed a fist to his chest. "Thank you for keeping Norak safe. Thank you for your service all these solar cycles. We're honored to have you."

Elder Kai whirled to the small crowd that consisted of El Lara, Magnetti, Aleeya, some soldiers, plant-beings from El Lara's garden, Warcat, and Nari. The two cats sat in the corner watching two plant-beings dance.

Elder Kai clapped his hands, getting everyone's attention. "I have an announcement to make. The Elders and I have been discussing some important changes. Necessary changes that are needed to strengthen Norak. The recent events have shown us the leadership we have available within our government." He placed a hand on Kazstrom's shoulder. "Kazstrom has demonstrated his ability to lead, to see through to the truth and maintain that integrity despite what others may say. He's unafraid to ruffle the feathers that flock with injustice. He recognizes lightbulb moments and illuminates a better path. He deviates from the main path to find a more direct course. He's willing to be right enough to be disliked." Elder Kai met Kazstrom's eyes.

Kazstrom knew the last statement referred to the incident with his nephew.

"True deeds of valor and fortitude deserve respect. And deserve to be rewarded." Elder Kai tapped a fist to his corra.

"We all need to help each other through the unavoidable conflicts that show up," Kazstrom said. "I couldn't have done this without my warrior brothers, sisters, mentors, soldiers, and pet friends. Or without Teegan."

Elder Kai nodded. "We have eliminated the two General positions. They are no longer essential. It is my honor to inform everyone that we have created a new Prime General position. We're offering it to Kazstrom, if he accepts."

Surprised, Kazstrom sucked in a quiet breath. Did he hear the words correctly?

Teegan placed a soothing hand on his arm. Magnetti and Aleeya came up beside Kazstrom and patted his back. El Lara gave him a warm smile.

Elder Kai continued, "Kazstrom defeated both Bannon and Moraku, which he would have been required to do during the General competition. Kazstrom has earned this position. Will you take it?"

Kazstrom had given up on the promotion because of what

the desire for power did to Bannon and Moraku. Kazstrom didn't want to repeat that.

But as he glanced around, he saw faces that believed in him, supported him, and loved him. He could be the agent for change. He could use his power to do good. It was his choice.

"You are the change you've been waiting for."

He turned to Teegan. In her words, in her eyes, he saw everything he ever wanted and found his answer.

With that belief, he replied, "I accept."

Celebration erupted in the courtyard.

"I'm so proud of you. It's what you've been wanting all along." Teegan kissed him.

"Yes, but the foundation of what I do and why I do it has all changed," he said. "Love has healed me and inspired me."

El Lara congratulated him and lured Teegan away for a female chat.

Kazstrom celebrated with Magnetti. "You know what this means, right?"

"What are you talking about?" Magnetti asked, sipping his Sirian Martini.

"It means I'm promoting you to be Captain of the Norakian warriors. You deserve it."

Aleeya beamed and gave Magnetti a one-arm hug. "Congratulations!"

Magnetti's mouth opened, closed, and opened again. His eyes sparkled. "Are you sure?"

"I've never been more certain. You've never failed me. You've shown all the skills required to take on those responsibilities. I trust you." Kazstrom placed a fist to his corra. "I'll announce it later. We'll have the ceremony in a few months when we can gather all the warriors back."

"Thank you, I won't disappoint you."

"I know," Kazstrom said.

Beaming, Magnetti got a second drink to celebrate.

"Just so you know, Elder Kai offered to take me to one of the GCOT conferences," Aleeya said. "It'll give me a chance to meet other cosmic beings. It's not until the next solar cycle, though. I'll tell you about it later."

"That's exciting. I can't wait to hear all about it," Kazstrom replied as his attention wandered over to where Teegan stood with El Lara looking at new plant species.

His life was becoming all that he'd wished for. He couldn't wait to share what he had planned for his love.

FORTY-NINE

Teegan

"WHAT ARE THESE?" Teegan pointed to a plant with transparent berries that looked like water droplets.

"They're freshenberries, they freshen your breath by removing unnecessary bacteria from your mouth, throat, and lungs. The berries are delicious in a salad. They have a great crunch." El Lara offered one to Teegan.

Teegan tried it and savored the sweetness. "It's delicious."

"So, now that you're staying in Norak, which I'm thrilled about, what are your plans? I remember you mentioned that you had worked at a bookstore when you were on Earth. Would you like to continue the work here?"

Teegan smiled. "That would be wonderful. I love working with books. I also love teaching kids too. But I'm not sure where I can find that kind of job here. I was going to ask Kazstrom later on."

El Lara wandered over to a tall tree with long leaves that sounded like wind chimes when they swayed with the breeze. "I know of a bookstore with a cafe that's looking for help. It's new. I offered to supply a variety of my herbs to them for teas and specialized drinks. I'm also donating some books I no longer need. I think that place is a great opportunity for you."

"Really?" Hope filled Teegan's voice as she tried to imagine what the bookstore looked like. "Where is it?"

"It's right next to the Cosmic Corra Orphanage. The building was for sale. Someone bought it."

Teegan couldn't believe it. "Do you know how I can contact the owner?"

"Kazstrom knows the owner better, you can ask him."

Teegan found Kazstrom alone, looking at the little pond with dancing water lilies. "El Lara mentioned that you know the owner of a new bookstore."

His lips curved into a smile. "I do. I know her very well." He leaned in and whispered. "It's you."

"What?" Her eyes widened as confusion, bafflement, and amusement entangled inside her. When his expression remained the same, she knew the truth. "You're not joking."

He shook his head. "I bought the building when I saw it was up for sale. You had said once that you would love to have your own bookstore one day. That day is now." He touched her chin gently. "And the orphanage needs a tutor."

A hundred hummingbirds thudded in Teegan's heart. "You did all this for me?"

"I take care of the one I love."

She threw her arms around him. "I don't know what to say other than, I love you. Thank you." Tears glistened in her eyes, blurred her vision, and streamed down her face.

He brushed the tears away. "You're welcome." He reached into his pant pocket, pulled out a gold bangle, and placed it in her hand. "It's your new communicator. You can reach wherever you are. I had it designed for you. The process took longer than I anticipated. The fortisium properties will alter to your wrist's size."

The intricate etchings on the surface resembled his cosmic codes. She slipped it on and the bangle modified itself to suit her wrist. She pressed a button, and a virtual screen popped up with his face. "This is a wonderful upgrade to my mobile phone! Thank you."

No one had ever shown her this much love before. She never imagined her desire for adventure would lead her to love and all of her dreams coming true. With two hands, she squished both sides of his cheeks and gave him a loud, embarrassing kiss. "You're just perfect. I have a thousand plans swirling in my head."

This endeavor would require her to learn about the authors from planet Terrakado. In addition, she'd need to learn how to read Norakian and the universal language. She had all the time in the world to do that. She wanted to alert Maverick and Steffani to let them know that she was safe. When she shared this proposal with Kazstrom, he said it wasn't a problem and that he could take her back for a visit any time.

More ideas popped into her mind. She could bring back some books from Earth to include in her store's selections. Excitement filled her as she saw herself working at the bookstore and going over to the orphanage to help out.

"The orphanage took care of you. I'd love to volunteer my time there." She gripped his hand. "Is tomorrow too soon to see the bookstore?"

"We can look right now if you want." He brought her hand to his lips.

"Yes, please! Let's go."

He chuckled. "So, tell me, what do you want to name it?"

"Something simple and to the point. How about Bound Together Bookstore & Cafe?"

"That sounds like a lovely beginning to a new adventure. Are you ready for more adventures?" Kazstrom asked.

"As long as you're with me, I'm always ready."

Teegan hooked an arm around Kazstrom, and they began the first chapter of the rest of their lives.

***

THANK **you so much for reading!** I hope you've enjoyed Kazstrom and Teegan's story! Read Aleeya and Kenzo's story now in **The Alien's Defiance!** https://callazae.com/books/

Don't miss out on any new releases. Sign up for my newsletter!

https://callazae.com/newsletter/

If you enjoyed this story, I'd love it if you'd consider leaving me a review on your favorite retailer website.

I invite you to join my Facebook reader's group, where I offer sneak peeks, giveaways, special perks, and other book news!

https://www.facebook.com/groups/callazae

"Love is the most powerful frequency in all dimensions. It creates many realities that can save us. Or destroy us."

Orphaned as a child, Aleeya is now a warrior with standards and expectations. When she witnesses a heinous crime, she defies orders to stand down even though she has no jurisdiction in that region. An attractive human shows her that her defiance is the key that unlocks her heart and everything that matters to her.

Kenzo, a bounty hunter searching for his brothers' killer, encounters a stunning star-being who tempts his heart. But the thirst for vengeance prevents him from love.

Can he defy his own darkness to find salvation in her?

For a complete list of my books, click here.

https://callazae.com/books/

AUDIOBOOKS are available for my Soldiers of Saedo Series!

Suggested Reading Order:

An Alien Rescue (#1)

An Alien Crush (#2)

An Alien Dare (#3)

An Alien Storm (#4)

(An Alien Storm: Ebook available. Audiobook Coming Soon!)

An Alien Lore (#5) - Coming Soon!

ACKNOWLEDGMENTS

Thank you to Laurie, Carol, Anna, and Jessa who helped my story shine. You are the shiny siSTARS in my galaxy. Thank you to my family who always give me everything I need to pursue my dreams. You are my entire Universe.

And thank you, dear readers, you give me a reason to keep writing. Without you, there's no one to appreciate the stardust within my creation. You have my utmost gratitude.

CALLA ZAE

ABOUT THE AUTHOR

I love writing sci-fi, fantasy, paranormal, and contemporary romance novels. I'm an artist, and I love to create visuals to convey my stories.

I live in Massachusetts with my husband who keeps me grounded to Earth and two creative children who think I have my own secret planet. They're onto something...

facebook.com/callazaeauthor

instagram.com/callazae

bookbub.com/profile/calla-zae

amazon.com/author/callazae

pinterest.com/callazae

www.ingramcontent.com/pod-product-compliance
Lightning Source LLC
Chambersburg PA
CBHW071746190726
48292CB00003B/881